Caring is Creepy

ALSO BY
David Zimmerman
The Sandbox

caring

is

creepy

a novel

David
Zimmerman

Published by
Soho Press, Inc.
853 Broadway
New York, NY 10003

Library of Congress Cataloging-in-Publication Data

Zimmerman, David.
Caring is creepy / David Zimmerman.
p. cm.
ISBN 978-1-56947-977-3
eISBN 978-1-56947-978-0
1. Mothers and daughters—Fiction. 2. Soldiers—Fiction.
3. Domestic fiction. I. Title.
PS3626.I49C37 2012
813'.6—dc23
2011041973

Printed in the United States of America

10 9 8 7 6 5 4 3 2 1

In Memory of Laura Hruska

"It's a cesspool, a spittoon, and the devil of it is, they set it in front of you in a fancy cup and make like it's champagne, so of course you drink it. My daughter never had a chance in a place like that."

—2002 radio interview about the Internet
with the mother of a teenaged kidnap victim.

"Allow me my phrases: there is a strange and deep thing coming, like a mouth, at the end of this."

—BARRY HANNAH,
"The Spy of Loog Root"

Caring is Creepy

The Game

The most dangerous thing I ever did was tell a grown man my real name. I typed it for him. Lynn Marie Sugrue. When it happened, it didn't seem like anything at all. Hardly something worth worrying over. Me and my best friend Dani were down in her basement bedroom on a night hot and thick enough to push in against the window screens. We were playing our favorite game of the moment, a sort of online combination of crank phone call and blind man's bluff, but it was really more of a scheme to try out being bad in a place we thought it wouldn't count. We just never expected to be the ones wearing the blindfold.

So this is August of 2005 in Metter, Georgia, population half of nothing. A million miles from anywhere good. So this is me and Dani, just turned fifteen and a couple weeks away from our sophomore year at Metter High. So this is me fucking up my life like you wouldn't believe.

New Identities

The trouble started with a gift. The day after my friend Dani's birthday, I found her moping down in her bedroom beside a pair of huge boxes. Dani's dad owns that used car lot out where Lewis Street meets the county highway—Big Dunham's it's called, the one where in the commercials a girl in a bikini goes around popping balloons on windshields, saying, "We're popping prices like you wouldn't believe." He'd been promising for years to buy her a car when she turned fifteen. Dani wouldn't be able to drive without an adult sitting next to her for another year, but this hadn't bothered her one whit. "I'll get to have plenty of practice for the license test," she'd say. A few weeks before her birthday, though, something happened to change Dani's mother's mind, something not even Dani would tell me about. Whatever it was she did, it made her mother decide poor little Dani wasn't quite ready for a car of her own. Instead, she got a new computer.

I took a beer from my backpack and waved it in front of her face to get her attention. "Cheer up, there's more naked men inside that plastic box over there on the floor than you could ever possibly look at."

Dani closed her eyes and shook her hair so hard it twirled around her head like a skirt, but she snatched up the beer all the same.

"Well," she said. "For scientific study."

"Sure," I said.

Dani had used the wholesome notion of scientific study as a

means of investigating all manner of nasty things over the years. We'd spent a good deal of the summer watching dirty movies filched from her dad's footlocker in the garage, pausing at the stranger parts and studying them like scientists. Once, she even got her mom to buy Judy Blume's *Forever* with the excuse that she needed to write a paper on the mores of suburban adolescents in the 1970s for her social studies class. I still shake my head in wonder over that bit of bullshit.

It took both of us to tug the computer free. The Styrofoam squeaked like a stepped-on mouse.

How could I have known then the kind of craziness that would come out of that box? Or that on that same exact day, maybe right around the same time, the boy who'd change everything about me, right down to my last clean pair of socks, was opening up his own box of trouble? Inside his box was the decision to leave his job, his home, his whole life. Inside his box was how he got caught sketching a stray dog on the back of a pink requisition form and was now pushing a mop as punishment. No more of this, he told himself. No way. I'm through. And I remember thinking how a new computer smelled like clean.

Dani tossed the instruction book and called her next-door neighbor, Wynn.

Wynn was a year above us. He was bony and stooped and had M&M-sized whiteheads on the back of his neck. He smelled like fresh-cut onion. As he sat at the keyboard, going through the start-up instructions point by point, I made a shadow-puppet alligator crawl across his back, showing Dani how any one of the whiteheads could burst at the slightest touch, like a grenade with a loose pin.

"I'm going to leave you two lovebirds alone," I said.

Dani pinched my arm, hard.

"And I'm going to stab you in the arm with a fork," Dani said, making an irritable V with her eyebrows.

But I didn't leave. I sat on the woven rag rug that covered most of Dani's floor. Hers was the kind of bedroom you'd expect to see on some Nickelodeon teen sitcom. It was the size of my living room and decorated in a color scheme of teal and silver. Dani used the word teal, anyhow—really, it was plain blue. The four-poster bed was blue, with blue sheets, and her two beanbag chairs were silver. She called this the hanging-out area and had hung posters of her favorite bands. In most, the musicians all had the look of long-distance truckers loitering in the parking lot of a Waffle House at 2:00 A.M. But in the newest one, there weren't any people at all, just a big blue box with the silhouettes of tan and white weeds. Dani had become obsessed with a band called the Shins. Jingle-jangle guitars, sad whispering boys, and the occasional rim shot. Hum-along music that snuck up on you and stayed in your skull.

When Wynn told us we were online, Dani stared through the wall and tugged at a strand of hair as he set up an e-mail account for us and bookmarked some sites he said he thought might be of interest, so I could tell something was on her mind.

"You like celebrity gossip?" Wynn asked. "Gaming news? There's this one site that's really great that has all these funny alligator-eating-pet stories from Florida. You want to see that?"

"Really," I said. "Florida?"

"Oh my God," Dani snapped, "will you two shut up about Florida? Look—" She squeezed her eyes shut until the lids wrinkled. Whatever it was she wanted to say seemed to be trapped like a hairball in her throat. Finally, she coughed it up. "Why don't you bring us to a site where we can . . . mess with people."

"What do you mean?" Wynn asked.

"Pretend to be someone else," she said. "Talk to them. Get inside their heads. Just *mess* with people, you know?"

Wynn wiped his hands on the back of his green corduroy cutoffs. "Who do you want to be?"

She looked for a few moments over at the posters in the hanging-out area. "I could be a singer in some band from Scotland."

"Come on, Dani," I said. "Think big. Why not a fifty-year-old gay guy with gorgeous pecs from Dothan, Alabama?"

"Or a pretty girl from Metter, Georgia," Wynn said. There were beads of sweat collecting in the wispy, little grandma mustache he looked to be trying to grow. It was gross and I really wanted him to wipe it off, but I didn't say anything. Dani had flung enough mean at him for three people. Earlier she had asked him if he thought about me when he jerked off and I thought the boy might faint.

"Oh, please," Dani said. She let loose with a lip-flapping sigh and made what I thought of as her fat face. She'd kill me if she ever heard me say this, but she had one of those Cabbage Patch Kid faces. Round and plump. And when she frowned, like she was doing now, she'd push her chin down and the fat would wrinkle up under there, making it look like she'd suddenly lost her neck. Dani wasn't what you'd call *fat* fat, but she wasn't even close to skinny either. She had beautiful black hair that came down to her shoulders and curled up at the ends in a flip and a button nose that turned up at the end too. When I was mad at her, I called her "pig snout" in my head, but the truth was she had a pretty nose. I wouldn't mind having it. Mine had a big bump on the bridge I hated. But her best feature, in my opinion, was her eyes, which were the color of a Rolling Rock bottle that'd been smashed on concrete. Green with silvery splinters.

"But why would you want to be someone else?" Wynn asked.

Dani caught my eye and grinned. Wynn looked back and forth between us, wearing a smile that looked like it hurt.

"What?" he said. "What?"

"Alright," Dani said.

"Alright, what?" Wynn said.

"Make me a fifty-year-old gay guy from Dothan, Alabama, The Peanut Capital of the World."

"With gorgeous pecs," I added.

And so Wynn showed us how to become a fifty-year-old gay guy from Dothan, Alabama. We were never quite ourselves again after that.

Asshole

My mother is a nurse and my father is an asshole. He left us when I was six. For the first couple of years after the divorce, he lived in Savannah and came up on weekends to see me. He paid his child support. My dad was an accountant at the Gulfstream airplane factory. "Your father makes a pile of cash," my mom would say whenever I asked her to get me something. "Ask him for it." Or she'd say, "You can go see *that* movie with your father if you think you can shake ten bucks out of him." Or, "If your father had half a heart, he'd get you some decent shoes."

"Your mother has an active imagination," is what he'd tell me when I asked him. "Rich, my ass," he'd say. "Gulfstream doesn't even have a union. At least not for accountants."

The last time I ever saw my dad was the Saturday he took me out to Tybee Island. In the parking lot, he swiped me a ratty orange life vest off of someone's boat trailer. He reached in and grabbed it and just kept walking toward the beach.

I was three weeks away from being eight years old. When Dad didn't call on my birthday, my mom tried to reach him and found his phone had been disconnected. She called his boss out at Gulfstream, who said he'd stopped showing up for work three days ago and hadn't left a forwarding address. He and my dad had been friends since high school, so my mom thought Mack—that was the boss's name—was covering for him. She said she hoped his wife did the same thing to him one day and for him to go fuck himself. She wrapped the phone cord around her fingers so tight they turned yellow.

The next day, Mack called back. There was a problem with Dad's accounts. The day after that, the police came to our house.

I asked what Dad had done to make everybody so mad at him. My mom said, "Your father's an asshole. He did what comes natural to assholes. He shit all over everybody."

The year I turned eight I learned how to do laundry, make Kraft macaroni and cheese out of a box, and smoke cigarettes.

I now divide my life into two parts—BDD and ADD—Before Dad Disappeared and After Dad Disappeared, and more and more I don't remember a lot about BDD.

I do remember Tybee Island, though.

He must of known he was leaving by then.

I wonder if he'd planned to tell me.

Or maybe he didn't know yet. And when he figured it out, it was too late to say anything.

His hair was curly and red and very thin on top. The sun turned his scalp the color of boiled shrimp. We treaded water out past the breakers, the gulls calling out threats to one another and the sunlight smashing into millions of pieces in the choppy water.

Learning the Rules

Dani and me went through dozens of cheesy adult social sites before we settled on **The Big Green Bus**. The description said you'd love it if you always saved out the green M&M's for special occasions because here was a site where everyone downed them by the handful. We guessed this was some type of reference to horniness. Officially, it was a site that listed evening entertainment in Chicago, but it also had a message board that you needed to become a member in order to see. The first few sites we'd tried were mostly filled with dorks like Wynn and other species of babbling idjit. Even when we'd pick out somebody that seemed halfway normal to send instant messages to, the guy would start right in with raunchy sex talk. "I'm jacking off right now thinking about you" or "I'm putting my fingers in your pussy and you like it." The thing was, we didn't like it. Not one bit. Dani and me didn't mind talking about sex, we liked to actually, it came up all the time, but not like we were actors in a made-for-cable porn movie. So we decided to try a not-so-obvious place to play.

The Big Green Bus was for "progressive adults in the Greater Chicago Area," whatever the hell that meant. Dani felt certain "progressive" meant perverted. One of the ways we tested a possible site was by trying to access it from her dad's computer upstairs. If her mom's anti-sex block let us view it, then we knew it was definitely a tame site for kiddies. **The Big Green Bus** got blocked. Just to see the home page you had to type in a birth date proving you were twenty-one or older and sign a release promising you were a "mature, professional adult." Its motto was: *A vehicle for single professionals to meet and socialize for a stop or two, or maybe go along for the long haul*—wherever *the bus might take you.* I couldn't decide if this was supposed to be funny or what. Dani thought not. It worried me who would be in here if this was supposed to be serious.

We threw out an opener on the message page—basically, *I'm lonely, young and female, help!*—and waited. It took longer than we thought it would. Dani made me refresh the page every few minutes. After nearly an hour, some guy checked out the fake photo Wynn had clipped from a website for preschool teachers called **The Peaceable Kidom**, and decided we were cute enough to ask if we wanted to instant message. Our name that night was Tabitha. Dani thought it sounded sophisticated. The guy's online name was Adguy1092, but once we started exchanging instant messages, he told us his name was actually Hank. He designed El ads in Chicago (Dani was convinced this was what city people called elevators until we Googled it).

After the very obvious **Rule #1: Don't use your real name**, we devised **Rule #2: Find out what your opponent really wants and determine why he thinks he can only get it online, so you can turn this against him later.**

Each time Hank provided an answer Dani didn't like (for example, Q: How many inches around are your biceps? A: Twelve inches), she would shout, "Lie!" and we'd stop for a moment to discuss a new approach. At one point her mom came down to see what the ruckus was all about. "It's a science game on the computer. They give you a bunch of true-or-false questions about stuff like dolphins and then the program rates your knowledge," she told a very skeptical Mrs. Dunham. Dani had gone to the trouble of providing an alibi should this moment come. As her mom came down the stairs, Dani clicked the little box at the bottom of the screen and up popped a photo of a dolphin munching on a dirty, yellow fish. "Some of these questions are so easy it's a little annoying. Sorry if I got too loud. I mean, really, who doesn't know a dolphin chews its cud like a cow? Why else would they be nicknamed sea cows? Jeez."

"I know, *right?*" I sounded like such a dumbass. When I panicked back then, I tended to imitate Dani. I even said, *"right?"* in a slightly higher pitch, something that used to drive me crazy when she did it.

"Sea cows," her mom said, "huh."

"Right," Dani said, "or that when they have to pass gas it comes out of their snort hole."

"You enjoying this game, Lynn?" Mrs. Dunham said, turning her skeptical squint on me. "About dolphins passing gas?" This last bit sounded more than a little sarcastic. I chewed my lip. Mrs. Dunham's eyes got even squintier. She yanked on Dani's earlobe. "You all aren't looking at naked sex pictures, are you?"

"No, ma'am," we said in a ragged chorus.

She let loose of Dani's ear.

"Well." She peered over Dani's shoulder at the photo of the dingy dolphin and its diseased-looking lunch. "Make sure you let Lynn have a turn, honey, and pipe down. Your father's going over his sales numbers."

Once her mom closed the door at the top of the stairs, Dani counted to thirty and then we got rid of Mr. Scabs the dolphin and went back to Hank, who seemed almost deranged by our short delay in answering his instant messages. We explained it away as a break for personal needs. Despite his growing clinginess, Dani had to work surprisingly hard to get him to admit why he really cruised around sites like this. Hank claimed to be tired of the singles scene, tired of going out to bars to meet people, and tired of going to work with a hangover. He'd only moved to Chicago for his job a couple of months before, so he didn't know anyone yet. Dani thought there was more to it than that. She was right. Finally, Hank admitted, he felt homesick for his hometown of Pana, Illinois, and these city women he met in the bars here intimidated him. "I'm always afraid they're laughing at me behind my back," he wrote. That's why he was so excited to meet a small-town girl like us. Dani laughed so hard the strawberry Yoo-hoo she was sipping on came out of her nose. I knew exactly how Hank felt. Well, almost.

"What a stupe," Dani said, unable to stop giggling. "Let's mess with him a little."

And thus we came to **Rule #3**, which was to be the rule that changed our aimless pranking into The Game: **Use the info you get from rule number two to make them do your bidding or simply to mess with their heads.** We decided to make Tabitha's life somewhat similar to our Algebra teacher, Ms. Oliff's, with some small adjustments. Like her being cool, for one.

Us: I'm twenty-five and there's not a soul in this crappy little nowhere burg to date. Everyone's either a kid or a geezer. I'm bored most of the time. Sometimes I sit up all night flipping through the Sears catalog and fantasizing about the men in the thermal underwear section.

Hank: I know the feeling. Even though I'm in a big city and there's lots to do, I don't have anyone to go out and do stuff with, so I end up at home most of the time. Sometimes I fantasize with magazines too.

"I bet you do, big boy," Dani said, snickering. "Probably spends all night in the bathroom with a copy of *Juggs*."

I considered pointing out she'd often done the same. Dani was fascinated by *Juggs* magazine. She even talked me into buying a copy from the Texaco station the summer before, and we spent an evening scrutinizing the various boobs on display, discussing their

design flaws. Six months later I discovered the magazine in her closet, tucked under her sweaters, even though she'd made a big pro-
duction of throwing it away in disgust the same night we bought it.
It looked wrinkled and well read. Some of the pages were marked
with dog-ears and had handwritten notes like *my boobs would look
like this if they were a cup size bigger.*

"I think we need to spice it up some," she said. "This is boring
the hell out of me. I think the problem here is he's a loser. I don't
believe I want to know his darkest secrets."

She sat down, scooched me out of the chair and set to typing.

Us: That sounds pretty pathetic. You live in one of the biggest
cities in America with lots of cool nightclubs and places to go. It's
not your imagination. Those women *are* laughing at you!

Hank wrote back that we were a nut-cutting, ball-busting bitch
and then put a block on our name and stopped sending messages.
We laughed.

"What the hell is a nut-cutter?" Dani asked.

"You," I said.

Rule #4

Don't get played.

The Bad, The Badder,
and The Ugly

ere are my mom's five ADD (After Dad Disappeared) boy-friends in the order they showed up:

1. Roy—This guy came into the emergency room one Sunday afternoon after an engine he was working on cracked the tree branch holding it up and broke five bones in his foot. He and my mom were only together for three months. I have no idea why it ended and I wasn't about to ask.

2. Joe Carey—I was never supposed to know about this one because he was married. Joe Carey was an insurance salesman. He came into the emergency room on a rainy Wednesday evening after slicing open his palm with a broken wine bottle, wearing a disposable diaper wrapped around his hand. He got seventeen stitches and my mom for about six months.

3. Keith—My mom discovered Keith rolling around and groaning on the floor of the emergency room one evening after he'd gobbled an enormous Mexican buffet dinner. He thought he was having a heart attack but was actually only suffering from heartburn. Three months later she told me not to mention his name again, explaining, "He's king of the rat bastards. I'll never eat a summer squash again." (I didn't ask.)

4. Duane—One day in November after school, there he was, sprawled out on the sofa drinking beer and looking at an

afternoon talk show. He had short black hair with a streak of gray above his left ear and eyes the color of rain clouds.

"Who the hell are you?" I asked.

He waited a full thirty seconds before he patted the cushion beside him and said, "I'm your new daddy. Come sit down over here with me and I'll let you have a sip of my beer."

I walked straight over to the hospital and found my mom. She told me he'd only be there a night. One night became a month. And like a bad roach infestation, she needed the help of pros to get rid of him—two orderlies from the hospital. He broke my favorite lamp as they dragged him out. It had a picture of a mermaid made from colored bits of stone.

5. Hayes—She met him long before he met her. Hayes was unconscious for several days, after running his truck into a ditch. When he came to, the first thing he saw was Mom changing his IV bag. "My old, sweet mama was wrong about me," he said. "I knew I'd go to heaven."

I tended to agree with his mama, but sadly, he was still here with mine.

Soap Opera Villain

Dani made me take the empty beer bottles with me. When the knock came, they were sitting in a plastic bag right there on our kitchen table. I should of tossed them in the grass on the bike ride home, but A) I was paranoid someone would see me and tell my mom or the police, and B) that's littering. I was still trying to think how I could dump them before my mom got back where there'd be zero chance of getting caught.

A decent breeze was blowing outside, so I'd left open the front and kitchen doors. Our window AC sucked rather than blew. It was a clear shot from the front door, down the hallway to the kitchen, and out the back door beside the sink, so I saw right away who it was. I thought about jumping over the breakfast bar that separated the kitchen from the living room, but it was too late. I'd been spotted.

"Your mama leave a package for me, cornflake?" Hayes asked through the screen door. He tapped again at the wooden frame with the Lucite cane he sometimes had a need for. He was the cutest of my mom's boyfriends, I'll give him that: short brown hair gelled up in spikes and a face like an oversexed soap opera villain. He must of done lots of sit-ups each morning because the times I saw him with his shirt off, his belly looked flat and tight and tan. On that day, however, he looked like the dog's dirty ass. When I let him in, he took off his sunglasses and his eyes were half hidden by puffy, greenish skin. His feet were bare and moist and blackened. Wherever he walked, he left behind gray moisture prints.

"I don't think she did, hoss," I said. I talked through my teeth, so he wouldn't smell the beer on my breath. I'd had four to Dani's two.

"Are you *positive*?" Hayes did a jittery little dance in the kitchen doorway. He lifted his arms and sent out whiffs of nastiness that smelled like the rotty juice that sometimes collects at the bottom of the fridge's produce drawer.

"If she did, she didn't tell me about it," I said, finding myself unconsciously imitating his weird jitter dance.

"I'm just going to go back and have me a look." He pushed past me before I had a chance to answer and kind of loped through the kitchen, favoring his short leg and wincing each time he took a step. I watched from the doorway and held my breath. He knocked over the sack of bottles on the kitchen table I'd tried to hide with newspaper, and I thought, Oh shit, now I'm doomed, but he didn't seem to notice or care. Hayes spent a few minutes rummaging about in the kitchen cabinets, before giving up to stumble through the living room, bumping into the shelves that held my mom's boat-in-a-bottle collection and almost knocking some down. He set them straight before going back into her bedroom. After shutting the door, Hayes commenced to tossing shit around in there and making a sound like a raccoon in a dumpster.

Our house was smallish, five rooms if you counted the bathroom, six if you counted the carport, and seven if you counted the little attic access between my closet and the living room. The front hallway, lined with elementary school photos of me from Kmart, led to a junction at the kitchen, forward took you past the sink to the kitchen door. If you took a right, you went into our biggest room, the living room, which stretched across the middle of the house from front to back like a saddle. From there, a worn trail in the carpet led straight past the couch, along the front windows, to the side hallway, a bathroom built for one, and on to our two non-spacious bedrooms. Mom's was on the left and had a good bit more moving-around space than mine. At the end of the hall, across from our rattletrap washer-dryer, was the door to my perfectly square, perfectly tiny sleeping box.

Five minutes of mayhem later, Hayes went limping into the bathroom, mumbling "fuck" over and over again like a prayer. What sounded a lot like my Suave Wild Cherry Blossom conditioner fell and rattled around in the shower. When he came out again this time, he had orange stuff on his upper lip. I thought for a moment he'd been drinking the liquid soap. Then I noticed the prescription cough syrup bottle in his hand. Hayes tossed it with a clatter into the sink.

"Bad cough," he said.

"Ah," I said.

I didn't remember him coughing once since he'd come, but if he had a craving to gulp syrup, it wasn't any skin off my behind.

"When's your wrinkled old ma get off?" he said

I didn't answer, since I'd heard her tell him this information twice already over the phone. I sat on the couch and looked at a man wrestle an alligator on the television. Hayes sat down beside me, stretching his back until it cracked. "Yu-up." He turned this into two long syllables. "So you playing the silent game with me here or maybe you just need a couple Q-tips? Huh? What's the good word, Little Flipper?" He made a dolphin sound. I edged away from him on the couch.

Without looking away from the TV, I told him she'd be home tomorrow morning. This was a trick my mom had taught me after I'd complained about him bugging me. "Just stop paying him any mind," Mom told me, "and he'll quit after a while. He just wants a reaction, any reaction."

"Okay," he said, almost to himself, and yawned wide enough to make his jaw pop. "That's alright. That'll work." He sat there for a few more seconds, breathing loudly and tapping out a complicated beat with his fingers on the back of the couch. Eight loud, wet sneezes came out, one right after another. Then he jumped up all of a sudden, banging his knee against the coffee table.

"Well, I'll be shoving off then." He limped over to the hall and looked about in a dazed way. I knew what he wanted.

"On the floor in the kitchen." I pointed to where his cane rested under a chair. "See you," I said.

"Yeah." He furrowed his forehead at me. "Thanks."

The hole in his muffler must of grown a good bit bigger, because I could hear that crap Toyota truck of his until it got out to the state highway. Hayes had a tendency toward moodiness, worse than my mom sometimes, but even for him this was whack-a-doo behavior. I wasn't quite sure what to make of it, but I knew better than to ask my mom for an explanation. I figured I'd be better off not saying anything at all unless she asked.

Types

Dani put her Shins CD in my mom's boom box. I'd been resistant to it at first because a senior girl at school had got her into them. An ex-cheerleader burnout named Barbara Ann that Dani idolized for some reason. Dani's Shins thing started with a Zach Braff movie, *Garden State*, that Barbara thought was pretty intense. She got so worked up over it she must of watched it a dozen or so times. The Shins were one of the bands on the soundtrack, so Dani bought the album. I didn't care all that much for the movie, or Braff's show. Even my mom hated Braff's goofy hospital show. In my experience, people at the hospital looked worn and grumpy. No song-and-dance numbers, just kids crying. It came as a surprise, then, when the album grew on me. I sometimes found myself humming along without realizing it.

"So," she said, raising an eyebrow, "what's your type?"

"I'm not sure I have a type," I said.

"Of course you do," Dani said. "Everybody has a type. You might not know what it is yet, but you've got one. Believe me."

Dani and me were sitting around the kitchen table at my house drinking stolen beer and looking at her rock star collection. My mom worked a double shift that day and wouldn't be home until seven the next morning, so we could do pretty much whatever we wanted. In this case, doing whatever we wanted meant drinking my mom's beer and talking about boys. The week before, my mom had come across a sale at the Quik & Eazy convenience store in

Statesboro, which everyone called the Quick & Sleazy. They were getting rid of their whole stock of a beer called Wanker. Each bottle had a different picture of a girl in a bikini on the label. For some reason they were selling it for $8.23 a case. I imagine there must of been something wrong with it, but it tasted alright and it gave you a buzz. My mom went ahead and bought ten cases of Wanker and stacked them up in the carport. She had to make two trips in her little '89 Ford Festiva to get it all home. So now we had hundreds of beers, but no cereal or bread. For breakfast I'd roll pressed ham and American cheese into little tubes and eat them with my fingers.

"So what's your type, then?" I said.

"I have complicated taste, so I actually have more than one type, but all my men pretty much fit in the same category."

"All your men?" I laughed hard enough to make beer fizz into my sinuses. Dani frowned. "Alright," I asked, "what category?"

"Well, for example, I only like men with brown hair. The darker the better. But not black hair, because you don't want someone who looks too much like you do, and not blond hair, because I'm a Leo almost on the cusp of Virgo."

"But, wait, I thought you liked Eminem? How's he fit in if you only go for brunettes? He's got blond hair."

"See, that's where it gets complicated. Eminem has blond hair, but it's bleached blond. His actual hair color is brown, so he fits into my type."

"How do you know he has brown hair? Whenever I've seen it, it's always yellow." I opened another warmish beer. It foamed over and made a mess of the tablecloth.

"It's *so* not yellow," she nearly yelled. "It's platinum blond."

"What do you go by then? The eyebrows?"

She calmed herself with a sip of beer and settled into the vinyl cushion on the kitchen chair. "That's a good clue, but you can't always tell for sure from the eyebrows. Sometimes they're lighter or darker. Look at my eyebrows."

I did. She'd plucked them into arches that gave her face a startled look. When she really was surprised, they looked like hand-drawn rooftops over her eyes. There was nothing realistic about them. In fact, one was just the tiniest bit higher than the other. But I saw her point—her eyebrows were a couple of shades lighter than her head hair. With the August sun pouring through the window onto her face, they seemed almost brown while the hair pulled back into pigtails was shiny black. The color of wet tires.

"Do you see?"

"Yeah," I said. "They're almost brown."

"Exactly. If my hair was bleached and you didn't know any better, you might think my hair was brown."

"So how do you know then?"

"I'll show you." She opened her rock star collection and flipped through it.

The rock star collection was a three-ring binder filled with sheets of heavy black construction paper. She organized it alphabetically by band, and then by the individual members of the band. Each page was covered with photographs of rock stars clipped from magazines or printed up from websites. Beneath each picture was a handwritten explanation of the photograph: name of the rock star, band, date of the photograph, location, and the name of the magazine or fan site it came from. She had subscriptions to about eight music and movie magazines. Sometimes she also added a personal note like, "Eddie has looked much better in other pictures, but this one shows off his wrists. They are amazing and tan and strong here. However, those dark circles under his eyes make me worry about his health. Drugs?" The binder we were looking at that day was volume two. She'd been collecting rock stars since before I met her, and by the end of eighth grade, she had filled up her first binder. Nearly three hundred pages, back and front. She hardly looked at the old one anymore since she believed her taste in music had matured a lot since then. The first volume was mostly filled with boy bands from the nineties. "I only put men in the new collection," she'd told me. All in all, there must of been at least two hundred pages and ten times that many pictures in volume two. You could spend a whole day looking at it, and we often did.

"Look here." She turned to the Eminem section, which had grown to almost twenty pages. "I've got a couple of pictures where you can just barely see his roots and they're brown." She jabbed at a photograph of him crouched down by a burnt-out car. He glared at something outside the frame that seemed to make him very angry.

I took a big gulp of beer and narrowed my eyes for a better view. "I don't think I see."

"Look closer." She tapped Eminem's head with her thumb and clucked at me. "At home I use a magnifying glass, but I forgot to bring it."

We bent our heads together, noses almost touching the page.

"Do you see it now?" she said, her forehead wrinkled up in serious concentration.

"Yeah, I think so." I didn't.

"It took me a while to find that one. I can't tell you how relieved I was. I'd started to worry he might not be my type."

"But he is?"

"Definitely."

"How do you find out what your type is?"

"The most important thing is they need to look similar to you, but they can't look exactly like you. So, like with you, you're a dish-water blonde with light brown eyes. Your type can have darker or lighter hair or eyes, but they can't be the same. Also, they've got to be at least five inches taller than you."

"Why five?"

"Well, the actual rule is your head can't be taller than his nose. Five's just a nice round number."

"Oh," I said, wondering whose rule this was. I picked two of my mother's cigarette butts out of the ashtray. Mom had a tendency to smoke four or five drags and then jab them out like she was killing something, so there were always a lot of smokable butts. I used to be able to steal a pack now and then, but I'm pretty sure she figured out I was doing it. About two months earlier, she'd started hiding her cartons.

"Give me one without the lipstick, please," Dani said, pointing to the ashtray. "This is gross enough without having to feel like I'm kissing your mom."

We swapped cigs and I opened up another beer. I'd drunk two over the last hour and already I could feel my tongue getting thicker. A cloud passed across the sun and the kitchen darkened for a moment. The sudden change of light made me dizzy.

"Your type," Dani said, moving her frown from my peeling purple toenail polish up to my nose, "also has to be at least three years older than you."

"So, could Andy Tyson be my type?"

Andy was a senior when we were freshman. I'd had a thing for him since Christmas last, when I saw him buying a paper sack of screws at the hardware store. Those tight jeans he wore really clinched it.

"Hell, no!" Dani scrunched up her face. "For one thing, you've got almost the exact same nose. I mean exact."

"I do?" This made me feel good and I must of looked it.

"I'm not sure that's something to be proud of."

"Fuck you," I said in my joking voice, which was higher and came out of my nose. She laughed, and so did I, but inside I kind of meant it. I knew she meant what she'd said about my nose.

"But the reason I brought it over was so I could show you my new section." She flipped to the back of the book where the construction paper was gray. "I started it on Tuesday when I was watching *E!* It's the dream man section. I'm trying to make pictures of all the variations of my types. When I get enough, I'm going to start a new collection book just for them."

The pictures in this new section reminded me of the paper dolls I used to play with as a little kid. The kind where you color the clothes with crayons and then cut them out. The clothes have tabs on the sides, so your paper doll can change outfits. Dani had taken rock stars and actors and cut them into pieces and then put them back together. She didn't mess much with their faces, but she'd given them other people's hairstyles and arms and legs, and in one case, a different neck. They creeped me out a little bit.

"They look weird," I said, risking Dani's bitchiness.

"I'm still getting the hang of it," she said, with an expression a couple of face muscles away from a pout. "If you want me to, I'll see if I can figure out what your type would be." She squinted at me carefully. "Maybe a blond. Your hair's really almost brown. Like something brown that's been left out in the sun too long."

"Thanks," I said.

"I didn't mean it in a bad way," she said.

A Tupperware Box Full
of Fresh-Sucked Pills

woke up in my living room at twilight the following day. I'd left a puddle of drool shaped like a dog's head on the armrest of the couch. Dani and me had played The Game the night before until the little window above her bed went from black to pink to orange. I only dozed for an hour or two at the most before Dani's mom woke us up so she could take Dani to her dental appointment. The last thing I remembered after coming home was turning on the tube. It was still on. A woman with hair the color of a tongue explained that the juice of several carrots and a handful of what looked like yard clippings would remove any and all blockage from your large intestine, up to and including the mouth of the anus. She actually said that. The mouth of the anus.

I clicked off the TV and heard three distinct thuds over in the other condo in the duplex. Or at least it sounded like next door, but maybe—nah, I thought, our house was empty when I got here. Nobody could sneak by while I was sleeping, could they? I wondered what Mr. Cannon, our hundred-year-old bachelor neighbor, was up to over there.

Then something fell over and crashed. This time I knew for certain the sound wasn't coming from Mr. Cannon's side. Did whoever it was that made that sound hear me click the TV off? Shit. I looked around for something heavy. An old wine bottle with a candle stuck in it sat beside me on the end table. I hefted it once and tiptoed down the side hall, flipping open my cell phone as I went and dialing 911, so all I'd have to do was press send. The glow from its screen made the darkened hallway blue. I paused next to the squeaky spot in the flooring beside the water-heater closet when I heard another bang. This one sounded like somebody slapping the bottom of an empty metal trash can, and this time I knew without a doubt it came from my mom's room. The door was ajar. A shadow moved across the crack. Four steps more. I put my thumb on the send button. Someone snuffled his nose and hummed a broken piece of a song. I knelt and peeked through the doorway. The dark shape of a hunched-over back sat at my mom's vanity. An arm moved up and down with slow, deliberate jerks. And each jerk ended with a soft crunch, like somebody grinding broken glass into pavement with his heel. When the shadow turned to the side, I saw who it was.

"Hayes," I said, loud enough to make him jump a couple inches off the seat. I snapped the phone shut. "How long have you been back here? What the hell are you doing?"

Hayes crossed the worn, green carpet to shut the door, but I beat him to it, wedging my foot in the gap right as he grabbed the handle.

"Little Flipper." He tried a couple of different smiles out on me before he settled on one that made him look like he had to go to the bathroom. "Right. Shouldn't you be in bed? School comes early and all that." He looked down at his wrist, but he had no watch. "I didn't even realize you were here."

This was such an obvious lie I didn't even respond to it. I went up on my toes to get a better look at what he'd been doing in there. He shifted his body to block my view. But I caught a quick glimpse anyway. A pile of crumpled Ziploc bags and two brown plastic serving trays from the hospital covered one side of the vanity table. On the other side was my grandma's old wooden mortar and pestle and a Tupperware container with a long, yellow cigarette burn on the lid. Hayes turned his face away and spit something into his hand, gave it a quick glance and then dropped it into the front pocket of his red plaid cowboy shirt.

I shifted back and forth, but he moved with me. A sort of half-assed country two-step. "Doing a little early evening grinding, huh?" I asked.

Hayes made a noncommittal grunting sound.

"Mom doesn't mind you using all her stuff, I guess."

I leaned my body to the left as though about to take a step in that direction and then faked him out and went right. He moved to the left to block me, but I slipped on by, smiling all the while. Once I stepped into the light, I saw a pile of orange pills and green pills on one of the hospital trays and a little mound of white powder in the Tupperware container. It looked to be pill pieces he was mashing up in the pestle, but the crunched-up bits weren't orange or green.

"Doing some freelance work for the pharmacy? I'm glad you finally found a job." If Mom knew about this shit, I thought, she'd jab him in the ass with a serving fork, and with good reason. "So if I ask Mom about this, she'll know what you're up to? She don't mind you doing this in her room, huh?"

"Well, see . . ." Hayes kind of trailed off, nodding his head and chewing at his lower lip. "I'm in a bit of a jam here, Flipper. Your mom knows about the one part of this—"

I held up my hand. "Don't, Hayes," I said. "Ain't none of it any of my concern. Don't tell me about it. Please. Then I won't have to lie for you if anyone asks. I don't want to have any part in—" I waved my hand at the mess he'd left behind on the vanity table. "But I know one thing. Mom'd throw a huge fit if she saw your crap spread out like that. I can't even start to guess why you chose her bedroom to do all this in."

"I needed the wooden thing. You know, the—" He made a

grinding motion with his hand. "—the crunch-crunch thing over there. And you were sleeping and I didn't want to, uh, disturb you. Look, I'll finish up pretty quick and be out of your hair." He pulled the little thing he'd spit into his hand out of his pocket and polished it with the hem of his shirt. It was a pill with greenish speckles on it. It looked to me like he'd been sucking the color off the pills and then mashing them into powder.

"No, no, no. You got to get this project or whatever it is out of here, Hayes. I can't have the police coming in here, say, and finding you sucking on pills and then crunching them. That kind of bad thing. Mom would kill us both."

"Hey, sure, no problem, I get it." Hayes set to scooping up his stuff and dumping it into bags. He hummed that little tune again as he packed. The melody was cheerful and familiar and seemed to jolly him along a little. He picked up the mortar and pestle and stared at it for a long while in a blank way.

"Take it with you if you want. Just be sure to bring it back quick. Knowing Mom, she'll get a notion to use that thing after work tomorrow for the first time in ten years."

"Thanks, thanks. That's perfect, Flipper. I'll be out in a blink of a lamb's tail."

I walked back to the kitchen and stared at my reflection in the door of the microwave oven. I flashed on Mom being led out of the house in handcuffs. I leaned across the sink and took a drink of warm water from the faucet. Even then I knew this wouldn't be the end of it. As I examined a newly formed whitehead above my eyebrow, the front door banged shut. I listened for the sound of his truck, but he must of walked from somewhere.

The world outside turned a deep, dusty blue. Along the roadside ditch, fireflies blinked. Crickets in the bush below the window complained about the heat. Somewhere in the endless evening sky beyond the backyard trees, heat lightning washed the horizon with light. Gone even before I had time to name it for what it was. I said its name out loud afterward because the thought of it made me smile. "Heat lightning," I told the empty kitchen. Right then I remembered the tune Hayes was humming. It was one Mom sometimes sang in the shower when she was in a good mood: "Sunshine Keeps Falling on My Head."

L.L.

I met Logan Loy by complete accident. I became his friend on purpose. Dani and me were on the Internet when I first came across him, but we weren't exactly playing The Game. We'd just finished a very short and intense session with a man who claimed to be a history professor from Liverpool who was visiting America. After a few silly small-talk messages, he told us he was doing something very nasty with a peeled carrot and wanted us to try it ourselves and tell him about it. He kept calling us "honey bunch," which is what Dani's dad sometimes called her, and this freaked her out a little. Dani pushed me aside to tell him carrots were only good for feeding pigs and other livestock, so what did that make him? He wrote back, lightning fast, "You're a fatty, aren't you, honey bunch? You're the little fat piggy here. Not me." Dani's eyes welled up with tears. She jumped away from the computer as though it had snapped at her. He slipped in a few more messages before I could block him. "I'm going to tear a hole in your belly button and fuck your piggy fat. I'm going to hunt you down and kill you with my cock, honey bunch. Don't think I can't find you. I'm looking at you through your webcam right now."

This last part startled even me because Wynn had set up a webcam the day before, although we'd yet to put it to use. Dani covered the golf ball-sized camera with her hand and then unplugged it. I thought maybe we should take a break from the computer. When I told her this, she did something strange. Her face wrinkled up like a clenched fist and she pounded on the desk, shouting, "No, I'm not going to let that nasty man ruin my game!" She shouted this so loud her mom called down the stairs to see if she was alright. I suggested we try something a little different.

All this had Dani wired tighter than a broken jaw. I thought she needed distraction. Since Dani had been going on and on about wanting to see The Shins in concert, her favorite band from that soundtrack album, I hunted down their website.

"Look," I said, "they're all dressed like superheroes and lying in bed together."

Dani pushed me aside and scrolled around looking for nearby concert dates. Per usual, she got hung up on the message board. There were only a few people leaving messages, but in no time at all, Dani had them sending her private messages.

After about ten minutes of this, Dani finally went to the bathroom and I took over. She'd waited just a drip too long to do it. As she waddled away, I noticed a small damp spot on the seat of her pants, and when she came back, she'd changed into shorts. I never said anything, knowing it'd cause an explosion of denials and a long period of silent treatment if I did, but it cheered me a good bit to see. The very moment I sat down, a fan named L.L. sent me a private message. He asked me my name and where I lived, and for some reason, I really to this day have no idea why, I broke the first rule of The Game and told him the truth. It turned out that L.L. lived in Savannah, about an hour's drive from Metter.

"Are you going to the concert in Charleston next week?" Logan typed.

"That sounds great, but I don't have a car right now." And probably never will, I thought.

"What do you look like?"

I hesitated. Who's talking here? Me? Dani? One of our combo dealies? Again, I told the truth. "Dark blond hair. 5'2". Brown eyes."

"I wish I could see you right now. It's hard to imagine what you look like from six words. That's the worst part about trying to talk this way."

"I agree. Plus, everyone lies," I typed, smiling. "Even though it's impossible to imagine and you could be lying, what do you look like?"

Dani returned while I waited to find out. When I explained about L.L., she really lost it, telling me we had an agreement to always, always follow the rules and I'd broken the most important one. She said she felt betrayed and her face turned red again.

According to the clock on Dani's computer, Logan Loy took exactly four minutes and twenty-three seconds to write back, which felt like an especially long time with Dani yelling at me the way she did. When his response finally came, it said, "5'11". Blond hair. Blue eyes. 165 lbs. 25 yrs old."

That's when Dani changed the angry little tune she'd been singing. Or screaming.

"Oh, shit," she said. "I can't believe it."

"What?" I said.

"He's your exact type."

"That's if he's telling the truth," I said.

"Well, of course," she said, stiffening up a little, "there's always that."

"I don't know," I said. "I thought you told me I wasn't mature enough for someone that old."

"The type is flexible when it comes to the age question, as long as it goes up and not down. The opposite is true of boys' types. But according to his stats, this one's perfect. You've got a keeper here."

"What about his face? For all we know, he could have a face like an elephant's ass. Or like Wynn's."

"There's always that, too," she said, using her *oh-the-things-I-must-put-up-with* voice and rubbing her eyes the way her mom did after she took off her reading glasses. "You're always such a glass-half-empty person. Look at the full side for a change, and with this guy, it's so far so full."

Now that she'd decided it was a good thing, Dani was about five hundred times more excited than I was, but I'll admit to being pretty interested in this L.L. person. As usual, completely unsure of myself about romantic questions, I took her advice to the letter. Literally. I asked him if he posted on this message board a lot. He said it was his first time, but he came to the website every once in a while to check on the concert schedule. I told him our story. Well, part of it, anyway. But for once, everything I wrote was true.

"Make a date to meet here again. Tomorrow evening," Dani said, hopping up and down on one foot and squeezing her earlobes. She'd been wearing her chunky, painfully heavy turquoise earrings all afternoon.

I asked and he agreed. Dani let out a shriek. I'll admit to feeling more and more excited each time this business with L.L. went another step further. He wanted to know my e-mail address. Dani and me looked at each other. We used Wynn's e-mail address every time we set up fake accounts, and one day we'd even used it when we ordered shoes with Dani's mother's Visa card while she was out shopping at the Piggly Wiggly. At the time it seemed funny. We imagined Wynn getting all these sexy or angry e-mails from guys we'd flirted with and then devastated in **The Big Green Bus**. It was Dani's stated policy to never give out our real e-mail addresses to people we met online. But we weren't officially playing The Game, and then there was also the fact I'd already told him my real name and hometown.

"Tell him you'll give it to him tomorrow if he meets you, and then we can go ahead and make a new one now. Just in case he's a freak," Dani said.

Logan told me he was about to go on-duty and he looked forward to messaging with me the next day. And that was it.

"On-duty?" I asked her. "What do you think that means?"

"Maybe he's a lifeguard. Who cares?" Dani shrugged. "You have an electronic date. You have an electronic date," she sang, giving me a giant hug and dancing me around in a circle. She smelled like fabric softener and fresh hair spray.

"You make him sound like a robot."

And that's how the serious fun ended and the serious trouble began. Sounds innocent enough, huh?

A Swallowed But

"I'll talk to him about it," Mom said. Twin clouds of smoke gushed out of her nose. She crushed out her cigarette after taking two drags and rubbed her eyes with the heels of her palms. I hadn't seen her in two days and this seemed important.

"That's it?" I asked.

"What do you want me to do, sweetie?"

"Mom, he was sucking on pills and then crunching them up with grandma's old pestle. You don't think that's a little—" I grimaced. "—odd?"

I set down the plate of toast and poached eggs—barely cooked and wobbly with warm, raw yolk, just the way she liked them—and handed her a fork. She broke off the corner of her toast and dabbed it in the bright gold yolk several times until it popped and oozed.

"Just let me sit here a while and relax before you start hammering at me with all this." She took another bite of toast. "I think you need a new pair of school shoes. There's a sale going on over at the J. C. Penney in Statesboro."

"Mom, why aren't you taking this seriously?"

"I saw a real cute pair of sandals I think you'd like. But then they probably wouldn't do for when it gets cool. If the sale's good, maybe we could get you a couple—"

"I think you should break up with him."

She dropped her fork and folded her arms across her chest. The only sound in the room was the faucet *drip-drip-dripping*.

"How about this, Lynn? You just attend to your business and let me handle my own affairs. The way I see it, this has nothing to do with you and I don't appreciate taking romantic advice from a pimply teenage girl."

Almost without meaning to, my fingers found the zit above my eyebrow.

Mom slapped the table, making the saltshaker bounce and fall over.

"You hear?"

"Yes, ma'am," I said. And swallowed the *but* I wanted to add.

The Dreamiest Arms in
People Magazine

My dream man was pasted on a piece of blue construction paper. His hair was blond and swept back to the right. Dani cut it out jaggedly and so it looked more like a scare wig than real hair. He had the face of a hero from a recent action movie, but the eyes had been colored in blue with a marker. The arms were too long for the body and stuck out at odd angles as though he'd fallen from a great height and broken several bones. His muscles bulged under an Old Navy T-shirt and something else bulged under a skin-tight pair of Calvin Klein underpants. For some reason, she'd also given him shiny, black, tasseled loafers she'd cut out and glued on top of his bare feet.

"His name's Dylan," Dani told me when she gave him to me. "Or should I say Logan?"

I rolled my eyes to heaven.

"Don't pout. It makes you look—"

I did not want to know what it made me look like. "He's got nice arms," I said, just to say something.

"They're what's-his-name's arms . . . uh . . . the drummer from that band you like."

"Oh, yeah, I can see the tip of the drumstick in his hand."

"I've put a lot of thought into this, Lynn. I used the stats from the talk you and Logan had the other day," Dani said. "And now maybe you found the real him. The real dream man, I mean."

"Yeah," I said, "maybe."

Cats and Dogs

t took a few days for Hayes to return the mortar and pestle. When he came, I was in the bathroom scrubbing the ring of soap scum off the bathtub, so I didn't hear the door. Mom never seemed to notice this brown ring of sticky muck, but I got tired of watching it grow each morning. I noticed a dark blob of shadow slide across the tile floor. But when I turned around, no one was there. I took off my rubber kitchen gloves and set them on the edge of the tub.

First, I noticed the mortar and pestle sitting on Mom's vanity table. It took me a moment to hear the scraping sound on the other side of the bed. I stepped around to see what was making it, and there was Hayes picking through the carpet on his hands and knees.

"Hey, dorko," I shouted, making him jerk up and hit his head on the corner of the dresser, "you drop your brain?"

"Ha, ha," Hayes said, rubbing the back of his head. He looked pasty-faced and agitated. "Ha. Say, Little Flipper, I might of mislaid something important here the other day. A white plastic package wrapped in duct tape about yea big?" He stretched out his hands the length of a cat's tail. "I was hoping maybe . . . actually, come to think on it, it might could be in a clear Ziploc bag. Anyway, I remember I put it in a safe place and now it's, well, too safe. But it's, umm, very—"

"Important?" I said, enjoying this way too much.

"Yeah." He smiled and rocked from heel to toe on his beat-up old cowboy boots, looking very pleased to see I understood. "Very. Man, Flipper, man, I can't thank you—"

"Nope." I edged forward a little. "Haven't seen anything like that. I would of noticed too."

"No, really, no fooling now," Hayes said, his eyes shiny with something that looked awful close to real tears. "You got to understand. I'm serious as shit here. I mean, this is important. To me. Shit. Fuck. I got to—damn it—"

"Finish making your pill flour?"

His eyes darted here and there, scanning the carpet. "If I hadn't of lost that package, it wouldn't of needed doing. And now I'm all out of—" He gave me a crafty look, the type he invented when he thought he was getting one over on me. This belief in his own sneakiness appeared to cheer him a good bit.

"What was that stuff you were making?" I asked.

Hayes explained the pills were some type of hormones for dogs. Dog relaxers, he called them. All the while, he kept picking up bits of lint, lost buttons, and even an unpopped popcorn kernel, holding them up to the light and then chucking them over his shoulder.

"So why were you sucking on them? Aren't you worried you'll start growing fur and some sort of weird dog muscles?"

"It's the easiest way to get the coating off, so I can crush them. If you're careful, they don't even get all that wet. You just brush them off with your shirt and then you're good to go." Hayes gnawed on his thumb for a second before deciding to pull the dresser out a few inches. This was work that required grunting. Whatever he was looking for, it didn't seem to be back there. He left the dresser pulled back from the wall and moved on to the vanity.

It still sounded hinky to me. But I knew Hayes really did breed dogs. Under normal circumstances, that's about all he wanted to talk about. He trained rat terriers. Mom said he actually fought them against rats.

"Looky here," I said, bending over and snatching one of his dog pills off the carpet under the vanity.

Hayes slid over the bed with both hands out. His eyes got big and hungry. I closed my hand around the pill and stepped back. He made a swipe at it, but I jumped away.

"Come on now, Flipper. Give it here!"

"That ain't no way to behave. Calm down, Mr. Grabby Hands."

I opened my hand and looked at his pill. A dull green thing about the size of an Advil with the number 80 pressed into one side. I cupped both hands around it and shook it like a pair of dice. Hayes's eyes followed every movement of my hands. He smiled, but it looked like it took a lot of work to get those lip muscles curling. As I was about to sit down on the bed beside him, he grabbed my wrist and tried to pry open my hand.

"Ow!" I shrieked. "Stop, you asshole. You're hurting me." I kicked him on the shin as hard as I could and his grip loosened long enough for me to slip away. I was out the door and into the bathroom in a flash. The lock clicked into place barely a second before his hand shook the knob.

"Sorry about that, Flipper. I didn't mean to hurt you," Hayes said through the door crack. "It's only I need it back. It's kind of important."

The bathroom door had one of those easy-to-pick locks. The kind you can open with a bobby pin. I didn't have much time before he'd get in.

"Please, Flipper. Just give me the pill."

"You had a whole mess of them the other day. Why you need this one pill so bad?"

"I told you, I hid the main bunch real good and I seem to of forgot where. Either that or the trash man got it when he carted off the sofa on my lawn. I might could of tucked them there for safe-keeping. I don't know. Anyway, those you saw were set aside for something else. Then when I lost the big stash, I had to crush the set-aside ones for the buyer along with a bit of baking soda to fill out the bag some. You know, for it to look like a respectable count. But it weren't hardly enough pill and too much soda besides. I need more pills. Way it stands now, that shit ain't fit for nothing. Believe you me, I tried."

"*You* tried? You ate some of the dog drugs yourself?"

"On a dog. He ate it. Didn't much like it as far I could tell. Barked all night." Hayes poked at the lock with something metallic.

"You bust in on me, Hayes, and I'll flush it. I swear I will."

The scratching stopped. Hayes thought so hard, I could hear his last five brain cells overheating on the other side of the door. They made the same sound my mom's transmission did when it was on the fritz. I rubbed my thumbnail up and down the edge of the jamb.

"You hear that, Hayes? It's your pill. It seems to want to take a swim. Tell me the truth now."

Hayes took a breath, held it for two or three toe taps, then let it out with a defeated grumble. The pills, according to him, were really to dope the dogs, so they would lose their fights after he bet against them. If he crushed the pills, it made it easier to slip the stuff into a poor dog's water bowl. Somebody had offered him big bucks for a bunch of these pills.

"God," I said, "and you lost them. Maybe it's for the best. Seems like a low-down business."

"Yeah, well. If you ain't noticed, I'm a little short on folding money these days." He sighed. "The drugs don't hurt them none. The dogs, I mean."

This story, I figured, was just sleazy enough to be true. I pushed the pill out through the crack under the door. His plan seemed to me a mite too clever to of started its life in Hayes's itty-bitty brain. The number of normal brains in his circle of pals numbered exactly zero. I hope you know what you're doing, Mom, I thought. If it *was* you who put this idea in his head.

"There," I said, "give this to your dogs with my compliments."

"God bless you, Flipper."

Sweet Talk

That night, we found out Logan was in the Army. And that his name was Logan. ("Logan?" Dani asked me. "Isn't that a kind of berry?") He was stationed at Hunter Army Airfield and worked in a huge hangar where they trained him to fix helicopter rotors. That's what the on-duty comment meant. I told him I was fifteen, even though Dani told me I should lie and tell him I was eighteen, and he didn't seem to care all that much. He wrote age was unimportant if two people got along.

"Very true," Dani said. "If it wasn't for his blond hair, I'd think he might be my type."

Dani pressed me to ask more questions, and to do it faster. She'd had trouble with the computer that afternoon and been forced to call Wynn and ask him to come over and fix it, and now she was afraid it could go out again at any moment. But I didn't want to rush. I liked the rhythm of how we were talking. Almost right from the start, all of it was romantic. Not romantic as in, I-can't-wait-to-hold-you-in-my-arms kind of talk. It just seemed like everything we discussed always came back around to relationships. An exchange would begin with him talking about his car and how old and crappy it was (Dani was already planning for him to come get us and take us out on the town in Savannah, so one of the first things she had me ask him was if he had a car), and then a couple of messages later he explained how he got his first real kiss in that very car back when it was still his dad's. Dani wanted me to ask him if he used his tongue the first time, but I wouldn't do it. "I bet you he didn't," she kept saying.

When I asked him why he joined the Army, he said it was because he'd been so mad about the towers getting blown up, but then a little later he admitted it was also because he wanted to go to college and didn't have the tuition money. The Army promised to help pay his way. Later, Logan told me he always said that bit about the towers when he first met someone because it sounded better. The more he told me about his reasons for signing up, the more complicated they got. A lot of it seemed to have to do with his father and his hero brother. Logan said he'd already been on one tour in Iraq, and almost as soon as he got home, the Army told him he'd have to go back for a second one.

"So, he's a war hero, too," was Dani's reaction.

We only got to exchange messages for about twenty minutes because he was using someone else's laptop and they kicked him off to play a video game where you were a giant ant and you had to herd aphids, or some such, but before he said good-bye, he gave us his cell phone number.

"I can already see us drinking frozen daiquiris down on River Street," Dani said. "This is beautiful."

Dani was all set for me to call him right away—she had visions of daiquiris dancing in her head—but I reminded her of one of her own rules. *Always wait three days to call.*

Crazy Spell

On the day after I learned L.L. meant Logan Loy, it got up to one hundred and two degrees by lunchtime. This always meant more accident victims over at the hospital. According to Dr. Drose, people had a tendency to go loony with the heat because it broiled their brains. During the winter, a tense situation might stay tense—say, for example, an out-of-work husband cooped up at night with his overworked wife—but during a hot summer spell, this same situation would pop—the pop in this case coming from the same husband's fist making contact with his wife's nose, or from the skillet of a work-frazzled wife on the husband's skull. What it meant in my day-to-day life was that there were twice as many patients to attend to and Mom hardly ever came home, and when she did she'd be in some weird zone like she was now, sitting in front of the TV and spooning nacho cheese dip straight out of the jar while drinking a cup of coffee and smoking a cigarette—all at the same time. I'm not kidding. I saw her take a drag while she chewed.

"Lynn, honey," she said, as I opened the refrigerator. Her voice had a tight sound to it. I thought she might of noticed the missing beer.

"Yeah?"

"If Hayes comes by—" She jabbed out her half-smoked cigarette and gulped down the rest of her coffee.

"Uh-huh."

"Do me a favor and don't let him in the house."

I stopped rummaging in the crisper and turned to look at her.

"You all break up?"

"Jesus, Lynn."

"Well, then, how come?"

"I'd just prefer him to stay out of the house when I'm not around."

"What? He steal something?"

Mom ignored this.

"You sure you all ain't breaking up?" I couldn't help but smile.

She pushed herself off the couch with a groan, picked up her purse, and stretched both arms above her head. "He's just going through a spell." She inspected her reflection in one of the glass doors of the china hutch, making a face like she was intent on scaring something inside there. The gravy boat, maybe. She wiped away a smudge of stray lipstick from a front tooth with her thumb.

"I think he's taking them dog pills himself," I said. "Cross my heart, I could of sworn I saw fresh fur growing on the back of his neck the other day."

She gave me a look and picked up her quilted cigarette bag. "Just don't let him in, alright? You think you can handle that?"

"When are you going to be home again?"

She opened the kitchen door and stepped out. "I have no idea, honey. Delia had to go to Brunswick for her uncle's funeral and I'm covering her shift."

"There's nothing to eat here."

"In the coffee can on top of the fridge, there's some money. Use that to buy a frozen burrito or something at the Texaco station."

I pulled it down and popped the plastic top off. "There's only a handful of change in here."

"Lynn, please." She made her *bad teenager, heel* expression. Then she shut the door and was off.

Phony

I let it ring three times before I picked it up.

"Hey," a man said. It was a voice I didn't recognize, so I waited for him to say something else before I answered him. "Hello." The pitch of his voice went up a little on the *o*. "Somebody there?" The man spoke in a gruff, southern accent, definitely a Wiregrass accent, so I thought he might be someone my mom knew.

"Hey," I said.

"Hayes there?"

"What?" I said.

"Hayes. I'm looking for Hayes. He there?"

"No, sir."

"You know when he'll be back?" The man coughed. It was a cough that sounded about twenty thousand cigarettes deep. "Ma'am?" he added after a cautious pause.

"He doesn't live here, sir."

"That don't matter. He's over there a lot, ain't he?"

"Sometimes." I let out a breath, wondering if I'd made a mistake admitting this. "I don't understand what you want." I forced myself to leave off the *sir* at the end.

"How about," he said, "you just give me the address where you are."

"If you're looking for him, why don't you go to his house? That's usually what people do when they're trying to find somebody. Not call a stranger's house asking after street addresses they have no business with."

This made him laugh until he coughed again, and then he coughed until he brought up something he felt the need to hawk and spit. The thick, wet sound of it came out of his mouth and through the phone lines. Then he hung up.

Doing It

"**I** think I'm ready to have sex," Dani told me.

"With who?"

"I don't mean I have someone picked out. I just feel like I'm ready now. I'm old enough. I might even need it." She went over to her bed and lay on her back. Her hair spilled onto the quilt like a black puddle of oil and she stretched out her arms and sighed.

"How do you know?"

She closed her eyes and kicked her legs up in the air, pumping them like she was riding an invisible bike. The springs in the mattress made a soft ping sound each time she kicked out a foot. "I can feel it."

"In your head?" I got up and sat beside her on the bed. Her pedaling made me bounce.

"No, of course not. I feel it right there." She stopped her imaginary bike race and pointed to a spot right above her belly button.

"Your stomach?" I said, carefully.

"Somewhere inside there. Maybe it's my womb. It's a kind of tickly-itchy feeling. I can't quite explain it."

"Your womb itches?" Something about this cracked me up and I giggled.

"Don't act like such a baby. I'm serious. I think it might be, I don't know, unnatural maybe."

"Well, my womb doesn't itch."

Upstairs, her mom stomped across the living room. A faucet turned on and off.

"I don't think I'm supposed to want it this much," Dani whispered to me without moving her lips and then glanced up at the ceiling as though her mom might be squatting on the floor, listening with a drinking glass pressed to the linoleum.

"But you haven't even done it before. How do you know that's what it is you want so bad?" I put a hand on my belly and tried to feel around inside my womb with my mind. "Maybe you're just constipated again, like when you had to get the enema treatment."

Dani sat up to pick a piece of pink sock fluff out from between her toes. "Ever since I kissed Wayne Keegan last month, I've been feeling like this."

"You told me his mouth tasted like cheddar cheese."

"That's the mystery of it." She put a fist under her chin. Her look said: *I am now assuming a thoughtful expression.* "It wasn't Wayne, exactly. Just the act of kissing. I think it started a chemical reaction. You know, inside. Now it will never stop and I'll have to keep doing it and doing it."

"Well, don't do it with Wayne Keegan. He'll tell everyone."

"I didn't say I was going to do it with anybody. I just said I wanted to. Sometimes, Lynn, you're so literal. I can't believe I even try with you."

"I'd want to do it too, but only if the right guy came around."

"You're just saying that. You'll probably stay a virgin till you're thirty." Dani closed her eyes and shook her head. Her mom did the exact same thing to Dani when she was frustrated with her. I had the urge to tell her this, but then the half-fight we were having would turn into a whole fight and I wasn't up to fighting with Dani that day.

"I do, *too*," I said, not sure at all if I did. "Really. Just not with someone from our school."

"Of course not," Dani said, sitting up and becoming even more serious. "I told you before, your type shouldn't even be in high school. Your type is at least a college sophomore." She studied my face like an *Us Weekly* photo spread. "Have you even looked at that sheet I made you?"

"That's what I'm talking about. If I did it, I'd want a college sophomore. Maybe some guy from Georgia Southern."

"Hah!" Dani said, flicking me on the knee hard enough to sting. "I knew you hadn't read it. I was testing you. I said your type was a college freshman. You're not mature enough for a sophomore."

"And you are?"

"Sometimes," Dani said, closing her eyes again and shaking her head, "I don't think you get me at all."

"You know, Dani," I said, and then it slipped right out, "your mom does that exact same thing where she closes her eyes and shakes her head like that." I did a little imitation. "Exactly the same as what you're doing now. She did it to you at dinner tonight when you told her—"

Dani made a loud, shrill sound.

Three-Day Rule

I broke the three-day rule out of boredom and general all around twitchiness about this Hayes weirdness, and then more boredom heaped on top. The house felt stuffy and smaller than normal. The window air conditioner in the living room wasn't working right again. It made coughing sounds and the air coming out was barely cool. I watched TV. I read my mom's back issues of *Cosmopolitan* from the stack in the bathroom. I walked in circles and talked to myself. I was about driven crazy with nervous energy and nowhere to put it. If you looked at it this way, and I did, I had no choice but to break the three-day rule.

"Specialist Loy," he said when he answered the phone. His voice sounded softer than I expected. And kind. I'm not sure if I can explain what a *kind* voice sounds like. Sort of even and deep. In the background a man yelled, "You sunk my fucking battleship!" Two or three other guys in the room laughed at that. I didn't say anything right away. I just sort of let his voice sink in. "Loy here," he said after a moment. The second time he spoke he sounded impatient, not irritated, more like he was pressed for time.

"Hey," I said, "Specialist Loy."

"Hey." His voice changed again. It became even softer and there was a hint of something new in it. Playfulness, maybe. "Who's this?"

"This is, uh—"

"Lynn?"

"Yeah."

"Really?"

"It is." I flopped down on the couch and put my bare feet up against the wall. The kitchen phone's cord stretched tight as a laundry line.

"I didn't expect you to actually call."

"Why not?" I pinged the cord with my big toe and tried to imagine his face. A medium-sized forehead and dark, well-defined eyebrows. A nice, straight nose and good-sized lips. A dimple in his chin. No, no, scratch that, I thought. No chin dimples. It ruined the picture.

"I don't know," he said. There was a muffled crash on his end. I heard him tell someone to take it outside.

"Do you have a roommate?"

"Yeah, but that wasn't him. Just some guys from down the hall throwing a football around."

I didn't know what to say. My belly felt like it was full of buzzing radio static. I sat up straight and put my feet on the floor. I watched the moisture prints on the wall shrink and vanish.

"Lynn?" His voice got just the teeniest bit higher. "You still there?"

"Yeah, yeah," I said. "Sorry."

"You know, you sound a lot like I imagined you would. What are you doing?"

"I'm bored. I'm stuck in the house today."

"I wish I could drive up there and do something fun with you, but I've got to do some bullshit scut work. Excuse my language. I got in trouble this morning."

"In trouble for what?"

"Oh, it was stupid." He let out a long breath. "I failed room inspection three times this week, so now I've got to go rake pea gravel up on the roof of the armory."

"Was your room really messy?" I pictured dirty socks on the floor and wrinkled uniforms tossed over the back of a chair.

"No, my sergeant just has it out for me. He has ever since I got transferred to his unit. I never even got discharged. As soon as I came home, they just reassigned me. I got stop-lossed, you know?"

Logan explained why this stop-loss business was bullshit. For a year they'd been telling him he'd get out on such-and-such a day. Less than a month before he was set to leave, they showed him the fine print on his contract, which basically said the Army had him as long as they needed him. All his plans were ruined in the time it takes to drink a Coke. He'd already signed up for a graphic design course at the DeVry Institute. His dream was to illustrate graphic novels. To top it off, nothing Logan did was good enough for his new sergeant. This last time he got in trouble it was because his bed wasn't made right. The sergeant couldn't bounce a quarter off it. If he messed up one more time, the man threatened to "section his ass." I couldn't help but imagine an ass being pried apart like a grapefruit.

"A quarter?" I asked, thinking of my bed.

"He has it in for me. I'd leave today if I could."

"Why don't you then?"

He groaned. "I wish it were that simple. I'd be in a world of shit if I just up and left. Take a lesson from me. Always read the small print before you sign your name to something."

"You couldn't just run away? Go to Canada or something? No one could say you were a coward. I mean, you already went once, right?"

"I guess." He paused for a second, like he might actually be thinking about it. I only said it for something to say. I didn't expect him to take me serious. "But here's the thing, if they caught me, I'd probably go to jail. At best, they'd give me a dishonorable discharge and with that on my record it'd be impossible to get a decent job.

Worst of all, they'd cancel my G.I. bill and then it's bye-bye tuition money and bye-bye DeVry Institute." He sniffed twice and clucked his tongue. "But yeah, if I wanted, I probably could skip. It wouldn't be all that hard. If this fucking sergeant doesn't get off of my ass, I just might."

"What'd happen? Do they send a pack of hounds after you?" I bayed like a bluetick and Logan Loy laughed.

"I don't think they'd come looking for me, unless I pulled some stunt before I left or maybe stole equipment. A gun, say. But if I was driving too fast or something and the cops pulled me over, they'd haul my ass in. No doubt. After forty-eight hours I think they put out some kind of a bulletin." He lowered his voice like a TV announcer. "Keep on the lookout for Logan Loy, five foot eleven inches and a hundred and fifty pounds. Blond hair and a tattoo of the word *Mom* in a heart on his left arm."

What he said wasn't all that funny, but it stirred up a couple happy bumblebees in my belly and set them to buzzing about down there. I laughed because he wanted me to, and knowing he wanted me to made me happy. A good sign, I thought. He ain't afraid to sound foolish.

"What about you?" Logan asked. "You skipping out on school today?"

"School doesn't start till next week."

"One more week of summer, huh?" Logan laughed some more. "That was always my busiest week. I tried to cram in all the stuff I'd planned on doing during the summer but hadn't gotten around to yet. Maybe I can come up and see you before you have to go back? What do you think? Would that be cool?"

"Yeah." I closed my eyes and tried not to shout my answer. "Very cool." My heart swelled—

"I was thinking like a picnic or something. You into that? It's not too lame for you?"

"Not lame at all."
—and swelled—
"How does Friday sound?"
—and then it popped from sheer happiness.

Serial Killer

I had saved a really long cigarette butt for after my shower and I was about to light it up, actually had it in my mouth and was picking up the lighter, when Hayes smashed his face up against the screen door and yelled, "Lynnie, sweetie, honey!" With his nose smushed up against the screen like that, he looked like a serial killer. I didn't say anything at first and I don't think he could see me since the blinds were down and it was dark in there. "Whatcha doing, Little Flipper?" He made a couple of dolphin squeaks per usual. "Why don't you let old Hayes in?"

I stayed right where I was on the floor by the coffee table. "My mom said you weren't allowed in the house because you're having a spell."

"Having a what?"

"A spell. That's what she said. Spell. S-P-E-L-L."

"The only spell I'm having is one of unemployment. And I believe that'll be coming to an end here shortly."

"You get a job or something?"

"I have some prospects."

After the accident that wound him up in the emergency room where he met my mom, she helped him get a job "managing" the pharmacy of a Drug Rite over in Statesboro. He was not actually a pharmacist, but something called a pharmacy technician, which, to my mind, seemed like the pharmacist's equivalent to a nurse's assistant. Maybe not even. More like a hospital candy striper. All a pharmacist does is count pills. What does the assistant do, hold the bottle for him? Anyhow, he was fired for reasons that were never fully explained to me (hmm, let me take a wild guess).

"I heard they were hiring over at the Crispy Chik," I said. "You know you look like a rapist with your face pressed flat like that?"

"In your dreams, Flipper," Hayes said.

"Nightmares," I said.

"Hey," Hayes said, putting his hands in his pockets and rocking back and forth from heel to toe. "Just let me in there for a sec to use the bathroom and then I'll take off."

"Nope. The order is, and I quote, 'Hayes is not allowed in the house when I'm not here.' The bathroom's in the house. So, no bathroom. Anyway, you drank the last of the cough syrup. If you really got to go, just tinkle out there behind the camellia bush."

His face drooped when I mentioned the syrup and he said, "Come on, now."

"I'm walking to the phone now. I'm picking up the phone. I'm dialing the nurse's station at the hospital."

"You go ahead and be that way, but don't expect no favors from me anytime soon."

When the thumps came an hour later, I thought it was Hayes back to pester me some more. I'd shut the door and locked it. There were just the two thumps, like somebody hitting the door really hard with the heel of his palm, and then nothing.

I crept to the window and peeked out. There wasn't anybody I could see on the stoop, unless he'd pressed himself right up against the door.

I went ahead and opened it. Not a soul on the front walk or anywhere in sight. Then I saw a little bit of shiny wet on the door-mat and crouched down to look closer. I touched it and rubbed it between my thumb and index finger. Red, I thought. Even then I didn't get it. But when I turned to go inside, I saw what was there.

Stuck to the door with green punch pins were two fuzzy, gray ears. I knew them for what they were right away. Terrier ears.

I thought about the man on the phone with the cigarette-burned voice. Two bluebottle flies buzzed in a circle and landed on the red, wet edge of the ears. First one, then the other. I thought to take the sad, little things down before those flies laid their maggot eggs inside, but I didn't want to touch them.

That man, I remembered suddenly, knew Mom was a nurse at the hospital and that we lived near it. I had a sudden picture of my mom's ears nailed to the door.

Angry Red Mouth Print

The only other person in the hospital waiting room was a great fat woman with an infected spot on her leg. The spot was greenish yellow and as big as a walnut. I tried not to look at her, but it was hard, as she kept squeezing at the lump and wiping off the drippings with crumpled-up Dairy Queen napkins. She seemed to have a never-ending supply of them in her purse.

When my mom finally came out, I saw right away she was aggravated. I found out later a boy with a jammed finger had bitten her on the arm and left an angry red mouth print.

"What do you want?" my mom said. She bit off the end of each word with a hard chomp of her teeth. "I only have a couple of minutes."

I told her about the man calling for Hayes, which I hadn't mentioned before because it hadn't really seemed like all that big a deal at the time. More Hayes's problem than ours. The husky woman on the other side of the room stopped milking her infected lump for a moment, so she could listen in. She nodded at me and clucked her tongue like I was talking to her.

"I hope to God you didn't tell him nothing."

"I told him he had the wrong number."

"When was this?" Mom asked. She squeezed her lower lip with her fingers.

"Oh, a day or so ago, but that ain't why I came over and bothered you."

"Don't say *ain't*," Mom said, although she said it all the time. "It sounds trashy."

I lowered my voice. I told her about Hayes coming over today and then finding the ears.

"Jesus," Mom said, her face going pale. She squeezed her lower lip until it turned yellow.

"Sorry for pestering you, but—" Watching her get worried made me feel even more scared.

"I think you should stay at Dani's tonight."

"What's going on, Mom?"

"It sounds like a world of trouble to me," the woman with the infection said.

My mom didn't seem to hear her or pretended not to. "You go on over to Dani's and I'll call you. I expect Hayes just owes somebody money. It's none of our concern." She shook her head and frowned at my feet. "We really got to get you some new shoes. You can't start school wearing flip-flops."

Boats in Bottles

My mom's favorite thing in the world to do is to build model ships. Not just any ships—she likes the kind you build inside of bottles with tiny tools. She built her first one when she was eight with her grandpa. It came in a kit. We used to have a picture of her in our photo album with that first boat in a bottle. She's standing on top of a chair with the bottle pressed up against her chest like a baby doll, wearing Mary Janes and a blue-and-white polka-dot dress. Grandpa is standing next to her with his hand resting on her head. Because of the chair, they're about the same height. She has an expression on her face I've never seen in real life. She looks like someone just told her she'd become a princess, and in a few minutes, they were taking the whole family off to live in a palace. Since then she's built dozens of these boats. She had special shelves made in the living room to hold her favorites. They were arranged by type—schooner, clipper, steamboat, frigate.

The month she turned twenty-two, the year before she got married, she won a contest for building boats in bottles. It took place in Providence, Rhode Island. It was the first time she ever left Georgia. Grandpa drove her up I-95 in his nut-colored Chevy Malibu. She had the picture of herself receiving the award framed in black plastic and hung it above her bed. It could be another person, she looks so different in it. She has on what she calls her *Little House on the Prairie* dress, a sort of long sack with a busy-looking print, frilly cuffs and a high, button-up neck. Her hair hangs to her waist and it's brown and shiny, unlike now. These days she wears it in a short, frizzy bob. "I don't have the time to do anything with it," she'd tell me whenever I'd ask her why she didn't grow it out again. "It's not practical for a nurse." In the picture, her skin is smooth and she's smiling. Her eyes are clear and unlined. She looks beautiful and happy. But it isn't really the features of her face or the length of her hair that make her look different. It's more like the way she uses her face. When I used to look at that picture and then looked at what she'd become, I could see how much the way you feel about yourself and the world affects the way you look. You'd be hard pressed to even recognize my mom now, if all you had to go by was that photograph. Looking at it made me wonder how much different I'd look if I was ever just-won-a-build-a-boat-in-a-bottle-contest happy. Ever since I'd come across that picture, I'd been on the lookout for my own project, my own build-a-boat-in-a-bottle.

I didn't know it yet, but I'd already found it.

"I want to do something dangerous," Dani said. "I'm so bored, it's giving me an all-over body ache." As she talked, Dani clipped fur off an old stuffed elephant with toenail clippers. Fluff drifted around the basement. She started with the belly and worked up to the head. It looked like a dog after it's been neutered.

If I'd told her about the ears, maybe she'd of felt that was danger enough. But I hadn't. So I just asked her what she had in mind— rob a convenience store?

"It'd be better than sitting around down here in the damn bat cave." She got tired of the elephant's belly and began giving the end of its trunk a circumcision.

We kicked around a few other ideas. Skinny-dipping in Water Oak pond, going bowling in Statesboro. At last I suggested the barn.

Dani tossed me the elephant and sat down at the computer. "I thought you hated going out to Wayne Keegan's barn."

"It was just a suggestion." I picked up the elephant and stroked its sad, bare belly. "They're probably not even out there."

"No, they're out there," she said. Then she made a sharp little squeak. "We already got mail." She turned and screwed up her mouth.

"We only made the new Game e-mail address the other day. Only us and Wynn and Logan know about it. Is it from him?"

Dani shook her head.

I leaned over her shoulder. Sure enough, there were two e-mails in the inbox. Both were from someone called angryeyeball@ bazooka.com. The first had a message line that said nothing. The second said, "The angry eyeball has you in its sight."

"You open them?" I asked.

Dani shook her head again.

I clicked open the first message. It was a single sentence in a weird font.

> Your days of torturing men are over

"It's impossible. Wynn said people can't track you down like this, remember? I asked him about that guy who said he saw us through the webcam and he told me it was B.S. Are you pranking me, Dani?"

"No," she said, "I swear." From the quaver in her voice, I knew she wasn't lying. "Do you think it's from the . . ." She stopped, but I knew who she meant.

"Professor Carrot? No, and I don't think he was any professor either. Probably works the deep fryer at Krystal's."

"He might not be that far away from us. He said he meant to drive from Chicago to Florida. The man could be here already." She winced at me and squeezed her lips together with both hands like she was fixing to eat them.

"If he had a fast car," I said, trying to calm her some with a bad joke.

It didn't go over.

"Shit," she said, "shit, shit, shit."

I turned back to the computer and opened the next message. It read:

> I know your face. I know your house. I know what you do.

Today you wore a yellow shirt. Tomorrow you'll
wear a frown.

Dani let out a shriek. I covered her mouth with a hand and looked up at the ceiling, where her mom had been pacing across the kitchen talking on the phone. When she made that noise, the pacing stopped. Dani wore a blue T-shirt with a Spam label printed on the front. Nothing yellow about it. I shook her sleeve.

"See, this ain't yellow, Dani. I didn't wear yellow today. Whoever this is doesn't know shit. They're just trying to scare us." I smiled, feeling a bit relieved.

"No, no," Dani said in a high-pitched whisper, "I wore a yellow shirt this morning when I went jogging."

"I'll send the fucker a message he won't forget." As I leaned across her lap to type, Dani grabbed my hand.

"No, Lynn, that'll just get him wound up even more. That's what he wants. To get a rise out of us."

I tried to soothe Dani's nerves by helping her pick out an outfit. She always said she didn't know how she felt until she knew what she'd wear. Once she'd calmed down, we decided on telling Wynn about the eyeball messages tomorrow. For tonight, Dani decided, we'd go to Wayne Keegan's barn.

"So wait," I said, now regretting the hell out of my suggestion, "how do you even know those boys'll be out there?"

"I saw Jared today at the Piggly Wiggly. Anyway, they're always out there. He told me Wayne's brother was going to buy them some beer." Dani hefted a breast in each hand and jiggled them. "I think they're getting bigger. God, I hope so."

"What else is there to do?" I said, actually hoping she'd have another idea.

Dani made a circle with her hands and looked at me through it.

Amateur Night

Dani's dad sat in the living room drinking a Pabst Blue Ribbon tall boy and watching a PBS documentary about insects. As we passed the bay window, a huge brown spider chased down a mosquito tangled in its web and wrapped it in silk. Dani's family had a projection TV and the spider looked as big as a Saint Bernard.

Dani worried her dad would hear the truck start, so we opted to hoof it out to Wayne's barn. This meant a long walk through dark, empty streets and scrubby fields of kudzu and honeysuckle, the only sounds the screech of tree frogs and the twitchy hum of the streetlamps and the *tap, tap, tap* of the bugs making blurry halos above each pole. August nights in Metter smelled like jasmine blooms and garbage juice with a faint tang of creosote drifting underneath. Lightning bugs flashed yellow in the weeds along the road like tiny thunderstorms. Even though the sun had been down for hours, the air still felt as warm and moist as an armpit. We cut across the lawn behind the First Baptist Church to avoid any late traffic, but we didn't see a single car until we got downtown. A light shone inside the old train depot and a shadow moved behind the window of Jenkins Hardware. Dani and me struck out along the train tracks that ran through the center of town. A cat appeared, eyed us sullenly, and scuttled away into the shadows. Above it all, a tiny red light atop the water tower flashed on and off, giving us quick peeks at the message painted beneath it: METTER IS BETTER. To me, this always asked the question: *Better than what?*

Hell? Neither of us spoke. The quiet was too perfect to break with anything but the squeak of our shoes in the dew-soggy grass.

Right before we got to the gravel road leading down to the Keegan place, a car came up the hill behind us fast. A big engine with a deep-throated growl. Dani grabbed my hand and yanked me toward the stand of young pines beside the road, but we weren't quite quick enough to avoid being spotted. The car slid to a stop on the sandy shoulder and idled for what felt an infinity. We froze, blinded by the headlights, two ditzy does. I scrutinized its silhouette, shading my eyes with a hand, but couldn't tell if it had a cop-car top. But no, an old Buick Skylark with these horrible spinning silver rims pulled up. The window came down with a glassy squeak. Dani sucked in a breath and squeezed my hand.

"Where you two ladies going—"

Another person sniggered.

"—on such a fine summer night?"

The voice sounded familiar—in Metter, every voice is familiar—but I couldn't match a face to it.

Dani could. She let loose of my hand and stepped up onto the shoulder, stumbling over a loose rock and holding out her arms for balance. "You scared the hell out of us, H.K."

Now I knew. H.K. Keegan. This was Wayne's older brother. Four years since he dropped out of Metter High and still wild as all get out. Every single one of the Keegan boys was trouble, but H.K. distinguished himself. I'd heard he spent three months in the county lockup for punching someone out in the parking lot of the Quick & Sleazy the year before. The man had told H.K. he liked his new tattoo. H.K. didn't believe him.

"You need a ride someplace?" H.K. asked Dani. "You and your friend there?"

That dark someone in the car beside him mumbled a couple of

things. I heard the word "jailbait." H.K. shaded his eyes and peered over at me.

"Well," Dani said, drawing the word out a second or so longer than necessary.

"Aw, come on. Get your butts in here. I won't have it said I'm not a gentleman."

Again, that sniggering from the other passenger.

The door swung open and H.K. pulled himself out. He stood about five foot eight, but carried himself like a much bigger man. Stringy, hard muscles and tattoos on both forearms. I noticed a tattoo of Woody Woodpecker on his neck. He made a small bow and gestured us into the backseat. Dani bent to crawl inside and he patted her on the ass as she passed beneath his arm.

When I hesitated, he took my arm and helped me in back—his touch was gentle but had firmness underneath that said, *You ain't going nowhere, girl*—then got in the front.

"I recognize you from somewhere." He tugged at an earlobe and made a short study of me in the dome light. "Yeah. You're Darla Sugrue's daughter, ain't you?"

"Maybe," I said.

"Your mama sewed up my arm one time." He lifted up his arm to show me a thick, pink smear of scar tissue behind his elbow. "Ran a little three-wheeler into a rusty strand of barbwire. Bled like a gut-shot buck."

"Must of hurt," I said.

"I weren't feeling no pain."

"Where you all going?" the guy in the front passenger seat asked. He wore his hair clipped down close to his scalp. I thought he might be twenty-five. A cigarette dangled from the corner of his mouth. Planted squarely in the middle of his left eyelid was a small, pink nub of a wart. He winked and the wart looked to be waving at me.

"We're heading over to you all's barn, H.K.," Dani said, "to hang out with Wayne and Billy and all them." She grabbed my thigh and gave it a painful squeeze.

"That ain't no fun," H.K. said, wheeling out on the blacktop and away from the road we needed to take to get to the barn. "Believe me, I know. I've spent plenty of nights out there eating bugs and drinking piss-warm beer. Come on with us. We're going to Bow Wow's. It's amateur night."

"Don't worry," the second guy said, "it ain't *that* kind of amateur night. You don't have to get your shirt wet or nothing."

"I thought Bow Wow's closed down," Dani said. "Anyhow, won't we get carded?"

"Naw," he said. "H.K.'s uncle Marty runs the place now."

"That's Ealey," H.K. said, jabbing his thumb at old wart-eye in the passenger's seat.

"Hi," Ealey said, suddenly sounding shy. He wore a black T-shirt with the words MAXIMUM GRUNTS written in red across the chest.

"I thought your uncle was still—" Dani stopped, looking unsure, as though she might of crossed a line she shouldn't of.

H.K. laughed at her. "He got out on Christmas Eve, and let me tell you what, he hit the ground running."

H.K. tore through the gears, making the engine whine and cry uncle. Dark trees whipped past the fingerprint-smeared windows in a blur. Thin trash pines and palmetto bushes. On the curves, me and Dani went bouncing from door to door, sliding across the seat and bumping heads. Beer cans and take-out bags from Forkin' Pork BBQ rattled between our feet.

"Can I have one of those smokes?" I asked Ealey.

He lit one with the tip of his own and passed it back over the seat. The filter was wet. He said, "Sorry if I nigger-lipped it."

I'd driven past Bow Wow's a thousand times, but I'd never been inside. It was an unpainted cinderblock building set back about a hundred yards from the two-lane county highway under a droopy, old live oak covered in Spanish moss. Somehow, even the Spanish moss looked ratty. There was no sign that said Bow Wow's out front. There wasn't even a real parking lot, just a raw red clearing of packed clay full up with patched-together, primer-spotted trucks. Just beside the turnoff, a floodlight pointed at a sign with the words AMATEUR BOXING TUESDAY NIGHT—$50 ENTRY/$500 PURSE spelled out in black removable letters, like the kind they use on church signs to spell out Jesus slogans. We stepped out of the car. I could hear the screaming and the music.

H.K. nodded to the doorman, a huge guy with a glistening shaved head and a wifebeater stained with little brown blobs of what looked to be some sort of gravy. When the man gestured with his chin at us, H.K. counted four bills into his oven-mitt hand. The doorman smiled at Dani, showing her a mouth of teeth so perfect and white they almost seemed fake. Inside, a rush of smoke and beer-sour breath hit us full in the face. The shouting was such I couldn't hear a word H.K. said until he yelled it right in my ear.

"Beer?" he asked.

It took a few seconds to get an idea of the place. Bow Wow's looked twice as big on the inside. A long plywood bar set atop dented aluminum kegs ran along a good part of the left wall. Three bartenders raced about behind it, setting up Dixie-cup shots and pouring draft beer. Just inside the front door there were three pool tables with green glass shades hanging from the ceiling above them. Men with cigarettes screwed into angry mouths leaned over the red felt and slung their cues. A good hundred people were packed into the building. Mainly men, but here and there I spotted a brightly colored miniskirt. In the center of the room, set up about three feet off the ground, was a platform lined with double strings of yellow nylon rope. From somewhere up in the ceiling, several spotlights shone down on it painfully.

That Makes Quite a Stink

.K. came back with two beers and shouted something that sounded like, "Do you want to go to church?"

When he saw me frowning at him and obviously not understanding what the hell he'd said, he grabbed my free hand, the other being firmly connected to Dani's nervous palm, and dragged us across the room. Ealey had vanished into the crowd, an easy trick since everyone looked like him. H.K. took us over to a door marked private at the end of the bar. The noise dimmed a bit when he shut it behind us, and I went completely blind. It took a few seconds to see we were in another room about half the size of the one in front, and instead of a raised platform in the center, there was some sort of pit lined with yellow sand.

He handed me and Dani our beers.

"It's where they fight the dogs," H.K. said. "You want to see something that'll blow your little girly minds, come to one of these dog fights. Shit, man, they're vicious as all fuck."

"Do the dogs die?" Dani asked.

"Them dogs love it. Believe me. They live to fight," H.K. said, warming to the topic. "I'm thinking about running a couple myself once I get the money."

"Do those terriers fight with the rats here?" I asked.

He grinned. "How'd you know about that?"

"Rats?" Dani's mouth shrank down to a pink, lowercase *o*.

"Places like this, Dani, they put these fierce little dogs down there in the sand along with a mess of rats." I pointed to the pit. "People bet on how many rats they can kill in a certain amount of time."

"Ewww," Dani said, making a face like she'd just licked the floor of the room out front. "How *do* you know about that?"

H.K. made a snarling dog out of his hand and nipped Dani's neck with it. She squealed, jumped back and bumped me, knocking both our beers to the ground. H.K. shook his head.

"Don't go anywhere. I need a fresh beer anyway." He put his hand on the door. "I'm serious. Don't move."

When the door swung open, you could actually see smoke and oniony armpit fumes roll in like a dirty wave. Dani apologized, something she only does when she's nervous.

I was about to say maybe we should make a run for it, but then a different door opened, on the wall behind the dog pit. Dani made a soft, high-pitched sound and grabbed my wrist. Before she had a chance to really get scared, I pulled her over to the corner and down behind a stack of folding chairs. Three men came out of what looked to be some sort of office on the far side of the room. Dani breathed fast against my neck. The office door opened again and a fourth man came out. When these men stepped into the light, I saw one of them was Hayes. I gritted my teeth and pushed myself as far back against the wall as I could, which wasn't much. *Please don't see me. Please don't see me.* The words ran over and over in my head until they became nothing but sounds.

A second, smaller lamp went on in the other corner of the room, and a cone of dusty, yellow light lit up a long, rectangular card table I hadn't seen before. Set up on top of it was a giant jar of pickled pigs' knuckles. The kind you see in little country gas stations sometimes. Chairs scraped cement. Hayes and two of the men sat. The biggest of the three, a balding guy with a big, bushy mustache the color of a carrot and a nose that resembled a beet root, leaned forward in his chair and held a bag of something up to the light. From where I crouched beneath the stack of chairs, the rest of his features were just a smear of shiny pink, but his shoulders were broad and thick and his hands were each the size of a boiled ham. The man's body looked to of been put together using huge portions of various foodstuffs, a meat version of the cars parked out front.

"Hungry, Hayes?" this man asked, sounding cheerful and good-humored. "Get you one of them knuckles. Burns here tells me the first four hairs on his ball sack sprouted out directly after eating one. Don't care for them much myself."

"No," Hayes said, in a strangled voice, "thank you." He sat directly under the light and I could see him more clearly than the others.

One of the men laughed. "I've heard it said human meat tastes a good bit like hog flesh."

Hayes's face was red, going on purple. He looked like he was holding his breath.

"Shut up, Travis," the big man said. His voice wasn't loud, but it carried clearly across the room. He breathed noisily through his mouth in an unpleasant way. The room went quiet for a moment, then he slammed his hand against the table three times. "What the fuck are you trying to pull here, Hayes? Huh?"

"What?" Hayes said, jerking in his chair as though startled out of a doze.

The big man flicked the Ziploc bag with a meaty finger.

"It's bulk," Hayes said, in a meek voice I'd never heard come out of his mouth before. "That's how they keep it in the hospital. When they need to use it, they dissolve it in distilled water and load it into needles or IVs or some shit." He said the word "shit" so quietly I barely made it out.

"I never heard of nothing like that before," the standing man said. I couldn't make out this guy's face at all, but he had on an old-fashioned, sky-blue Members Only jacket like the one my father wore in pictures from the eighties, except Dad's was gray.

"Me neither," the big man with the mustache said.

"It's the exact same shit you asked for. There's nothing different from this batch than the stuff I lost when I wrecked the truck. Just in powdered form. I ain't ever heard of them keeping it stored like this neither," Hayes said, but he didn't sound too sure of himself. "But that's how she explained it to me. It's worth the same. Same as what I brought up from Florida."

"Bullshit," someone said, "that was a hundred and fifty grand you lost us then."

The man sitting across the table from him opened the big jar and plucked out a pig knuckle before going back into the office. Despite the stifling heat, he wore a heavy leather bomber jacket, and when he passed under the light, I noticed blue tattoo smears running down one side of his neck and a triangle of dark-pink skin on his cheek just below his left eye. After a minute or so, the man came back with a plastic water bottle, a small black pouch, and what looked like a single-element hot plate. He set the hot plate down on the floor beside the wall and plugged it in. I didn't see any coffee pot. None of the men said a word about it. He stood again and unzipped the black bag, pulling out several shiny metal objects. The three others leaned in and watched. He took the bag of powder and fussed with it a bit. Then he did something with the water bottle. I couldn't make out what he was up to. A lighter scratched and flickered. The man held it under one of the pieces of metal for a moment and then set it all down on the table. None of the men spoke. They seemed almost hypnotized by the process. Finally, Triangle Cheek stepped back, rolled his hands toward the stuff on the table with a flourish, and cleared his throat.

"It's ready, Marty." Once he stepped out of the light, all I could make out was the red baseball cap he wore. His face became a black smudge of shadow.

Marty turned out to be the big one with the mustache. "First, you're going to try this shit yourself, Hayes, so we're sure there's nothing nasty in it. Then Burns here"—he thumped Triangle Cheek on the arm—"will give it a go and tell us what we've really got. Want to admit anything before it's too late? I surely wouldn't want you to get a hot shot. At least not till you paid us back."

The man in the Members Only jacket nickered like a horse.

"Shut up, Travis," Marty said.

Why was Hayes going to try the dog dope? I squinted at the brightly lit table of men and tried to make sense of this business. And then I got it. That weren't any dog dope. Dog dope! What a dumbass I was.

"Sure," Hayes said, but he didn't sound sure at all. I even felt a little sorry for him. "But use this arm."

The door to the bar swung open. H.K. balanced three beers in his hands and grinned blindly into the dark room. I stared at his face as hard as I could, trying my best to warn him off. He squinted for us in several directions.

"The fuck you think you're doing in here, H.K.?" Marty yelled.

H.K. jerked back, dropping one of the cups of beer. A few stray droplets splattered my cheek.

"Uh, sorry there, Uncle Marty. Didn't know you would be, uh—"

"You dumb shit!" Uncle Marty lowered his voice to a middling shout. "If I've told you a hundred times, I've told you a fucking thousand. Get your ass out of here, 'less you want it kicked out through your mouth."

H.K. turned and left in a hurry, sloshing beer everywhere. As he passed our hidey-hole, he muttered "shit" five times really fast, but I don't think he saw us. Dani squeezed my upper arm and nudged me in the direction of the door. I shook my head without looking at her. Not now. All four of the men were watching him go.

"Here, use this," Hayes said in a creaky voice. He broke the end off a cigarette, peeled back the paper and tore a piece of filter fluff loose. "You draw it up without a filter, you'll shoot me full of grit."

The man called Burns, the one with the triangle cheek, leaned over him for a moment and blocked my view. His arm moved in and out of the light, dropping the bit of fluff into a spoon. Uncle Marty put both elbows on the table, cradled his chin in his hands, and leaned in close to study the results of all this. The short of it was Hayes grimaced and then shut his eyes. Something of an anticlimax for me. I don't know what I expected. Hayes turning blue, maybe, and frothing at the mouth. Instead, he appeared to be napping.

"He ain't dying from it, anyway," Burns said, "so at least we know it ain't poison." Then he sat down at the table with his back toward our side of the room and rolled up his sleeve. He tied off his upper arm with a piece of black cord and kept it tight by pulling one end with his teeth. I'd seen my mom do something very like this to people at the hospital a hundred times.

"So?" Uncle Marty asked.

Burns shook his head. "It's something, but it's a long fucking way from the Oxys what this asshole promised. This is like the weak shit you get from the doctor for a fucking headache. I just barely caught a whiff of a rush. That or he cut some real dope down to nothing."

Marty grabbed Hayes by the collar of his shirt and shook him. "That what you did, fuck-o? Step all over the product? What were you, holding some back and thinking to sell it off yourself?"

Wasn't he already selling it? It seemed a strange thing to say, considering.

"Shit, no, man," Hayes said. Once Marty stopped shaking him, he plucked the soggy shred of filter out of the spoon and dropped it into a small, Ziploc bag he took from his shirt pocket.

"Don't worry, we'll give you a souvenir of tonight's fun, if that's what you want," Marty said, yanking Hayes so hard the chair legs squeaked.

One of the others laughed. "You don't get it, Marty. This dickweed's holding onto it, so when he's run through his supply, he can cook up the whole collection of filters and get maybe one half-assed hit."

"Christ," Marty said, drawing out the word. He jerked Hayes back and forth one more time and let go. "I don't know whether to cry or bitch-slap you."

Travis, whose face was now just a dark blob, reached over and flicked Hayes on the nose. His voice was sing-song and sarcastic. "I'm of the opinion that dickweed here cut this all to shit and back, so he could use it himself. The greedy fuck tried to burn his friends. Again. Sad, sad, sad. Look at his other arm." He wrenched up Hayes's sleeve and jerked his arm into the light. "It ain't the first time he's had a sample."

"Even this sorry fuck couldn't pound that much dope in two weeks," Marty said.

"That's if he even had it to start with." Burns folded his arms across his chest.

"No, he's got it alright," Marty said. "I already heard about it being missed at the hospital."

"Hey, Marty, dude, man." Hayes spoke very quickly. "Maybe there was a mistake. Maybe we just got the wrong stuff. We didn't, I mean, she didn't know what exactly you all wanted. She ain't used to doing this."

Great, Hayes, blame it on Mom. If it really was Mom. I still held out hope that it wasn't, even if all the evidence pointed to yes. I couldn't believe she'd do it.

Dani's mouth pressed right up against my ear. "Can we please just—"

Wanting to know fought with wanting to leave. I shook my head.

"If that's true," Marty said, "I still don't understand why the shit came in a sandwich bag and not some hospital jar."

"They keep it in a big plastic tub over there. We took a few big-ass scoops. If we took the whole jar, they'd know it was missing. Then she'd be looking at jail time for sure."

"Bullshit," Travis said. "First you told us you'd get two jars"—he held up two grubby fingers—"each with five hundred eighties in them. Then you say you're getting us a hundred Fentanyl patches and one jar. Now this useless shit. What the fuck, man?"

Burns stood up and punched Hayes full in the face. His fist made a wet, meaty sound when it hit.

Travis stood and went back into the office. He returned with a large, table-size paper cutter. The kind they have in the art room at school. Travis set it on the card table and worked the blade of the cutter up and down a couple of times. It made an ugly screeching sound each time he pushed it home.

"Lucky for you," Travis said, "I sharpened the blade today with a stone. Unscrewed it from the housing, took it off and *schweep*, *schweep*, *schweep*." He rubbed his thumb down the length of his forearm each time he made the sound.

"What?" Hayes asked, shrill and desperate, his head going back and forth between Marty and the man with the cutter. "What do you want? You don't have to do this. I'm just saying, man, you don't. What do you want? I'll tell—"

Marty grabbed him by the shirtfront again and shook him. A snap popped off his red plaid cowboy shirt, shining for a moment in the light, and then clattered onto the table, rolled to the edge and stopped. "No need for telling me shit, Hayes. We had it figured out pretty good before you got here. Just thought we'd give you a chance. Could be, I told these boys, Hayes might even of done what he said he'd do."

The other two laughed good and hard at this.

"But no, not our buddy Hayes. He hates the easy way." Marty took Hayes's chin in his hand and shook it slowly side to side. His voice changed. It lowered to a growl. "You ain't too hard to predict. You really think we wouldn't notice you cut this shit all to hell? A powder jug? Jesus Christ, Hayes." Travis grabbed Hayes by the shoulders. Marty and Burns leaned over his chair and did something to him with a piece of orange electrical cord. "We made some promises too, Hayes, and you're fucking them up. You got a day to bring me what you promised. Or a hundred and fifty grand." He flicked the Ziploc bag and powder puffed into the air. "This don't count for shit. Take it home, for all I care."

"He'll need it," Travis said and laughed. "This is really going to sting."

"We can't get more that fast." Hayes sputtered as he spoke. "Like you said, they already suspect—"

"If you already sold it, why don't you go buy some more?" Travis asked. "I know a guy you can call with a connection at the hospital. Oh, wait, shit, that's you. Never mind."

Burns laughed.

"No, man, it ain't like that." Hayes squirmed in his seat. "Here's the honest-to-God truth—I just, I just fucking lost it. Sure, I held back a handful or so for my own private use, but I put all the rest of it in a special place, so nobody'd find the shit. I hid it in an old couch in my driveway when I was drinking, and then, well, shit, by the time I remembered about garbage pick-up day, the truck'd come already and dragged it off. The whole stash gone. I about cried. But if you wait, like, say, a month, I can—"

Burns patted Hayes on the chest. "Get bo here, trying to negotiate while tied to a chair."

Marty laughed. "Hayes, there ain't nothing more to talk about. I don't care if you sold it or lost it or shoved it up your dog's ass. But I have a pretty good feeling it's around here close. So you best put on your remembering hat. Travis only wants to make sure you don't forget your promises this time. You took a big pinch for yourself and replaced it with trash. Now we'll take a pinch of our own. See, we're at the stage where either you do what you said you would or—"

Hayes broke in before he had to hear the other option. "If you really want it, you got to give me a little more time. It's impossible to get it by tomorrow. We only have the chance every two weeks. See that's when the hospital pharmacy does its inventory. The old man in charge, he's getting forgetful. The day after he does the inventory, his son or daughter-in-law comes in and does it over, and they sort of fix all the mistakes. The only time we can do it is that night after the old man counts—"

Marty clamped a hand over Hayes's mouth to shut him up. "You got a week. No more. And since you got a tendency to forget your promises, we got something here to keep your memory jogged."

"I hope you don't play the guitar," Travis said, pulling on a pair of yellow kitchen gloves like the kind I used to clean the bathtub. "You'll be missing a couple of notes."

Burns yanked Hayes's arm flat and duct-taped it down to the top of the table, winding the tape across the corner and around one of the legs over and over again. Hayes struggled and grunted, but it did no good. Someone slapped him and he quit. No one spoke a word. Travis wiped his forehead with the crook of his elbow and squatted to pick up the hot plate, which he set on the table beside the paper cutter. Its cord stretched tight. Then, with a surprising amount of care, he slipped Hayes's hand onto the flat wooden base of the cutter, made a fist of all but Hayes's pinkie finger, and slid this last wiggling finger under the blade. It looked like a thick, pink worm. Marty nodded twice. And before I could even catch my breath, Burns hopped up into the air and brought the cutter down on the finger with all his weight. The blade crunched. The finger flopped across the table, curled once and lay still. A single squirt of blood burst from the stump, like a tight string of bright red yarn. Hayes made horrible, garbled shrieking sounds. Quickly, and in a single motion, Burns lifted the mangled hand and brought the bleeding knuckle down on the orange circle of the hot plate. The stump squeaked and hissed. I turned away and leaned my forehead against the wall and tried not to make any noise as I cried. Dani retched a little and buried her face in the crook of her elbow. Hayes screamed and screamed until someone muffled his mouth.

"Shit," Burns said, "that makes quite a stink. Smells like burnt hot dogs."

"We're gonna hold onto this for you," Travis said. I looked up in time to see him drop the cut-off finger into the jar of pickled pig knuckles. It plopped into the cloudy vinegar, making a smoky trail of pink as it swayed gently to the bottom.

I couldn't sit there any longer. A muscle in my leg twitched and cramped. I grabbed Dani's hand and jerked her to her feet. Shadows covered most of the back wall. I hoped they'd cover us. We tiptoed six very long steps. Then pushed through the door and tumbled into the crowd. Behind us, Marty shouted that H.K. was looking for an ass-whipping. I tripped over Dani's feet and fell into someone. A woman with greenish hay for hair shoved me toward the bar and hissed at me.

H.K. grabbed both my arms and put his face right next to mine. "Jesus fucking Christ, what took you so long?" His sideburns were dark with sweat. He'd chewed a little red drink straw practically to shreds.

Dani made a few sounds, none of them words.

"Never mind." H.K. pulled us by the arms through the crowd.

At the door, he backhanded Dani on top of the head, but not all that hard, and said, "I got a hundred bucks on Johnnie Gilbert Cook and 'cause of you I'm fixing to miss the whole fucking thing."

As he hustled me and Dani across the parking lot, he told us several times that whatever the hell it was we'd seen back there, we hadn't seen it. The tires smoked and squealed when he slung the car around on the county highway and pointed us back toward town. Nobody said a word. Dani held a hand against her mouth. With the other she made four fingernail marks on my wrist. The mascara smeared around her eyes made it look like she'd been the one back there boxing. *God*, I thought, I hope Hayes didn't see me. Before we could tell H.K. where to drop us, he pulled the car into the gravel track leading out to the Keegans' farm. The same place he found us. He flicked his cigarette at my leg and gunned the engine, spraying us with orange dust and bits of pea gravel.

"Damn, damn, damn." Dani walked in a circle around me, wiping her face with the back of her wrist and smearing the mascara even worse. "Well, I haven't had any fucking fun yet. I ain't going to let that asshole ruin my night. We might as well head to the barn."

She stomped over the warped plank that crossed Turkey Creek. Before I could shout out a reason for us not to, she disappeared under the trees. I followed.

The Barn

Wayne Keegan's barn wasn't really a barn at all. It was a tottering sharecropper's shack in the middle of an unused field full of blackberry brambles. A Coleman lantern hissed in an open window. The shadows of two heads fluttered on the weeds beneath it like a couple of bulb-drunk moths. But from the sound of the voices, there had to be at least two or three more people inside. Dani and me paused at the edge of the long rectangle of light from the window. Blaring hip-hop made the clapboards buzz and shake. In the space between songs, there was a gunshot sound. The two of us jumped. Wayne Keegan said something stupid. A girl cackled. A new song came on. The Shins.

"'Caring Is Creepy,'" Dani whispered, smiling for the first time since we'd been hijacked by H.K. and squeezing my arm. "That's an omen."

"Yeah," I said, thinking, the song fit us to a T this summer. We weren't building anything, like the song said, we were just chucking around bricks. It worried me some that Dani had made this our anthem. I'm not sure I understood all the lyrics, but I didn't like to think we were dying over and over like the person the song's addressed to, but maybe we were. I wondered if tonight was another one of those times. Dani had taken the title for a motto. She wouldn't care until it killed her.

"Jesus," Wayne shouted, "will someone please shitcan the fag soundtrack!"

We exchanged grimaces. Before I could suggest we turn around and go home, Eminem started yelling something angry. Inside, the boys let out several loud whoops of approval. Dani took four steps forward and then stopped and glanced back at me. She looked like she'd just learned the truth about the Easter Bunny. I couldn't help but follow her.

BARN Rules

1. No one allowed inside unless WAYNE is here
2. No Pissing in Barn
3. ~~NO GIRLS~~
   ~~No Girls~~
4. Everybodys got to say a cuss before coming in
5. Never say the word Pink
6. ~~No More fucking KoolAid~~
7. No Fags allowed
8. No Fat Girls
9. You break the rules you got to leave

10. WAYNE IS BOSS. Don't do what he says you got to leave

11. Josh Barnum $ Danny Edenfield $ ~~Bill Varnet~~ aint allowed

$ Derek clark

12. Girls got to take off shoes

13. Jenkins can <u>Never</u> take off Shoes

14. All beer labels go on walls

Signed,

Wayne

Boss of the Barn!!!

Russian Roulette Truth

Dani took off her shoes, shouted, "Bitch!" and went inside. I craved a beer, even a lukewarm one, so I muttered, "Shit," and walked in behind her. Hazel Kinney, Dani's worst enemy since the sixth grade, sat on the floor swigging from a brown bottle of beer. Wayne and Billy Varnel and a kid named Jared sat across from her. Billy waved a very real-looking pistol at us and laughed when we ducked. After a couple of lame jokes about barnyard animals, Wayne, the boss of the barn, explained they were playing Russian Roulette Truth and the realistic pistol was only a starter pistol full of blanks.

The rules went something like this: On your turn, you put in a blank, spun the cylinder, held the gun next to your head, and pulled the trigger. If it didn't go off, you took a drink. If it did, you had three choices: they could ask you any question they wanted and you had to tell the truth, you could take a dare, or you could go up in the attic with the last person who got shot.

We found out Jared jacked off three times a day minimum and Wayne had never had sex with a pig. Some of us doubted that last one, and when we said so, Wayne turned tomato head and stuttered something about us not knowing what all he did with his cock in private. Billy admitted to once letting a dog lick cheese spread off his dick. After that, Wayne took to calling him cheese dick. I drank three beers and felt better.

On my third turn, the gun went off and I chose truth. I told them I got my period in the seventh grade. This was a lie. I didn't get it until ninth grade. Dani, who knew the truth, winked at me. Barely twenty seconds passed before the gun went off again. Billy, who had the hygiene habits of a goat, chose to take me up to the attic. Of course. My ears still rang so loud I couldn't hear a word he said. Billy trapped me in a corner and got a mouthful of hair before I slid out from under his sweat-greasy arms and escaped.

On the seventh or eighth time round, the gun went off against Hazel's head.

"You ever been lezzy with another girl?" Billy asked her. There was a scratch on his face from where he'd fallen after I'd pushed him in the attic, and I felt like adding a little length to it.

"Well," Hazel said, drawing out the *e*. "I've never actually done anything myself, but I've noticed Dani is always staring at me when we're changing for P.E."

"That's just 'cause Hazel's got a giant ass," I stage-whispered to Wayne. "Looks like someone tied a piglet around her waist."

Hazel either didn't hear or pretended not to. Dani kept her mouth clamped shut and tried to strangle her with her eyes. Wayne and Jared laughed. Then Billy laughed, but by that time he was so drunk I'm not sure he even knew what he was laughing about.

"That reminds me of what you told me about your brother," Dani said.

"What?" Hazel said. She stood up.

The room went quiet.

"You know, how you said you like to watch him through the crack in the bathroom door when he's taking a shower."

The boys laughed. I wondered if this was something Hazel had actually told her when they were friends. It seemed possible. Hazel was trashy.

"Fucking cunt," Hazel said. She ran across the room and grabbed Dani by the hair. I got up to help Dani, but Jared grabbed me by the elbows and held me back.

"You got to let them fight it out," Jared said.

"No, I don't. Let loose of me."

Dani's crate tipped over backwards and they rolled around on the ground. They weren't really hitting each other, just scratching and biting. Hazel got a slap in and then Dani tore a fake fingernail off clawing at Hazel's cheek. She left a long red gash. After a couple of minutes, they stopped cussing at each other. It was all grunting and screaming. Both of them cried and dripped mascara. They kept at it for a good ten minutes at least. Finally, Hazel clocked poor Dani in the eye with her beer bottle. It made a hollow clunk. She stopped fighting. Her face went greenish gray. The lantern continued to swing. None of us said a word for a very long moment, but our shadows shrank and swayed and grew as the lantern moved. Dani pulled her knees up against her chest and sobbed.

"Alright, now. Leave off," Wayne said. Hazel had reared her foot back and looked ready to kick Dani in the head, but Wayne managed to pull together sense enough to stand up and grab her first. Jared let me loose.

"Get the fuck out of here, you bitch, and take that dyke with you!" Hazel screamed at me. Wayne still held her, so I slapped her as hard as I could. It made me happy to see I left a handprint. She kicked her legs up in the air trying to get away, but Wayne held her and smiled at me.

"I like to see a little spunk in a girl," he said.

"Man," Billy told his left foot. "Girls fighting."

I helped Dani stand up and we left without saying another word.

Jared stood in the doorway and called after us, "Don't be like that. We didn't even get to mess around yet."

The walk home was silent but for the sound of Dani's head slowly swelling larger and larger. We swiped a venison steak from the basement freezer and Dani fell asleep with it melting on her face.

About Busted Up
My Poor Boy's Head

I didn't sleep that night. When the alarm on my cell phone went off, I crept into her closet, flipped on the light and huddled under a row of dresses bagged in dry-cleaner's plastic. Logan picked up before the first ring finished. All it took was the sweet sound of his trying-hard-to-be-a-tough-guy hello for my stomach to settle some and my no-sleep headache to ease off a notch or two. Still, I could hear right away the boy was in some kind of mood.

We talked a lot about the Army and how much he hated it now. When Logan first signed up, he said he was all gung-ho. But then he got over there and it stopped making the same kind of sense. Or any kind of sense at all. They stuck him on something called a forward operating base in the middle of nowhere, way out in the desert. What were they protecting? Nothing. A tiny three-house town. One of the things he noticed straightaway was the kids. They didn't appear all that different from the ones at home. Nor did their games and basic boyish hijinks. In fact, one kid in the village near his base bore a strong and eerie resemblance to his cousin Holt. This troubled him. Logan had no stomach for shooting people that looked like his own kin. The TV had prepared him for towelheads in white, billowing dresses. Men wore pants here like everywhere else. For the most part, he found the war boring. Another surprise. Soldiering mainly consisted of cleaning things and using swear words and long strings of letters to describe normal objects.

But this all changed after the attack that killed two of his friends—Krantz and Petersen. Nothing was the same after those two died. Nothing. They were driving in a convoy through a small town near their base. Narrow, twisted streets with a thousand places for the enemy to hide. An IED bomb blew up under his friends' vehicle and then someone tossed a bottle full of gasoline from a balcony above. He'd watched these boys burn to death from a Humvee ten feet behind them. Only one of them managed to get out. He ran across the street with his head on fire. Krantz. He was dead before he fell to the ground. And even though they'd killed the man who threw the gas bomb, the world stopped meaning what it did before. The sun didn't even look the same to him. He got hit by shrapnel in that attack. Nothing all that bad, he said, a little cut on his shoulder. Ten stitches. He wished his body had been torn up even worse, so it'd match outside with how he felt inside. Logan told me he couldn't concentrate on anything for the rest of his time over there. It was all he could do every morning just to pull himself out of his cot and zombie through the day. Every day, the same old shit—sand and sun and shouted orders. Logan paused for a moment after telling me all this, and then said, "Blood smells different out in the sun like that."

I arranged Dani's shoes according to color.

"Sometimes," he said after this three-year pause, "the sun will shine off a windshield someplace, like the parking lot at the PX on base, and my mind will do this fucked-up thing where I see some plain Toyota as the Humvee Petersen and Krantz died in. And now, Lynn . . . I don't know. I can't even take elevators anymore. No thanks, I'll take the stairs from now on. Does that make sense to you? Why wouldn't I want to get stuck inside an elevator?" He let out a ragged, breathy *ahhhh* sound. "You must think I'm crazy."

"Nah, man," I said. My heart twisted and turned over on itself like a wrung-out washrag. "I don't think nothing like that, Logan.

You a had a shit-poor time over there is what I think."

"Fucking right," he said softly and did a pretend kind of laugh. "Once I get going, it's just like *blech*." He made a puking noise of sorts.

"If it's got to come out, it's got to come out. You can talk to me about that stuff all you want." So he went ahead and told me a few more things. How he wished he had a dog—he'd always had a dog since he was a boy. How he missed eating barbeque at the restaurant in his hometown. How bummed he was about not being able to take the illustration class he'd signed up for. He explained how his fiancée broke up with him two weeks after he got back from Iraq. Wrote him a Dear John letter and tucked it under the wiper on his car. It sounded to him like she'd gotten it off the Internet someplace. How-to-break-up-with-a-vet-dot-com. She ended up marrying a guy he used to play football with in high school, one of the crew he ran with back then, drank beer with. "This is a guy who used to yell and scream about how he wanted to kill him a whole shitload of towelheads. Course, he never signed up for shit." The news about the wedding hit Logan in the head like a big, pointy rock. His exact words. "They even had the nerve to send me an invitation. That's why I went out there with the bat. Left a surprise for them in the parking lot."

"A bat?"

"It was nothing," he said. "Just being stupid. I didn't hurt anybody. I thought about smashing out the headlights on their limo. I couldn't even do that. I left the bat on the hood and went home."

We had another one of those long, uncomfortable moments of silence. When this kind of awkward pause happened at home, my mom would say, "Somewhere, an idiot has been born." But I didn't know him well enough yet to make a joke like that. Finally, he said, "So, about that picnic?" We made plans to meet that Friday at Guido Gardens, a religious park at the edge of town, and go out into the country somewhere nice for the picnic. I could have kept listening to him for hours, but Dani's mom started moving around upstairs and I got nervous and told him I had to go.

I checked on Dani, who was still asleep. Her fight with Hazel had left her with a big black eye and a bite mark on her arm that looked like a Doberman had been gnawing on her. Maybe she could wear a long-sleeved shirt, but her eye was a mess no amount of makeup was going to hide. And you can't wear sunglasses at breakfast unless you play in a rock band. She looked worse than awful—like a halfway rotted eggplant. When her mom saw that, she'd be grounded for the rest of her life.

I didn't bother leaving a note.

The Mystery
of the Snitch in the Night

"So, anyway," Dani said. "Someone phoned my mom this morning and said they saw us last night."

"Who?"

"That's the crazy thing. I don't know. They called while Mom and me were having breakfast. Dad had gone to work already. But what really gets me is they lied."

"They lied?"

The AC had crapped out completely sometime in the early afternoon, and there's only so much a box fan can do, even if you move it around with you from room to room. The air felt as thick as cream of mushroom soup. Every inch of my body was coated with greasy sweat. But when Dani said this, it seemed to cool and congeal into a clammy paste. I chewed off a hangnail.

"Yeah, whoever this was said they saw us in Statesboro."

After this last bit of bad news, I accidentally swallowed the tiny bit of skin.

"How would we get to Statesboro?" I asked her. Statesboro was about twenty miles away.

"That's what I told my mom. She thinks we went with some older boys." Dani let out a long, nervous laugh. "Close enough to the truth to rattle me when she told me. This person said he saw us in the Waffle House on Main Street. I told my mom to call the Waffle House and ask, but she won't."

"He?"

"A figure of speech, Lynn. Ever hear of those?" She made a snuffling sound. I had a mind to hang up on her. Then, between breaths, she dropped the sarcasm. "Actually, I have a feeling it was a *she*."

"You don't think it was the same one who sent the e-mails, do you?" I didn't want to believe this was possible.

"Uh-uh." Dani munched on something as she talked and this made it hard to understand what she was saying. "My mom knew this person, whoever it was. She said she wouldn't tell me who it was because she didn't want me trying to get back at them. And now I'm grounded for an extra fucking month. I'm not supposed to use the phone for a month either. She even hid my cell charger. I bet it was that bitch Hazel that called. My mom knows her. I'm starting to think Hazel's behind the e-mails too. I don't know how she did it, but I know it was her."

"I don't know," I said. "That sounds too smart for Hazel. Plus, we got the e-mails before you all fought."

"I'm going to get that bitch." In the background, a door squeaked open. I heard the hum of a refrigerator. "My mom let Wynn come over because I told her the Internet was messing up again. I showed him the new e-mails. All he did was babble a bunch of nerdish at me. But he's coming over later to try and figure them out while I watch *Judge Judy*. I think he's cooking up a plan and—" Dani groaned. "Oh God, my life sucks. We're out of Diet Coke."

"Is the punishment written in stone?"

Sometimes Dani's mom would give in after a few days and let her off the hook. I guess it depended on how steamed up she was about all this. The Statesboro business sounded bad. It was one thing to wander around Metter, but Statesboro had college boys and every mother in town had a fear of Georgia Southern frat boys.

"Yeah."

"Is she going to call my mom?" I hadn't thought of this till now.

"I don't know," Dani said. "I told her not to."

I wasn't sure if I believed this. "Thanks."

"I said to her, 'This is just as much a punishment for her. Where else does the poor girl have to go?' But don't worry, she's only dangerous when she's first mad. Like a kicked dog. If she hasn't done it already, I don't think she'll—"

"I talked to Logan today." I grinned at the mouthpiece of the phone.

"You did?" Her voice went up an octave and she choked a little on whatever crunchy thing she was eating. This was very satisfying to hear.

"He said he can hardly wait to meet me." Not exactly true, but I felt inspired. "We're going on a picnic."

"Shit, got to go. She's back."

Will Hayes Go to China?

The phone rang again, and I picked it up because I thought it was Dani calling back.

"Hey, Dani, what is it?"

A man breathed heavily into the phone. Before that first breath was through, I knew who this was. The mean man who called before. I recognized the wheezy sound and the way he blew out air with a kind of grunt at the end. After his second noisy suck of air, I matched up the breath with the man. Not that it made me any happier to of figured it out. This was Marty. H.K.'s uncle, who ran the Bow Wow club. The boss creep. The head thug. The mouth breather.

"You tell Hayes I found his car." His voice had a flat sound to it, bored almost, as if he was reading from a piece of paper he'd already read a hundred times. "I'm taking it as mine and it don't count for nothing toward what he already owes, not even the vig. You hear me?"

That bad night flashed through my head again like pictures in a PowerPoint presentation. The paper cutter goes *whomp*. The little pink nub jumps across the table. The hand squirts red. Plain, old-fashioned fear turned my insides into goo.

"I don't speak for Hayes," I told him, trying to keep the wobble out of my voice.

"Shit. You tell him, you tell him this—" He made a long sound of disgust, like he was clearing his throat. "I ain't going to let this slide. You tell him that. He goes to fucking China—I don't care—I'll find him. You tell him it don't have to go bad for him. But, but, *but*, if he don't get with it, I'm going to send Butthole Gibbs after his sorry ass. Hayes will know what I mean. He's got two days."

Then he hung up.

This is the end of summer, I thought.

Guido Gardens

Pastor Guido was a local televangelist. Even though he was from New Jersey, most people liked him anyway. His wife's people were from Metter, so that made up for it some. In fact, I think my mom's aunt was his wife's second cousin once removed or something like that. He had this little TV show that came on once in the morning after the local news out of Savannah and once after the late news at eleven. *A Seed from the Sower*, it was called. Only fifteen minutes long. It always started with some lame joke and ended with a passage from the Bible.

Pastor Guido built the garden a couple years before I was born. My father took me there every year to see the Christmas lights. At the gate they'd usually put up a huge plaster birthday cake with electric candles that said, HAPPY BIRTHDAY, JESUS! Thirty-three candles. I'd count them each year. Once I asked my dad, "Shouldn't it be one thousand nine hundred and ninety-some candles." He said, "Shhh, these people are as serious as a heart attack."

The gardens were about forty minutes away from my house if you walked. Half that if you rode a bike. They were pretty in a loud way, like a Hawaiian shirt. Artificially colored streams ran along fiberglass beds and splashed from cement waterfalls and fountains. The whole place was only about three acres, but it was strangely shaped and filled with trees and covered pavilions, so it seemed a lot bigger. Someone told me once that if you walked every path it was exactly eight miles. The paths were made of brick and lined with black-eyed Susans and ferns and bright purple coneflowers. No matter where you were in the park you could hear Muzak versions of famous gospel songs playing out of hidden speakers.

I chose this place to meet Logan because there were lots of hidden nooks where we could talk and not be seen. The place I had in mind was at the very end of the gardens near the road. A wrought-iron bench beside a waterfall. It was surrounded by weeping willows and plastic statues of geese. It'd take a long time to find it if you didn't know where to look, and if you wanted to get out of the gardens fast, all you had to do was jump over a couple of bushes and you were out on Turner Street. A sign behind the bench said, PLEASE ALLOW ME TO COMFORT YOUR SOUL. I hoped Logan might do something very much like that.

A Red Shirt and
a Polka-Dot Dress

Two middle-aged women pushed into the restroom when I was at the tail end of cleaning up—in fact, practically just about taking a shower in the sink. With the heat index, it was pushing a hundred and ten. I'd had to pedal along a busy road for most of the way, so to really get an idea of how I looked, add a few cups of dust and grit to a bucket of sweat and pour that over the image of me in your head. By the time I finished washing, the sink looked like somebody had scrubbed a pig in it. I finished off my transformation by putting on Mom's old blue-and-white polka-dot dress, the one Dani said made me look older, and rubbing my neck with a perfume sample out of that month's *Vogue*. The women turned their fancy hats and pinched little frowns on me. As I stumbled out, the first one nearly knocked me into the wall with her breasts, which were so big and mushed together, they looked like a single, jumbo-size loaf of Wonder bread set up there above her bellybutton.

Clamped down on the head of the second woman was a hat with a fake flower bed glued to the brim. This fancy bit of headgear resembled a natural history exhibit I'd once seen on a field trip to the state park museum. All it needed was a stuffed owl. She clucked her tongue and, after a last headshake in my direction, said, "Gary told me he was overjoyed to see my mama. *Overjoyed*. But he can't fool me. I know that man like the back of my hand. He is *up* to something. Mark my words."

"You got to watch them every second, Carrie." The big-bosomed lady's voice boomed inside the tiled room.

And then the door banged shut.

I've wondered often about that word—*overjoyed*. People say it a lot, but it usually doesn't make sense the way they use it. If you overdo something, then it most often means you've done it too much, like overeating, which can keep you up all night groaning and clutching your belly or send you racing to the toilet. Does a big, greedy gobbling of joy give a person some other variety of indigestion? Joy lives mainly in the head, right? So then it stands to reason a day of overjoying will end in a night of headaches and sinus trouble. Since joy is a feeling that generally escapes me, it's a rare day I get the opportunity for joying of any kind, much less overjoying. I suspect the term that best applies to my usual state is *underjoyed*. The day I met Logan for the first time I was afraid to hope for anything as extravagant as joy. I wished I had real breasts instead of these two little hen's eggs with match-head nipples. I wished Dani'd been there in the bathroom to help me with the makeup. All I wanted was to avoid embarrassing myself. If I could manage that, it would be a good day. Joy could wait for later.

The gardens were almost empty, so it was hard to keep a lookout for Logan without him seeing me do it. The last time I'd been here was almost five years earlier, with my Sunday school class. I couldn't think of any easy place for us to meet before I took him back to the little nook at the south end of the garden to talk, so I told him to wait for me at the gate. He said he'd wear a red shirt.

I sat on a bench about a hundred feet from the entrance. Across the goldfish pond, three solemn men in dark suits talked quietly. Every once in a while I'd hear one of them quote something with a scripture sound to it. *Thees* and *thous* and the like. It was a quarter after four and I was sweating again, even though I was in the shade. The gnats found me right away and launched an invasion into my ears and up my nose. I sang peppy radio songs in my head and tried to think of nothing. School started in a matter of days, but I couldn't quite make myself believe it. Sitting there, waiting to meet up with a soldier I might later even kiss (fingers crossed), made the idea of high school as distant and unreal to me as a family sitcom from the eighties rerun on cable. Metter High School seemed like some other world that didn't have anything to do with what was happening to me now.

At four-thirty, Logan showed. I'd about given up. He was shorter than I imagined, and wiry like the boys on the track team. I'd pictured him with a military buzz cut, but his hair came down below his ears. The only thing I didn't like was a mole on his cheek that looked like John Boy's from *The Waltons*. My mom liked to watch *The Waltons* on cable, and whenever John Boy's mole came on the screen, it always made me leave the room. The one on Logan's cheek wasn't quite as big, but you definitely noticed it. He held a blue box in his hand wrapped with a white ribbon. Something went suddenly wrong with my inner organs, and I thought I might have to make a dash to the restroom, but I didn't.

I kept walking toward him until he saw me and waved. We were still too far apart to say anything and I didn't know what to do with myself. I forgot what I usually did with my hands when I walked. Did I usually swing my arms or hold them by my sides? I couldn't keep looking him in the eye that long. I waved and looked down. My face felt like melting wax.

I thought he would shake my hand when we met, but he hugged me instead. It surprised me, but I liked it. All of my inner organs really went into overdrive then, churning and squirming and making dangerous noises. I wanted to say something clever or funny, but my head was an empty egg. I felt all thin shell.

"Hey," he said. "Sorry I'm late."

"Okay," I said, immediately thinking, Why did I say that? What the hell does that mean? Okay? Dani would laugh if she heard me. He must think I'm retarded and I've only said one word!

"You want to walk around?"

"Okay." It was all I seemed able to say right then. Maybe if I concentrated really hard, I could add one more word to my vocabulary. Like *sure* or *great.*

He took my hand, which probably felt like pickled pig's knuckles, and we walked along the outer path. The flies buzzed very loud at that moment, and although the sky was the color of skim milk, the sun shone so brightly I could barely see. He talked. He said I looked better than he imagined, older. He liked my hair and my polka-dot dress. He told me he'd had some problems leaving the base. Literally five minutes before he planned to leave, his asshole sergeant assigned him to do something really big that afternoon. I can't remember what. See, Logan's presence took up so much of my attention I could barely hear what he said. I do remember he asked me if I listened to the Shins a lot. For a long moment, I had absolutely no idea what he was talking about.

He hummed a song.

"Oh," I said after a moment, "right, yeah, the band. I only really know the songs from that movie soundtrack. My friend plays it a lot. I do like the creepy caring song, though."

Logan laughed.

A bus of nursery school kids unloaded at the visitor center and the gardens filled up with screaming children. It seemed oddly late in the afternoon for them to be there. Everything in the garden suddenly felt bigger and louder and brighter than normal. My voice warbled when I talked. I told him I liked his red shirt, but I hadn't really looked at it. His eyes changed color when we left the slanting afternoon light and walked in the shadows under the trees. He had very white teeth. His lips were thick but not too thick. Full, I think is the word. He said a lot of things. Things I can't remember now. I could barely concentrate on walking. I forgot how to do the most basic things, like breathe and talk. We circled the garden three or four times before he gave me the package. By then I'd forgotten he had anything with him at all. The package was small, about half the size of a CD case but thicker, and it felt light when he put it in my hands.

"What's this?" I said. The package made me even more nervous than I was before.

"Open it." He smiled and his teeth looked very bright in the sunlight, like polished bits of stone.

I took off the paper carefully, peeling the tape back instead of tearing it, as though I meant to reuse it and not just chuck it in a trash bin like I did. This was something that irritated me to no end when my mom did it, and there I was doing it too. The box inside had a gold foil sticker that said, LEVY'S JEWELRY, in raised, bumpy letters. He watched my face very closely and this made it even harder for me to use my hands like a normal human. Lying inside on a mattress of white velvet was a thin gold bracelet with a charm shaped like a puppy.

"See these little loops?" He pointed with his pinkie, as though the gold was so delicate a larger finger might wreck it. "You can add more charms later on if you feel like it. I didn't know what kind of animals you liked. This guy's smiling, which I thought was pretty good. The penguin looked mad or . . ." Logan seemed to run out of words there. He smiled an apology. Without even thinking, I grabbed his wrist and squeezed it once before realizing and yanking away.

"Thank you," I said. My tongue seemed to fill up my entire mouth and spill out over my lips. At least that's how it felt. I could hardly get the words out around it.

He took the bracelet and draped it over my wrist. It was hard not to shake as he fixed the clasp. I made a fist to keep my fingers together, but my hand still trembled. In the bright sunlight, the bracelet looked like a squirt of burning lighter fluid on my wrist. Once he got the bracelet on, he leaned over and kissed the inside of my wrist. It surprised me so much I almost pulled my arm away again. A couple of little boys ran past us yelling, chased by a girl in pink shorts waving a branch as long as she was. Logan gave me a serious look and took my face in his hands and kissed me on the lips. He didn't open his mouth when he did it. He just pressed his lips against mine, like a kiss in a black-and-white movie. Logan had a nice, soapy smell. But hiding right beneath was something spicy and sharp that reminded me of nutmeg. It was the kind of smell to fill your belly with raw blue swirls of electric current. And his lips left behind a clean, mint taste.

"I know it ain't much," he said, holding my wrist with both hands and tapping the bracelet with his thumbs, "but I wanted to bring you something."

Boone's Farm

ogan had an old, mint-green Grand Marquis. The backseat was big enough to hold my bike, but we put it in the trunk. An Army duffle bag rode shotgun with the seat belt holding it in place. He tossed it in the back and helped me into the car. I wondered about the bag but didn't say anything. The air conditioner was broken—he apologized for this three times—so we put the windows down. Something was wrong with the automatic window on my side. He had to get back out and yank on it a few times to make it come down even halfway. He told me his father had given him the car when he joined the Army, and he tried to take care of it as best he could, but it was old and there was always something that needed to be repaired. While he was over in Iraq, his ex-fiancée drove it. She hadn't thought to change the oil once in an entire year, and this had added to its sorry decline. Even I would of known to do that.

Logan turned left on Lewis and we drove through Metter, crossing over the interstate and going a ways out into the country toward Cobbtown. The cotton fields along the road were dark green and powdered with orange dust. The bolls themselves had only barely begun to burst into white. I leaned back in the seat and watched the neat red rows of clay flicker past between the lines of cotton plants. I gave up my head to happy, empty looking. The sun-baked air blew my hair out straight behind my head. We topped a small rise, and on the other side, the hard sunlight of the cotton fields ended and the swaying, speckled shade of the pine tree farms began. Tall, straight trees rose up on either side, darkening the asphalt and filling the car with the sticky, medicine smell of rising sap. We passed the rusty ruins of the old turpentine factory. A donkey and a cow chewed grass in the building's blue shadow. I threw them a wave, but neither one bothered to look. The clover in their pasture must have been juicy and sweet. All their wishes had been granted. They had no need of me and my cheerful teenage waves.

"Where are we going?" Logan had to shout because the wind roared in through the windows. Even with the air fluttering my hair here and there and keeping it up off my neck, the car was still hot. Sweat puddled up under my legs, so they stuck to the vinyl seat, and a dribble dripped down the middle of my back.

"I don't care," I said.

"Okay," he said. And then, after a couple of seconds, "I'm not going back."

"What?" I wasn't sure I'd heard him right. At first I thought he meant Metter and I wondered briefly if he meant to kidnap me. The idea didn't bother me much. It sent another zing of electricity through my frazzled nerve endings. No Metter High for me next week.

"I wish I didn't have to go back to Hunter. I can't stand it there. I hate it worse than anything I've ever hated. And the idea of going back to Iraq—it just—" He banged his fist on the outside of the door. It made a hollow thump. "I don't think I can do it."

"What would you do instead?"

"I don't know. But I'm sick to death of the Army. I did my bit. Nobody can say I'm not patriotic. There's plenty of other assholes who could go instead of me."

We were quiet then, thinking about this. We drove past Dean Martin Taxidermy with its huge JESUS SAVES sign and pasture out in front. A couple of fat black sheep leaned together back to back, so still in the shade of a cypress tree they looked like great big rocks. I wanted a cigarette. We passed the little gas station at the edge of Cobbtown and I wondered if I should ask him to stop and buy me a pack. Logan beat me to the thought.

"Do you drink wine?" he said.

"Yeah," I said.

"I think some cold wine would be good."

There were no cars coming, so he made a U-turn in the road and drove back to the gas station. It was a little cinder-block box with peeling white paint and a window made of glass bricks. On one side of the gas station, a row of pecan trees kept the service island shady, and over past the trees, two tireless rust heaps were parked forever in a patch of jimsonweed and buttercups.

"Mind going in the store for me? I'll give you the money. I don't really like crowded little places like this."

The store looked empty.

"Logan, the problem is they know me here. I ain't twenty-one." I asked him to buy me a pack of cigarettes, rummaging in my purse for bills. He waved them away. I watched the muscles in his back flex and relax as he walked into the store. They looked hard and well kept. Just then, I wanted more than anything to touch them.

A few minutes later, Mr. Jenkins, the owner of the hardware store in town, pulled up next to Logan's car. I tried to slink down in the seat, but he saw me.

"How you doing, Lynn?" he said. Mr. Jenkins was just this side of fat and his T-shirt was a little too small, so you could see a bare strip of white belly above his belt.

"Alright, Mr. Jenkins," I said.

"Last Friday before school starts, huh?" He smiled that superior little smile adults always use when they're talking to teenagers about school. Like, *hah, I don't have to do that shit anymore, but you sure do.* "Who you out motoring with?"

I treated him to one of my sweet girlish smiles, dialed down a notch or three. My little-girl-on-the-way-to-Sunday-school smile. "My cousin Logan," I said. "He's stationed down in Savannah and he came to visit us for the afternoon."

He looked me over for a moment, squinting. "My little brother Jeffrey is stationed down there. You remember Jeffrey, don't you? I wonder if your cousin knows him. What'd you say his name is again?"

"He might," I said.

Before I could say Logan's name again, the bell on the door clanged. I sucked in a breath between my teeth. He came out of the store toting two white plastic bags. Bottles bulged against the sides and Mr. Jenkins looked at them.

"Your cousin here tells me you're stationed down at Hunter."

"Yes, sir," Logan said, his back going all stiff and soldierly. I couldn't help but smile at this transformation.

"Maybe you know my brother, Sergeant Jenkins?"

"I don't, sir. But Hunter is a big base."

"That's true," Mr. Jenkins said. "What was your name again, son?"

"Charlie Davidson, sir."

Mr. Jenkins squinted hard at me then, and it wasn't nervousness that made me think he was suspicious this time. "Your cousin told me your name was Logan."

That little shit, I thought. Why'd he ask Logan what his name was if he remembered?

Logan smiled. It looked like a perfectly natural smile. I was impressed. "That's what my family calls me, sir. It's my middle name."

"Well," Mr. Jenkins said, "I would tell you to tell my brother I said hey, but since you don't know him—"

"If I ever meet him, I'll tell him, sir."

"You all have a nice day." He looked down at the bag of wine bottles again and then over at me, raising an eyebrow. "Be careful now."

Logan started the engine and pulled out with a spray of gravel. His eyes were dark. "If he says anything to his brother, I'm fucked. He'll know in a second who I am and that I was off base without permission."

"You know his brother?" This seemed an impossible coincidence, and an awful one.

"My sergeant. The one who made me late meeting you. He thinks he's some kind of hardass but he's really just a pissy little REMF."

"REMF?"

"Rear Echelon Mother Fucker. Means those guys that stay behind the wire where it's safe. Or in his case, at home."

"Is this going to get you in more trouble?" I said.

"I'm in trouble no matter what," he said. "Now it might just come a little quicker."

"I don't think he'll say anything. He's probably already forgotten about it."

"Probably not, but still—"

"Don't worry about it now." I touched him on the arm with one finger.

"Nah," he said, pointing to the sky, "you're right. On a day like this? I'll worry about it tonight."

When we got back on the highway, he gunned the engine and we flew across the countryside like a big green buzzard.

A Half-Collapsed Barn Covered in Kudzu Vines

"Where does this go?" Logan asked, slowing down the car and pointing to a road of packed orange clay that wiggled off into the pines.

"I don't know," I said. "I've never been out that way before." I shaded my eyes with a hand. "But I think it belongs to the McWhorters. Or at least it used to. Nobody's planted anything here since I was little."

"Good," he said, and we pulled off the highway, raising an orange cloud behind us. The trees beside the road were wide and tall and the road itself had sunk down four or five feet below the fields from a couple hundred years of wagon wheels and pickup trucks, so it felt like we were driving through a tunnel of green needles. Sunlight freckled the clay. A crow pecked at the body of a smaller bird in the ditch beside the road. And somewhere back behind the trees a cow lowed. Logan drove slowly now, taking the curves carefully and glancing over at me and smiling every couple of minutes. I bounced in my seat and grinned back, pleased to be me at that moment, in that car, with that boy. I didn't want the ride to end.

We turned a bend and found a cow standing in the middle of the road. Logan tapped the horn once, but she wouldn't budge, so he wheeled us down into the ditch and drove around her. He said something too quiet to hear. The cow never moved an inch, but she turned her head to watch us pass, chewing and chewing. I wondered what she saw.

"Are you worried?" I said.

"About what?"

"About leaving."

"Yeah," he said, "but I had to get out of there. Even if only for the day. Maybe I should do something and get myself chucked out. Do something crazy. The big problem is my family. They'll never forgive me for that. My dad's a Vietnam vet. Two tours. He's going to think I'm a pussy. I wouldn't be surprised if he takes it into his head never to speak to me again."

"Really? But you already went over once."

"That don't matter to him. The only time he was ever all that nice to me is when I told him I'd enlisted. This would screw up everything." He sounded more angry than sad.

"Where would you go if you left?"

See there, how already I wished he would stay with me? Although I didn't know it then, I'd started tying little invisible strings of trouble to each of the veins going into my heart. Each lie, each selfish intention—another dainty little knot.

"I'll burn that bridge when I cross it."

Logan drove the car into a clearing of high grass beside a half-collapsed barn covered in kudzu vines. The door squealed when I pushed it shut and I had to bump it with my hip to make it click. The grass came up past my knees and tickled me. He pulled an old green blanket out of the trunk and slung it over his shoulder. Beside the barn was an overgrown pasture filled with cornflowers and goldenrod. We walked to the edge of the clearing and he spread the blanket out in the shade of an old camphor tree.

"Ready to celebrate?" he said.

I smiled and sat down next to him. He pulled a bottle out of the plastic sack, all sweaty and slick with cold, and unscrewed it. He took a swig and passed it over to me. It was berry-flavored Boone's Farm and it tasted like Kool-Aid.

"Sorry," he said, "I forgot to buy cups. Some picnic, huh? I meant to bring all this stuff, but it was all I could do just to get to those gardens before you thought I'd forgot about you and left."

"I don't care."

We passed the bottle back and forth a couple of times and he looked at me as though he was on the verge of saying something, but he didn't. He just looked.

"In the barracks all anyone ever does is bullshit and drink beer," he said finally. "So, I hope I don't sound stupid." Him saying this made me like him even more. It felt like he'd opened a window curtain and let in a gush of sunlight.

This is *her* August afternoon. Young Lynn's, *before* Lynn's. Her prized possession. Looking back, I know now that day stood up on its tippy-toes and peeked over into September and all that came with it. Hints of trouble floated here and there like motes in sunshine. That younger Lynn might not of known what her August day saw over the edge of the month, but, feeling as she did right then, she sure as hell wouldn't of given her afternoon back even if she had.

Don't ask me if I'd do it now.

We drank the wine, and sip by sip he told me about his family and his life in the Army. He was the youngest. He had two sisters and a brother. All of them were married. His brother was a Ranger stationed in Kabul, Afghanistan. The hero of the family, who hadn't done wrong since the day he first put on his Pop Warner football helmet. No matter that Logan played just as good, maybe better. His sisters made babies, he told me with a frown, and that's about all his father expected from them. Five grandkids so far and more on the way. His father owned an Army surplus store in Virginia Beach and traveled to gun shows to collect antique pistols. His mother taught tatting at the local sewing shop. They'd moved away from Savannah while Logan was overseas because his father worried the blacks were invading his south-side subdivision.

Logan had recently gotten the rank of specialist. That's why they stationed him down at Hunter Army Airfield, where they were training him to fix helicopter rotors. Because of his shrapnel wound, he wouldn't have to go out to some forward operating base and do movement-to-contact missions anymore or patrol urban streets, but he'd still be over there. This new training, he said, was all but over and he'd be shipping out in a matter of months.

"My dad was proud of me when he heard. Sent me down a bottle of Wild Turkey and a case of beer," he said, "but it don't mean fuck all to me. I'm twenty-five years old and my biggest accomplishment is a little iron-on patch." He laughed like laughing was something you did when you were angry and took a long gurgle of wine. I watched the bubbles fight each other to get to the end of the bottle, and when I reached for it next, I accidentally on purpose touched him on the neck. His skin felt soft but hard with muscle. Tense and corded.

I told him about my family and Dani and school. But only when he asked me. Mostly, I asked him questions and listened. It helped me control my misfiring nerve circuits. Whenever the conversation slowed down, I asked him another question. Butterflies floated about in the clearing eating flower perfume. Logan caught one with a cupped hand and set it down on my knee. It rested for a moment there, stretching its baby-blanket-colored wings, and then took off. I hadn't eaten since breakfast and the wine went straight to my head. Like I'd poured it in my ear. It made my stomach tingle and my mouth want to laugh for no reason. At that second, Logan looked to me like the most beautiful man on earth.

In August, it doesn't get dark until after eight, so we drove around for a while talking. I made sure we never got too close to town. I didn't want anyone else to see us. By then I did all the talking and the words came out as fast as the wine went down. Dizzy now, I felt the words spin out in circles around my head. I told him I wanted to be a social worker and help children with bad parents, which was funny since I'd never thought that before. It only occurred to me then.

When the fireflies started flashing along the road, I had him park his car in the hospital's side parking lot, which was never full but never all the way empty either. We walked on either side of my bike, each of us holding a handlebar, and cut across the strip of grass between the lot and my backyard. I kept a careful eye out the whole time, nervous somebody'd drive past and see us, but no one did. The house was dark and my mom's car was gone, which worried me some since I thought she was working that night and she almost always walked to work. But there was nothing I could do about it, so I tried to push the idea from my head. That was a whole different soap opera and I wanted to keep it on a whole different channel. The last thing I needed was for Mom to drive up unexpectedly and see me getting out of some strange boy's car, or at least strange to her, so it was just as well she was off somewhere and I'd had him park so far away.

"What—?" he wanted to know, but I shut him up with one last kiss. No tongue, just a fearsome squashing of lips.

"Thanks," I said and made to shut the screen door, but he stopped it with a hand.

"When can I—?"

I needed him to be off and away before Mom came home. I'd used up all my extra talk, small or otherwise. At the same time, I didn't want to make Logan think, well, whatever it was he'd think if I dashed off into the house without some last swapping of *see you later*s and *call me*s. I didn't know how to tell him it had been the most perfect day of my life without sounding like a sappy fifteen-year-old girl. But he wouldn't know any of that unless I said something. I muttered and stuttered and said, mouth so full of smile I could hardly get the words out, "We can do this again whenever you want, soldier. But it's late." I put my thumb and pinkie up to my ear and waggled them in the universal sign for call me, and then felt so dumb for doing it, my face probably looked like I'd dunked it in ketchup. "I mean, this was the best day of the summer. Call me tomorrow and—"

Now it was his turn to steal away the last of a sentence. "Wait, I almost forgot." He reached into his pocket and pulled out something white—a scrap of paper. "I have something else for you. I made it when you were off in the trees . . . uh . . ."

Peeing, he meant.

"Thanks," I said quickly and snatched the paper out of his hand.

I tossed him my best sexy smile, the one I'd been practicing in the bathroom mirror, and skipped into the house, screen door bouncing behind me. Really. I skipped. I couldn't help myself. Around the coffee table twice and then down the hall to my room and back. When my pulse stopped hammering in my eardrums, I looked at what he'd given me. An origami butterfly made from the gas station receipt for the wine. I have it still.

Heckle and Jeckle

At eleven o'clock that same damn night, somebody, or some-bodies, had to go and ruin my day of black-eyed Susans and Kool-Aid wine kisses by ringing the doorbell. Nobody was home but me. The only light in the house came from the TV, and it was on mute. Hardly ten seconds passed before they rang again. I crawled to the front door on my hands and knees. The hallway was as dark as the inside of my stomach. I didn't hear anything at first, and then a man said, "I saw her leave before. Around dinnertime. Maybe they both—"

"Will you hush?"

One of the two of them slammed on the door with a fist. The sound of it filled up the hallway like shotgun blasts. I held my breath and waited. It was quiet for a time, and then the first one started up complaining again.

"After all this waiting around, I could eat a bite or two myself. What you think about barbeque? I hear there's a good place up the road. Just off I-16. I think it's called the Forking Pork. My cousin went there before and he said he ate the shit out of their pulled-pork sandwiches. I could seriously go for some pulled pork and—"

"Ever hear the expression, never trust a man with an ass wider than his shoulders? Well, you're one fucking sandwich away from untrustworthy, bo."

"Wenzell, come on, man. Don't give me that—"

"What I tell you about using that name? Just quit, before I pop you one. I didn't choose the damn thing and the hell if I'm going to let you use it."

"I'd like to see you try."

"Uh-huh," the Wenzell man said, and the way he said it, all freezy and evil sounding, I'd of kept my mouth shut about the name, the Forking Pork, and everything else. The hungry one must of agreed with me. Neither said nothing for a while.

Then the hungry guy came on quiet and apologetic-like. "Sorry, I forget. What you want me to—?"

"Wait. Hush up now, Travis." The second man, who didn't like to be called Wenzell, made a hissing sound and lowered his voice. "You hear that?"

"No.'

"The car is—" The rest of what he said was a grumble. Neither of their voices sounded like the one I'd heard on the phone. The mouth breather. I tried to picture Marty from when I saw him the other night at Bow Wow's, but his face wouldn't come.

"Yeah, that's probably right. I don't expect he walked here," Travis said. His voice was higher pitched and easier to hear.

Something crunched outside and then the flap on the mail slot lifted. I held my breath again and concentrated on being invisible. *No one can see me. No one can see me. No one can see me.* The man looking through the slot breathed heavily, but not the way Marty did on the phone. This one had a slight wheeze. I hoped to God he couldn't see the blue flicker from the TV.

"No nothing," Travis said. "If he's here, then he's quiet as a Goddamned mouse. We can tell Marty we waited till . . ." He paused. "Around midnight. I don't believe he's here. Even Hayes ain't stupid enough to hide out in the first place we'd look."

He obviously don't know Hayes, I thought.

"Marty thinks he is." Wenzell coughed and one or the other of them rubbed his feet against the brickwork, making a couple of sandy scrapes.

"Well, the man can come out here and wait himself, he thinks that. I'll tell him to his face." Travis giggled. It was a very unpleasant sound, and I was glad I couldn't see him while he did it.

"Uh-huh. I'll be believing that shit when I see it. You always talk big when it's just you and me."

"Let's go get us some food," Travis said, his voice turning whiney. "We been here for fucking ever. They're gone. Vamoosed. I still don't get why Marty won't let us bust in here and check for sure."

"Marty says there's always cops coming over to the emergency room. He said, unless it's a real dark, overcast night, somebody might see something."

"Bah. The hospital is a half-mile up the hill. Nobody can see us." Travis sniffed and spat. "Wait, you hear that sound, Burns?"

Neither of them said anything for a second.

"I don't hear shit," Burns, the non-Wenzell, said. Then I remembered the name from that horrible night at Bow Wow's. I couldn't remember the man's face to save my life. Only that ugly pink triangle scar on his cheek and the red baseball cap. Unless these were different Burnses and Travises, I had nearly the whole nasty cast on my doorstep.

"That's the sound of my stomach eating on itself." Travis made his horrible giggle again, like a ten-year-old troll girl.

"That be the case, bo, you ain't got nothing to worry about for a while. You could live off that belly for a month or two."

"Fuck you."

"Fuck you yourself."

"And if you don't quit with that bo shit, I'll take up calling you

Wenzell again. I noticed bo is what you always call people you're fixing to punch. Don't be calling me that. It's like you calling me bitch or something."

"No, you dumbass. It ain't nothing like the same thing," Burns said. "For somebody so ugly, you sure are sensitive."

"I'd like to see you say something like that to Butthole."

"Bah." Burns paused for a couple beats. "Who?"

"Butthole Gibbs. You know. The one who laid down the law over in Jasper that time. Marty might bring him up to do a job on Hayes."

Burns grunted and said, "Nuh-uh, I don't recall nothing about that."

Travis told him last fall the Higgins brothers held up a high-stakes poker game. The night they came, there was almost forty grand on the table. The man who ran the game called up Marty after it happened, pissed off because he paid Marty to provide pro-tection, and so Marty called Butthole and said for him to fix the ones who did it. The older Higgins boy's mask slipped when he was scooping the cash up off the table or they might of gotten away clean. Half the room had a good, long look at him by the time he shoved it back in place. A week later and he was in the hospital, a stuttering idjit with half a dozen broken bones. Butthole split his head open and all of elementary school fell out. They never found the younger one, but Travis heard he'd poured lighter fluid in the kid's mouth and set him alight. The oddest part of all, according to him, was that Butthole lived forty minutes away in a little house in Garden City with his mama. Every Sunday morning he bought her a fresh bouquet of pink carnations and took her to the early service at Second Baptist. Supposedly, even his mama called him Butthole.

The two stopped talking. A car rolled slowly down the road. I'll be damned if I didn't hear them scramble behind the holly bushes next to the door. As the headlights strafed the windows, their shadows hunched and fattened against the blinds. I hoped to God it wasn't my mom coming home. Somewhere close, gravel crunched and a bad muffler farted twice and then the engine quit. A car door slammed. Maybe next door. Then a man started humming an aimless tune. Mr. Cannon. His screen door creaked open and shut, bouncing three times before it came to rest. I smiled to think of those two getting jumpy over Mr. Cannon, who always put me in mind of a pink trash bag filled with mashed potatoes.

"We best be getting on soon," Travis said. "That was close."

Baby's Got a New Pair of Shoes

The first thing my mom said when she came home an hour or so later was, "Did you try on your new shoes?"

"No," I said.

"Try them on. Let's see."

"Mom, did you get my message?"

Mom frowned.

"I told Carla it was urgent."

She jammed one of the sneakers on my left foot, but it was a right shoe. "Hmm, that don't fit like it should," she said. "I hope I got your size. Eight, right? Hurry up now, I've got to go back and finish my shift."

"Are you listening to me, Mom? It's important." I pinched her on the thigh. She thumped me on the forehead with a finger. I took the shoe from her and put it on the right foot. "Mom," I said.

Mom let out a little whoop when she saw the shoe fit.

I put my face right up to hers and said, "Mom, some scary men came by an hour ago. I tried to call the nurses' station three times, but it was busy. Didn't Carla say nothing to you? She said she'd tell you."

"No, Carla didn't tell me noth—" Her face froze. She dropped the other shoe in her lap. "What'd they look like?" she asked in a tight voice.

"I didn't see them. I only heard them through the mail slot." I told her what they'd said, especially the part about Butthole. "One of them was called Travis."

"Travis?" Mom said, pinching the tip of her nose. "I don't know."

Either the name rang a bell and it worried her, or it didn't, and this worried her more.

Advice

"He came," I whispered to Dani. I was sitting on the seat of the toilet with the phone to my ear. My mom was still up watching TV.

"I hope he didn't ruin your dress." She made a smirking sound, a cross between a croak and a snicker.

"Oh, please."

"Is he a hunk or a gunk?"

"Can you hear that?"

"What?" She sounded suspicious.

"It's only just the sound of my heart melting." I laughed when I said it, but it felt true enough.

"Oh, Lord Jesus," she said and groaned. "Well, your heart sounds like a bathroom sink running to me. What's the scoop?"

"Longish blond hair, good nose, muscles but not gross Schwarzenegger ones. Smells good. Nice kisser."

Dani squealed. I held the phone away from my ear. "Did you do it?" she asked.

I said nothing. The jealous sound in her voice made me smile extra wide at myself in the steamed-up mirror. I ran a brush through my hair and examined the blackheads on my nose.

"Well, did you?"

"Sure. Just like you said. Right under the giant shrub shaped like Jesus' head."

"You did?" I think she almost believed it, not that she'd admit it in a billion years.

"No, we hung out in a flower patch behind an old barn and drank wine. I mean, come on. What do you think? It was our first—"

"Second, if you count the online one."

"—and anyway," I said, ignoring her, "I'm not doing it for the very first time in a weed patch, squishing bugs with my bare butt."

"I thought you said flowers." She made a *got you* noise. "Think you'll do it next time?"

"We haven't scheduled a next time yet."

"Oh, but you will, I know it. Now you've had a taste of the forbidden fruit, there's no turning back."

"What movie is that from?" I said, thinking his kisses tasted more like forbidden Boone's berries.

"None." She laughed, a bright, tinny sound. "I've been reading one of my mom's Scottish time-travel romance novels. That's how bored I am, cooped up in the house all day."

I knew for a fact she read them all the time. And loved them.

"I don't know if I'm ready to do it yet," I said, chewing my cheek and wondering if this was true. "Probably not."

"When you *do* do it, make lots of sounds."

"Why?"

"Men like it."

"How do you know?"

"I read it in *Vogue*."

"I thought you said not to."

"Only at first, when he tears the flesh of your hymen. Afterward, yes. Double yes."

I yelped at this.

"Be more realistic come mating season or you'll sound like a piglet." Then she cleared her throat in a way that told me something serious was coming up next. "Something happened."

"Oh, shit," I said, "not another e-mail."

"No, maybe something worse, or I don't know, Lynn. Maybe you're right. Maybe I should tell my dad."

"You don't have to tell him the whole story."

"I saw somebody spying on me through the bat cave window."

"*What?*" I nearly yelled.

"Yeah, I was painting my toenails around nine thirty with this new ice-blue polish I swiped from my mom and I heard this sound, this—" She ran her fingernail along the side of the phone so it made a hollow scraping sound. "When I looked up, I could swear I saw the shadow of a head and I screamed. I must of sounded pretty scared 'cause my dad came running down the stairs. When I told him, he ran out there lickety-split with his shotgun."

"Damn," I said in a hushed voice. "Did he—"

"No, but he thinks he found footprints. There's a new flower bed beside the window and the landscaping guys did something up there the morning before so the dirt's all loose."

"Jesus Christ."

"I know. Dad called the police and they said they'd have someone circle the neighborhood a few times tonight."

"Can't they do anything else?"

"No, it pissed my dad off like nobody's business. He raved and ranted about how he's going to blow the guy's head off. The police can't do nothing at all unless we catch the guy red-handed or he actually does something."

"Like—"

"Yeah, tear me a hole I can't fix."

You Did What, Now?

I went to bed after talking to Dani. Early Sunday morning, the cell phone rang under my pillow. The clock said 3:30 A.M. I near about ignored it, not being in the mood for any more Dani drama. But when I looked, it was Logan Loy.

"Lynn Marie?" he said, not sounding quite right. Even though I loved that he called me by both my names (nobody but my mom did that and usually only when pissed off), I also felt something hard and prickly doing angry laps around my stomach lining.

"Yeah?" I said. "Is something wrong, Logan? You don't sound—"

"Remember I told you about that sergeant? One who knows that old man we saw out by Cobbtown? His brother or cousin or something?"

"Mmm-hmm." I thumbed away some sleep from my eye.

"Your nosy old man called him up. I'm looking at a buttload of trouble. He told me, tomorrow morning I've got to go up." He breathed in wisps and wheezes. "They're going to article my ass. I know it. I fucking know it. I'm dead, honey."

"Slow down, Logan. What do you mean, articled?"

"I hauled off and thumped him one. Just the once, but it knocked him clean out. Now I'm well and truly fucked. Backwards, sideways, you name it."

"You did what, now?" I asked.

Logan spoke so fast it was hard to follow what he said. I'm not even sure he heard me because he kept right on talking. "I lost my shit and ran. I'm on I-16 now, going near about ninety miles per hour."

"Man, you best slow down or the regular police will drag you in."

"You're right, you're right. I didn't even think of that. I knew you were a smart one the first time I talked to you."

Despite the circumstances, I couldn't help but feel a gush of pride. "What are you going to do now?"

"I don't know. Run."

"But where? You got friends you can stay with?"

"Uh. My grandma."

"Oh, Logan, you can't go there. That'll be one of the first places they come looking."

As it turned out, he was only about three miles from the Metter exit. I told him he might as well just come here for the night. He could figure out what to do in the morning. Nobody would think to look for him at my house. He wasn't all that sure about it, but I added that Mom wasn't home, and then all at once he was.

"You saved me, girl." He nearly sang this to me, like the sweetest gospel song ever sung and aimed straight into my ear.

Should I Really Let Logan Loy
Spend the Night?

Yes	No
I'm ready to lose it	I'm not ready to lose it
He can protect us against creeps	He might be a creep
I'm lonely	He could be really crazy
He seems kind	It's only the one night
He might be faking it	Mom could find out
I'll do it before Dani	Dani might tell people
He's the sexiest thing ever	He might snore or have nasty feet
He's 25	He might think I'm a baby
I'm ready to lose it	I'm not ready to lose it

ogan said he'd only talk for a minute and he meant exactly that. He wanted to make sure I hadn't changed my mind and where I wanted to meet him. I told him to park where he did before. I'd be waiting.

"Are you ready for me?" he said. "I'm passing the town limits."

"I can't wait," I said.

"Good," he said. "I have a surprise for you."

Sort of Green

I hugged my knees and leaned against a pine tree. The late night air didn't move an inch. Like instead of oxygen, the air was made of chocolate syrup. Tree frogs sang sex songs one to one to one, from this end of town to the other. By the time I saw those headlights wash across the lot up on the hill, I'd near about lost control of my entire body.

"You alright?" he asked once he got closer. His smile was bright as beer neon as he swung his duffle off his shoulder. "You're looking sort of green."

"I . . . it's the streetlight."

With that, he folded me up in his arms. I never thought a man's sweaty pits could smell so good. Logan kissed the top of my head and held me out at arm's length to take a look at me. My huge, new feelings for him filled me up to the crown of my head. Any doubts I had about him staying flew out my ear right then.

"Are you sure this'll be alright?" he said, smiling and smiling. I gave him a dozen or two smiles right back. "It'd only be for the one night. I'll be out of your hair before the sun rises. I won't try anything unseemly. I'll be as quiet as a mouse."

"We just can't let my mom find out. She'd kill me. You too."

"Where you going to stash me? Under the bed?" He linked his arm through mine. "Remember, I'm a mouse. Mice are easy."

"Yeah?" I said.

"They require very little space."

So I told him about the little room behind my closet.

"Sure enough," Logan Loy said.

Princess Lynn Marie

ogan lugged in his green duffle bag and I hid it under my bed. I had to mash it down before it would fit. We sat down on top of the comforter and looked at each other. It was hot in the house, as usual, and sweat dotted his upper lip. It was all I could do not to kiss it away. I swayed on the bed. The room spun a bit.

"Where's your mom at?"

"I don't know. Work maybe. She told me when she'd be home, but I forgot." I really did. I searched my head for the answer, but it had completely up and vanished. It took every last one of my powers of concentration just to listen to what he was saying.

"You think I could take a shower?"

"Yeah, but you have to be quick."

"Don't worry."

Ten minutes later he came back with wet, ruffled hair and the smell of my chocolate ice cream soap on his skin. I got some blankets out of the linen closet and took a pillow off of my bed. We crawled through my closet over old shoes and under hangers jammed with clothes. Behind last year's too-small church dress, there was a door the size of an opened newspaper with a fake bronze handle that opened onto the attic access. The room was a quarter the size of my bedroom and the ceiling slanted down low enough for Logan to bang his head against if he tried to stand up. On the far wall, a small window would of given a view of the lawn if it hadn't been covered up and darkened by the holly bushes. Unpainted plywood covered most of the floor and only one of the walls was finished with sheetrock. Two-by-four studs and itchy pink insulation made up the rest. It smelled of stale ginger bread and old pine needles. Piled from floor to ceiling along the side closest to the living room were boxes of Christmas decorations and my old kiddie stuff, black plastic bags of worn-out clothes and junk my dad never took when he left. Dust covered everything and it felt twice as hot as the rest of the house, but Logan didn't seem to mind any, or didn't say so if he did.

I made a bed for him and we lit emergency candles and stuck them in beer bottles. He asked about a painting on the wall I did when I was about ten. It was a sloppy picture of me riding a brown horse in the princess outfit I wore for Halloween that year. Long pink scarves and an upside-down ice cream cone hat. He moved his blankets over beneath it, so he could look up at me while he went to sleep.

"Princess Lynn Marie," he said and laughed. It was a nice laugh and not one that was making fun of me.

I went and got him a plastic water bottle in case he got thirsty in the night. Logan smiled when he saw it and pulled out a bottle of Boone's Farm wine, saying he got it because I'd seemed to like it so much. This time I got us a couple cups to drink from. We drank while I told him about the games I used to play in the storage space when I was younger. Prisoner in Troll Castle. Or the cave of a monster snail who guarded over a treasure hoard. I used bottle caps as silver coins and my Cabbage Patch Kid, Penny, as the snail. Occasionally I traveled through space, stuck in suspended animation until I arrived on a blue planet populated only by singing whales. Other times terrorists with turbans kidnapped me but their leader, a sock monkey named Chief Biltmore, Esquire, was kind enough to provide cherry Kool-Aid and Ritz crackers. We sat quiet for a moment.

"Oh, yeah, I nearly forgot." Logan reached inside the lower pocket of his cargo shorts and pulled out something crinkly. Going down on one knee, he bowed his head. "These, my princess, are for you."

He held out a bouquet of paper flowers glued atop fuzzy green pipe cleaners, all folded dozens of times to look like tiny roses. They looked so real that for just the littlest moment, I was amazed they hadn't wilted in his pocket.

"I made the white ones from the certificate I got when they gave me my mosquito wings a couple years ago. The pink one's a parking ticket, and those blue ones are from the paper my dress uniform came wrapped in. They're like . . ." He stopped to kiss the knuckles on my hand one by one, then on the crook of my elbow, and a last, longish smooch on the base of my neck.

"Like what?" I asked.

He shrugged. I watched his eyes and they watched me right back. They looked to be worried, waiting, and maybe the tiniest bit afraid. It was this last possibility that thrilled me through and through.

"They're gorgeous," I said, to make this strange expression on his face go away.

"I'm going to kiss you now," he said in an odd, flat voice. The flickering candlelight made his eyes look sunken in, but not in a gruesome way, more like intense. He put his hands on my shoulders and we kissed. This time we opened our mouths and touched our tongues together. He didn't slobber or try to ram his tongue down my throat, like Billy had the night in the barn. He touched my cheek and my hair. I put my hands on his hips. Almost from the moment he touched me, the shaking started again. I don't know where it came from, but it took over my entire body and wouldn't stop. My teeth chattered.

"Is something wrong?" he asked, tilting his head back.

"No, no," I said, "it's just . . . I'm not . . ."

"Don't worry," he said, and he kissed me again.

Embarrassment gave me a fever. My face probably glowed in the dark. I closed my eyes and let my hands rest on his hips and tried to forget my name.

I don't know how long we'd been doing this when my mom came home. It didn't seem all that long, but I'd lost track of time. I jerked up when I heard the front door slam and banged my head against a two-by-four on the ceiling.

"What is it?" he said. He must not of heard the door. I'd been listening with half an ear the entire time.

"It's my mom. I've got to go back and get into bed or she'll think something weird's going on."

I crawled into my bedroom. My hands still shook so bad it looked like I'd swallowed some convenience store speed. A long bit of cobweb stuck to my arm.

Filthy

"What have you been doing? It's four thirty in the morning," my mom said, giving me an up-and-down look and shaking her head. "God, Lynn, what's that smell? It's like, like—"

I cut her off by pretending to fan my armpits at her face. Until this conversation started, I thought I'd sobered up some. Now I felt dead drunk and none too sure on my feet. She wrinkled her nose at me.

"Like what?" I said, keeping it short. I didn't trust my voice to do or smell as it should.

"You're all covered in grime and your hair looks like you haven't brushed it in weeks. What are you doing up anyway?"

"I got worried, so I couldn't sleep. I was waiting up for you."

"Where?" she said. "In a trash can?"

"A book fell back behind my bed." I spoke slowly and carefully. I must of sounded half-retarded. "It got stuck and I had to crawl under there and pull it out."

"Jesus," she said. "It looks like you've been rolling around in Mr. Cannon's charcoal grill. You should take a shower before you go to bed tonight." She reached over and plucked something off of my head. "You've got a leaf in your hair. When's the last time you cleaned under your bed? You growing trees back there now?"

"Where have you been?" I said, and then added, for the guilt it might stir up in my favor, "I really was worried."

She narrowed her eyes and went quiet a moment.

"I went to see Hayes." It was her turn to speak slowly and carefully.

"How's he doing?" I hoped to God she didn't hear the Boone's Farm wrestling with my tongue because I sure as hell did. Shut up, I told myself. Stop while you're still not grounded.

She didn't say anything to this. Instead, she went into the kitchen and got a beer out of the refrigerator. She sat down at the table and took her quilted cigarette bag out of her purse.

Paranoia kept me talking. Her silence spooked me. "Is he feeling better?" I asked, sitting down across from her. Suddenly, I had a wine headache and my eyeballs felt like fried grapes. Just like that, the fun part of the drunk was gone.

"You're sweating like a pig." She ran a finger across my forehead, examined it in the overhead light, and then wiped it on my shirt.

"It's hot in here. We need to get the window unit fixed."

"Not as hot as all that. Why don't you go take a cool shower?"

"Are you working in the morning?"

"No, thank God, Velma's taking my shift. I'm exhausted." So was the smile Mom gave me. "I might just sleep till noon."

"What did Hayes say?"

"He's still going through a rough patch." She gave the wall above my head an empty look. Her eyes went dull.

"You ain't going to help him again, are you? You promised you wouldn't."

"I didn't promise shit." Her eyes met mine. "This ain't none of your concern, Lynn."

"That means you are helping him."

She said nothing, but her eyes went from dull to full-on glare.

"I knew it." I tried to keep the sob out of my voice because I could feel it creeping in and clamping down on the muscles in my throat. "Mom, I wish you'd let loose of him. He's going to get you arrested or worse."

She squeezed the tip of her nose between her thumb and forefinger.

"Mom?"

"I told him he should run away." She lowered her head and picked at the label on her beer. I sat very still and watched her pick. Outside, crickets argued and shouted and told each other scritchy-scratchy lies. Inside, my mom's nails went *click, click, click* as she tore away the silver paper. "He said no. The dumb bunny is too scared to leave and too stupid to be scared to stay. He thinks he can handle it. I tried to tell him that if he stays . . ." Her voice trailed off and she looked too tired to explain what she tried to tell him. This wasn't the answer I'd hoped to hear, but at least Hayes wasn't here at the house anymore. And if he wasn't here, maybe the creeps wouldn't come here looking for him anymore.

"But you're not going to help him again, right?" I said, trying to catch her eye. "Right?"

Mom let out a sigh, blowing her bangs out of her eyes, and pushed herself away from the table. "If you're not going to take a shower, I will."

When I didn't say anything, she got up and went back to her room. I drank the rest of her beer. After a couple of minutes, the shower started running. I sat at the kitchen table and stared at the ashtray, wondering what I'd do if all this went wrong, how I'd find my dad if it came to that.

Sex Slave

"And?" Dani whispered. It was Sunday morning around eleven. Water ran in the background and something metal clanked.

I couldn't help myself. I'd told her everything. Or near about. We had a new half-ring system. Half-ring and she'd call me back. Logan Loy was still snoring softly in the storage room when I'd last checked on him.

"And what?" I asked.

"Have you done it?"

"Not yet," I said. "My mom's here. She doesn't have to work."

Dani's flip-flops went *smick-smack, smick-smack, smick-smack.* A door slammed and something rattled. "So he's stuck in there for another night?"

"At least," I said.

"Now you have your own personal sex slave in your closet. That's what I need while I'm grounded."

"Yeah, right."

"When he kisses you—wait, you have kissed him, haven't you?"

"Yeah," I said, embarrassed suddenly. "I told you already."

"Oh, right, you said it was like eating chocolate velvet pie." She snickered. I'd said no such thing. "So when he kisses you, does he move his tongue up and down or in a circular motion? And if in a circular motion, is it clockwise or counter?"

"Is this something out of *Vogue*?"

"*Cosmopolitan.*"

I thought for a second, moving my tongue in my mouth to remember. "In circles, why?"

"Direction?" Paper rustled.

I guessed. Who remembers stuff like that? "Clockwise."

More pages turned. "Ahh, that's very interesting."

"What? Come on."

"That means he's passionate, but prone to outbursts of anger, and has an artistic nature."

"You already knew about the art stuff," I said. "Has the eyeball bothered you again?"

"No, my dad stayed out all night on the sleeping porch with the shotgun."

"He see anybody?"

"Nah, my mom said he was asleep when she went out in the morning."

A cabinet door banged. Then I heard a toilet paper tube clatter, roll, and rip. A toilet flushed. I made a face.

"Are you going to the bathroom?" I said.

"Don't you just love cell phones?" She laughed. "I found out where my mom hid the phone *and* the charger. On top of the fridge. Can you believe it? Like I was three and couldn't see up there. I have to make sure I put it back is all. So how long is he going to stay, your Mr. Logan Loy? Or is it Private Logan Loy? Be careful. He could go to jail, you know, if your mom told the police."

"Forever," I said.

"No, they'd let him out after a while."

"I mean in my closet. I'm keeping him forever."

"Or at least until Mr. Jenkins's brother Captain Crook gets him."

"Clap your hands if you believe."

Dani clapped and laughed, but I stopped thinking it was all that funny almost as soon as it came out of my mouth. I could believe all too easy.

The Dangers of Girl Warming

After I hung up with Dani, I told Logan good morning and we kissed again, but only for a little while. This time the shaking wasn't so bad. I told him he'd have to stay all day today, since my mom wasn't working and he couldn't leave anyway. He smiled at me then, and it felt like a hot water bottle popped inside my belly. If Greenpeace had seen it, they'd have killed him to save the ice caps.

"Sure," he said. "I think I'd like that."

We messed around for hours and hours until my lips were actually sore. He never tried to get under my clothes, but he didn't hold off from various sorts of rubbings. By the end, I could of exploded into a million pieces if he'd touched me in the right place. And by then I wanted him to, but I didn't know how to ask.

Afterwards, I lay on my bed and went back over every word we said to each other that day and the one before and my heart beat so hard I could feel it in the tips of my fingers. My mom stayed up looking at the TV that night until three in the morning. The thought of him back there sleeping behind my closet, with my princess picture watching over him, kept me awake for most of the night. Was he thinking about me too? I liked knowing he couldn't come out of the closet unless I told him it was alright. I wasn't used to being able to tell someone what to do, especially someone older, and it felt nice. But it scared me a little as well, because I didn't know where all this would end. And scared because anymore I didn't want it to.

A New Boat

"Where did you get that bracelet?" my mom asked me Monday morning. I'd been wearing it since I got it, but this was the first she'd noticed. Since she didn't have to go in to work until noon, she'd started working on a new boat. Mom spread the pieces out all over the kitchen table. The room had a sharp chemical smell from the glue. The boat was called the Cutty Sark and she was building it in an old vodka bottle. She wanted to build it in a bottle of Cutty Sark scotch, but she figured the label would hide the boat, so what would be the point. I wasn't allowed to come into the kitchen when she worked on her stupid ships. She was afraid I'd walk too hard and vibrate the table and ruin it. I'd done this once when I was six, so ever since then she made me stand in the doorway to talk to her when she was working on one.

"Dani let me borrow it," I said. "For the first day of school." I waited for my chance to sneak some breakfast out for Logan. Mom had gotten out of bed early and was already working on the boat when I woke up. I made sure and brushed my teeth before I went back and saw him. I gave him my copy of *Harriet the Spy* and kissed him good morning. His stomach growled twice. Mom turned my attempt to get Logan breakfast into an obstacle course.

"Are you going over to see her today? To pick out your first-day-of-school outfits?" my mom asked.

"Who? Dani?" I said, as if we could be talking about anyone else. My mind was still back behind the closet. "No, she's grounded."

"What for?" she asked in her fake casual way, picking up a strip of balsa wood with a long, thin pair of tweezers. She dabbed the tiniest bit of glue on it and slipped it in through the neck of the bottle. She wore special magnifying glasses she'd bought at Wal-Mart, so she could see the details better. They made her look like a properly medicated mad scientist. But I noticed her hands weren't all too steady. She kept reaching in to place the little stick of wood and then stopping and pulling it out again.

"She got in an argument with her mother about something."

"That girl does have a mouth on her."

The house phone rang and we both stopped talking and stared at it like it might jump off the hook and bite us. I looked over and raised my eyebrows at her, but she shook her head and mouthed the word, *Wait*, as if the person calling could hear us even without the phone being picked up. The answering machine clicked on and my mom's voice informed whoever it was that we weren't home. It was Dr. Drose. Mom asked me to pick it up and went back to work on the Cutty Sark. She must of made a mistake with the piece she was placing because she cursed softly and pounded her thigh with a fist. I'd never seen her do that before. Then she took her tweezers and poked herself on the palm three times.

"Hi, sweetie," Dr. Drose said when I answered. "Is your mother home?"

Mom came out of the kitchen after she tried gluing the piece of balsa wood for a third or fourth time and still couldn't get it right. She snatched the phone out of my hand like I'd stolen it from her. "Of course," she said and nodded with a lot of energy. "I don't mind at all." And then after a moment or so, "Believe me, I could use it. Alright then, I'll see you." She smiled after she hung up. "That's a nice surprise."

"What?" I said. I smiled too. The secret of my closet boy hummed sweetly in my chest.

"Someone made a scheduling mistake and they don't need me for the next couple of days. I get a little vacation."

"Oh," I said.

"Why do you look so glum? Am I interfering with some plan of yours?"

"No," I said.

"Yeah, right," she said, examining my face like it was a restaurant check from a careless waitress. "What new scheme are you up to today, Lynn Marie?"

The phone rang again and my mother picked it up without thinking. She must of been distracted. Her voice changed completely when the person on the other end of the line said hello. "When? Are you sure it's not a clerical mistake?" she said, after listening for a little while. It was a man's voice. That much I could hear. I knew without her saying it wasn't a call from Dr. Drose. "Have you ever noticed it's always Carla who makes these little discoveries?"

I went into the living room and sat down, so my mother wouldn't think I was trying to listen in. The only thing separating the kitchen from the living room was a Formica-topped breakfast bar and three padded barstools. My mom turned and faced the window over the sink, but I could still hear what she said.

"How do you know this?" She shook a cigarette out of her pack and lit it. "That's ridiculous. He's a complete idiot anyway. That's why his own kid checks the med inventory after he does it." After three or four drags, she stubbed it out. "*Goddamnit*," she said, still grinding the cigarette into her coffee saucer even though it was completely out. I hated when she put out cigarettes on dishes. It seemed trashy and I was the one who always had to clean it up. "Just call me when you know for sure, okay? Right. And tell her not to butt into other people's wards. In fact, tell her not to touch anything until I get there. Good-bye." She put the phone back in its cradle and lit another cigarette. Smoke curled out of her nose.

She glared at the ship for a long moment and then walked back and sat down at the table.

"Was that Dr. Drose again?" I knew it wasn't. She'd never say Goddamnit to Dr. Drose.

"No," she said.

"Who was it?"

"It sure as hell wasn't Ed McMahon." This was an old joke of hers and it always irritated me when she said it. It was so stupid it was aggravating. This time she didn't even try to use her jokey voice. It came out flat and mean.

I slipped in and grabbed a Coke and a half-eaten bag of Wise potato chips before she could start working on her boat again, making sure to walk across the linoleum very softly. This was not a good time for a big blowup.

"I'm going to go read," I said.

"Fine." Mom picked up one of her tools and bent it against her chin a second before letting it pop back into shape. Then she shut her eyes and did it again. She was still doing this when I went back to my room. But before I even opened the closet, the kitchen door creaked and slammed.

The First Real Lie

"**D**o you think I can slip out and go to the bathroom? I'm about to pop." Logan leaned up against the wall with a pillow behind his head and *Harriet the Spy* folded on his chest. It was late afternoon and my mom had been missing now for several hours on some work errand. Logan had jammed the flashlight into the rafters above him, so it shone down on his head like a spotlight. All he had on were boxer shorts, but sweat dripped from his chin and darkened his side burns. The flap in the front of his boxers was open and I could almost but not quite see in. A dark, fluffy shadow of hair. I tried not to stare, but my eyes kept landing there like flies on something stinky.

"There's no way," I said. "My mom's in the kitchen. She'll see you for sure."

"When's she leaving? I mean, I've seriously got to pee. I thought you said she'd be at work by now."

"She usually is, but her work called up and said she had the day off. Tomorrow too."

"Shit," Logan said, "I'm beginning to think this wasn't such a great idea. There's no way I could slip out without her seeing me?"

"No way, Jose," I said.

"Could I maybe climb out your bedroom window? This is near about emergency mode. In a little while, nothing's done about it, I'll explode and you'll have quite a mess on your hands."

"Wounded in the line of duty."

"I'm serious." He pulled a pout.

"You can't. The window's nailed shut." These were the first lies I told Logan Loy, and even now I'm not entirely sure why I told them. Of course I wanted him to stay for a little while longer, but there was more to it than that. The scary part was I didn't even think about it. Not till afterward. I just lied and he believed me. "If she sees you, she'll call the police. The station's right down the street. You wouldn't even make it to your car."

"Shit," he said. His sweat smelled strangely spicy in that small, hot room, but I didn't mind. I kind of liked it. Since he was in my room and I was taking care of him, I thought of it as kind of like my sweat. And your own sweat never smells as bad as other people's.

"Look," I said, "I'll go get you a can and you can use that. It's all we can do for now."

You'd think it'd make me feel like a servant or something, fetching him stuff and taking away his piss in Coke cans, but I felt the opposite. He really needed me. And this felt as good as, maybe even better than, it did when he touched me.

Officially AWOL

"Least you can do is come in here and talk with me some," he said, giving me his best sweetie-pie look as I set up the screechy old box fan for him. I'd borrowed it out of my mom's room after she left to see about whatever was going on at work, but I didn't tell him that. He thought she was lying out in a lawn chair in the side yard. Again, I'm not sure why I kept lying. I was still waiting for something to happen. Just *something*. I thought I'd know it when it came. Something that'd make all this feel permanent and real after it ended and he had to leave. Right then it still felt like a daydream, some story I'd cooked up to amuse me and Dani one bored Tuesday afternoon in August.

"Alright," I said, and crawled over beside him.

"Do you like me?" he said. "I mean, do you really like me?"

"I do," I said. "That's why I'm keeping you prisoner in my closet. The evil princess keeping the brave knight in her tower."

"This is serious, right?" he said. "I mean what we got here. Us." He didn't act as confident as he did the day I met him. Today it seemed more like he was my age, maybe even younger, like he needed me to tell him everything was going to be okay. But I liked knowing he'd been thinking about this.

"Yeah, it feels bigger than anything I've ever—" I wasn't sure how to say it. I wasn't sure what *it* was. "More than anyone else I've ever met." I tilted my head away and stared at the wall. "What about you?"

"Seems like I left the base a million years ago. Here, I made you something." In his palm was a little orange animal made of paper. "It's a fox, on account of your being so foxy."

I took it. The closer I looked at it, the more intricate it seemed to get. The little beasty even seemed to be smiling. It occurred to me then that under different circumstances Logan and my mom would probably get on famously, them having a shared interest in making normal objects very small.

He sat up suddenly, his face serious. "What time is it?"

"It's almost three, I think."

As of eight this morning, he was officially AWOL. They'd probably put him behind bars if he went back. If they discovered I'd helped him, I wondered, would they put me in an Army jail or send me to juvie over in Bulloch County? Thinking this and holding his hand gave me a shiver of happiness.

He put his arms around my waist then and kissed me. I lost my balance and we fell back onto the blankets, a muddle of sweat-sticky arms and legs. His hands crept up under my shirt. This time I didn't need to tell him where I wanted them to go because they wanted to go there too. I wasn't wearing a bra because it was so hot and, to be honest, my breasts weren't really big enough for anyone to notice if I went without. We rolled over again and I could feel his excitement pressing through his boxer shorts. He took off my shirt and kissed my breasts. An electric tingle wriggled in from the tips of my nipples, through my belly, and down between my legs. When he tried to take off my shorts, I made him stop.

"Not yet."

"Why not?"

"Wait till later, when my mom goes to sleep," I said. I wanted to draw this out. I wanted his needing me to last.

"You're getting me all riled up," he said. "Being stuck in this little closet is hard enough without—"

"You're a soldier during wartime. The town has been invaded by your enemies. I have to hide you until it's safe. You ever see that old movie, *Summer of My German Soldier*?

"What movie?"

"It's old. From the seventies, I think. See, during World War Two this American farm girl finds a German soldier wandering around lost after he's escaped from soldier prison and she hides him. He's not really a bad guy. He got drafted and had to fight or they'd kill him or something, but he actually hates Hitler. While he's hiding, they fall in love."

"Yeah," Logan said, "I can dig that. How's it end? Does he get away?"

"Sure," I lied.

Nervous

I looked at the TV with my mom while we ate a Monday dinner of fish sticks and Tater Tots I'd cooked in the toaster oven. She'd come home with a strained face about an hour before, but hadn't said a word about where she'd been. The six o'clock sun peered through the blinds.

"Why's it you keep picking at the sofa cushion and kicking the coffee table like that?" she asked. "Are you worried about school tomorrow? I used to get so worked up before the first day of school I'd get these awful nervous farts. The worst you've ever smelled. They just slipped on out. Nothing I could do about it."

"Mom," I said, "when's all this trouble with Hayes going to be over?"

She was quiet for a while. "If he's done what I told him to do, it's already over."

"What'd you tell him this time?"

She blinked her eyes for half a second and then stared hard at the coffee table. "That stupid man."

Finally

didn't notice more than a few speckles. A lot more blood came out when I got my period. Even spotting makes a worse mess. The hard part was getting it in. He almost put it in the wrong hole. It did sting at first, pretty bad, but it wasn't half as awful as Dani made it out to be. Or as good. Part of the reason I felt scared was because Dani told me the man would have to tear through the fleshy part of the hymen with one hard jab of the penis before things could get started in earnest. She used those exact words—*tear through the fleshy part of the hymen*. Whenever someone said, I'm going to tear you a new one, that's what I thought about—losing my virginity. But it wasn't like that at all.

It was only in the shower after that I started to shake. As I washed his smell off my skin, I thought about how you were supposed to feel different afterwards, like a woman, and how I felt exactly the same as I did that morning, except maybe a little tender down there. I figured maybe it took a few days for the change to sink in. I studied myself in the mirror to see if I looked any different.

Logan went on and on so much about the bathroom when I got back that I told him Mom was in the front yard, so he could go, but only if he went quick. I emphasized quick.

He said, "Alright, farm girl."

My mom actually left off someplace while I was in the shower, but I had no idea where she went or when she would be back. That was fine with me. I'd heard stories about how a mother could tell her daughter wasn't a virgin anymore just by looking at her, but I doubted my mom would notice anything. I looked the same as ever, just wet from the shower and a little tired. I'd lost my virginity, but I kept the box it came in.

Before I finished saying, "Fine, you can go," Logan was jogging across my room headed to the bathroom. He stopped in the doorway as I tried to squeeze past and took my cheeks in his hands and studied my face. I thought he might be angry about something. That was how serious he looked. But he only kissed me and shut the door. I knew then that once he left my house, I'd never see him again. He might think he was going to come back and see me, even really believe it when he said it, but he wouldn't. This was all I was going to get.

Luckily, there were no windows in the bathroom, so he couldn't see my mom wasn't in the yard talking to Mr. Cannon. I'd of hated to have him think I'd lied.

I've Been Thinking

"Lynn, princess, listen," Logan said, his voice sharp and tense, when I went in to tell him goodnight. "I like hanging out with you and all, but I can't stay in this closet anymore. I'm going crazy."

This was so different from what I expected to come out of his mouth, I couldn't say anything for a long moment.

"It's better than jail," I said. "So just wait. My mom will go back to work tomorrow and you can get out."

"I've been thinking . . . ," he said.

"Yeah?"

"I've got this friend in Macon. I can go there for a while. I could visit you sometimes."

It felt like someone had poured Liquid-Plumr straight into my stomach. "That's so far away."

"It's only about two hours. I can visit on the weekends. There's a campground near here. I can stay in a tent and we can hang out together." He brought his knees up to his chest and put his arms around them. All he had on were a pair of blue striped boxers. "At least that's what I'm thinking right now."

"You'll leave and that'll be it."

"That's not true."

"Please don't leave tomorrow while I'm at school," I said. "Please. I don't want to have to visit you in jail."

"You couldn't anyway," he said. "The place they'd probably send me is in Leavenworth, Kansas." He pushed a bit of hair off my forehead and tucked it behind my ear. "I don't want to leave you. It's only I—"

"Take me with you," I said.

"With the Army chasing after me? That ain't no life for you."

"I don't care. I've never had nothing like this. I don't expect I ever will again."

He turned away. I took his chin and pulled his head to face me. His eyes shone and I kissed them closed, one after the other, and then again for good measure.

"God almighty, I wish I were someone else. I wish—" He stopped and kissed my nose.

"Who?"

"I don't know."

The Emperor's New Clothes

The alarm clock in my brain woke me up at five on Tuesday, the first day of school, even though I didn't actually have to leave until seven thirty. My real alarm clock was set for six. That's when I woke Logan up and told him I would wash his clothes.

"Strip," I said, and he did, tripping on his filthy boxers and blinking his eyes. He hardly made a peep about it, did everything I told him. I figured it was his Army training kicking in. Always follow orders and such like.

"It's not as if I need them in here anyway," he told me after he'd rubbed the sleep out of his eyes. "It's a fucking sauna. I've probably lost ten pounds from sweating alone."

"That's true," I said. "What do you need clothes for?"

My mom was still asleep, so I took his duffle bag and all his clothes and put them in three big triple-ply garbage sacks. Our neighbor, Mr. Cannon, had a huge trash can, the kind with the lid that flips up on plastic hinges. I threw the clothes in there, but I was careful to put some of Mr. Cannon's trash on top. Mr. Cannon worked for the county animal shelter and was hardly ever home anyway. I didn't think he'd notice.

On the bus, I sat next to Sally Bryant and she told me about a trip she'd taken to Jacksonville with her family the week before. I wasn't really listening. I had on my favorite pair of jeans, the ones with flared legs and rivets down the side, and I was thinking about Logan sitting around in no jeans and no nothing, reading my eighth-grade English *Johnny Tremain* book, trapped in the secret room behind my closet.

A Fistful of Trojans

I didn't see Dani until after homeroom. She handed me a fistful of Trojans. "You know I am *so* proud of you. What happened? Tell me everything. Did it kill when he first put it in?"

I told her about it. She nodded wisely.

"Well, it ought to last longer than a minute," she said finally. "I'll think about this premature ejaculation problem for you. I think we can fix it."

"Premature ejaculation?" I said.

The second bell rang.

Dani dug in her pocket and pulled out a plastic baggie. "After breakfast I went and checked for footprints myself. In the grass by the flower bed, I found this."

She handed me the bag. Inside was an ace of spades. I took it out and held it up to the light. There was a picture of Bugs Bunny nibbling a carrot on the other side.

Dani snatched it out of my hands and put it back in the bag.

"You'll mess up the fingerprints." She made an *ugh yuck* face at me. "Fucked up, isn't it? And that's not all."

"Dani, the second bell rang."

"Just look at it."

She handed me a second bag. Inside was a computer-printed picture of Dani from last year's yearbook, but the eyes had been rubbed out with an eraser. It gave me chicken pimples on my arms.

"Whoa," I said. "You found this outside your window?"

She had.

The Answer

I didn't see Dani again until the end of second-period lunch. She had third-period lunch and came into the cafeteria as I left. According to the clock in the cage up above the salad bar, I had exactly three and a half minutes before the bell. We went out on the breezeway.

"I got an answer for you," she said.

"An answer for what?"

"You know, it being too fast." Dani poked a stiff index finger through her fist a few times.

"Oh," I said.

"I talked to Barbara Ann."

"You didn't tell her it was me, did you?" I moaned. "Dani. Shit."

Barbara Ann Habersham was a bottle blonde with a body that made boys turn their heads as she passed in the hall. Back when she still wore a cheerleader uniform, they'd wait for her in clumps below the front stairs in hopes of a panty flash. I'd heard she dated a frat boy from Georgia Southern. She looked like a college senior, but she was only a high school one. I seriously doubt she even knew who I was. She'd been the youngest-ever head of the varsity cheerleading squad until she got kicked off the first quarter of her junior year. Some people said it was because she got caught smoking pot in her hotel room at a preseason exhibition game over in Tuscaloosa, Alabama, but I'd heard a few other people say it was because she got pregnant and had an abortion. Despite all this,

Barbara Ann was still popular. Maybe even more so because pretty people could do shameful shit and not even the teachers seemed to care. These days she was kind of like the queen of the burnouts and baddies. Still, I didn't much care for her to know all about my private sexual goings-on.

"Of course I didn't tell. I acted like I was only curious to know if it was *theoretically* possible to fix a hair-trigger penis." She made air quotes around the word "theoretically," one of her favorite bandying-about words, along with "homunculus" (as in, "we had a homunculus good time at that party") and "plethora," which she emphatically believed meant an enormous fat person (like, "look at that plethora on the bike over there, his butt's gone and swallowed the banana seat right down to the tires"). It didn't matter how many times I tried to shove a dictionary in front of her face.

"'Is there any cure for such a poor, sad condition as this?' That's what I asked her. I described your boy as a three-scoots-and-shoot kind of guy."

"You did not say that." I sucked in two lungfuls of air in one breath. "Did you?"

"Oh, please, *tranquilo* the hell out." Dani had just come from *Español* with Senora Pulawski. "The last person she'd expect it to be is you. She probably thinks it's me that's wondering."

"Thanks," I said. "And I wasn't wondering."

"I'm hungry, so I'll make this quick. Barbara Ann told me to take a hair tie or a scrunchie in your emergency-type situations, and wrap it nice and snug around the bottom of his dick once you're sure he's good and hard. That's key or it won't firm up in the first place. Are you paying attention?"

The bell rang.

"Dani," I said.

She ignored this. "Listen, Lynn, this is good stuff. You wrap it nice and tight, but not so tight it starts turning blue. The idea here is this'll keep the blood in there and the whole thing will last longer. Depending, it could be like two or three times longer. She wrote the instructions on a Juicy Fruit wrapper. Here, I've already memorized it."

Dani handed me the wrapper. It was folded up into a tiny square. I thought of Logan's sweet little origami roses and made up my mind to chuck the wrapper as soon as Dani left. As I put it in my hip pocket, she sighed in her most dramatic way. "I wish I could meet him. I hardly know what's going on and it was all my idea to begin with. You never tell me anything."

"He's probably leaving tomorrow, but he says he'll come back and visit me."

"Why tomorrow? I thought you planned to move him in for good." She winked.

"My mom's going back to work and he's sick of it in there. I'll admit it's pretty hot."

"I bet."

"I mean—"

"I *know* what you mean." She tossed me one of her more superior looks. "Still, while you've got him locked up in there, you should try to get him to stay as long as you can. I mean, what's a few more days at this point? And also, do you think he'll really come back? I very seriously doubt it. Think about it, Lynn, when's the next time you'll get a chance like this?"

"I've thought about that."

"Maybe you should tie him up? My dad has some real police handcuffs."

That made me laugh. The thing is, I did think about it. Not really. Well, I don't know. What I was mostly thinking was, *What the hell am I doing?*

Fashion Crime

ogan was asleep when I came home from school and I had to shake his toe before he woke up. Then I kissed him, even though he had some truly atrocious morning breath, or late afternoon breath in this case. He sat up and stretched. Sweat made a moist shadow on the blanket where he'd been sleeping. His skin stuck to me when we hugged and his unshaven face scraped my cheek.

"What day is it? It's so dark in here, I never know if a nap was all night or five minutes," he said. "I think I'm getting a heat rash."

"I'll get you some baby powder."

"Honey, sweetie, what I need to do is get out of here."

When he asked about his clothes, I told him I hadn't had time to bring them in that morning after I dried them, so I stuffed them all in a black plastic trash bag and tucked it behind the washer. My mom, I explained, must of found them and thought they were trash or some of my dad's old clothes and thrown them out.

"They're gone? They're really all *gone*?" His voice went from soldier to little boy to girly whine.

"Snap out of it, soldier boy. I looked in the cans out back of the carport, but they'd been emptied. She hasn't said anything, though. That's good at least, isn't it?"

"Some of them were clean!"

"I didn't know which were which, so I did them all. Don't worry, we'll figure something out."

"Oh, shit." Logan squeezed his eyes closed hard enough to make the lids wrinkle. "I didn't give you my car keys and my wallet, did I?"

"No, they're right over there in the corner."

"Shit," he said, but his voice was softer.

"Listen here now," I said, trying to keep the mad out of my voice. I knew that showing how angry I was would only rile him up that much more. And to no good account either. But I didn't forget about how he was acting. I only pushed it off to the side. "Don't fret over this. It ain't nothing we can't figure out together. Come over here and rest your worried brain." I patted my legs and he crawled over and put his head in my lap. I stroked his hair and lowered my voice, sweetening it up as much as I could. "My friend Dani has an older brother who left some clothes behind when he moved out to college. She's going to look for them tonight and call me. I think he was smaller than you, though." I pulled this right out of my ass. Dani's an only child. It was scary how easy it was for me to make all this shit up the way I did. By my count, this was lie number nine.

Logan pointed the flashlight down at his legs. Puffy red patches stretched from his crotch down along his inner thigh. He shook his head when he saw them. His cheek stubble rasped against my jeans.

"Shit." He poked at the red spot on his left leg.

This went a long way toward ironing out the wrinkles from his temper tantrum. Poor little guy, I thought.

"That does look like heat rash," I said. "Does it itch?"

He grunted. But I could tell my taking an interest and feeling sorry for him had already helped calm his nerves some.

I gave him a pressed beef sandwich with mustard and American cheese and a cup of Sunny Delight. Later, back in my own bed, it occurred to me that Desitin, the ointment moms use for soothing particularly angry flare-ups of diaper rash, might do him a world of good. I bet I could get some down at the Piggly Wiggly.

Some Nightmares
Smell Like Burning Plastic

That night, I woke up from a terrible dream about Logan. His dream yells kept bouncing around in my head after I opened my eyes. Then I realized. Those yells were real. Although muffled some by my hanging slacks and dresses, Logan's shrieks were clear enough out in my bedroom. Clear enough, I thought, to wake my mom.

"Please don't hurt her," Logan wailed. "Just leave her be."

When I shone the flashlight on his face, his eyes were clenched tight. The skin on the lids looked pinched and wrinkled again, like before when he was feeling sorry for himself over the lost clothes.

"Hey, soldier boy," I whispered, "I'm here now. Your farm girl."

Logan didn't wake up all the way until I pinched his earlobe with the longer of my two thumbnails. He jerked awake with a ragged, wet gasp, as though he'd just burst through the surface of the ocean after holding his breath too long. His eyes were huge and terrified. And he had a hard-on. The way it supported the weight of the sweaty sheets looked uncomfortable. I flicked the flashlight back toward myself to reassure him about who I was. But Logan still didn't see me. I planted a kiss on his forehead and hoped it'd grow in there and crowd out his inner crybaby.

"Bad dream," Logan said, as if there'd been some doubt on this count. "Hajjis were going to rape you."

"I had a bad dream about you too," I said.

"They took your breasts. Cut them off and burned them."

"Take a deep breath now."

Logan hummed a few notes and in a weird, wavering voice sang a few lines about how he'd have to think things over before he—I think this is what he said—smashed it through his skull.

"What the hell?" I said. But the tune was almost familiar.

"That damn song was playing in my head. And everything smelled like burning plastic." He clenched the muscles in his jaw and neck into hard, tight ropes. "As soon as I get to liking something, it gets taken away in my dreams."

Then I got it. "Caring Is Creepy." The lyrics had changed somehow in his singing—been warped, like everything else.

"You mostly have nightmares about bad things happening to people you love?" I slipped that love in there as an experiment. When he didn't say anything about this, I put a hand on his forehead. He was burning up. "I think you got a fever," I said.

Logan's Car

I saw it happen while I waited for the bus Wednesday morning. I'd just said good-bye to my mom and was watching her walk over to the hospital when I noticed the tow truck. A yellow light flashed on its roof and I recognized the guy driving, but I couldn't remember his name. He graduated at the end of my freshman year and went to work for his dad. A horn beeped again and again as he backed the truck up behind Logan's car and made the ramp slide down. It didn't even occur to me at first what the guy was doing. By the time I finally did realize, I was like, *Oh, now I won't have to lie anymore.*

I thought of telling Logan right then, but I would of missed the bus.

And Logan wasn't going anywhere anyway without his clothes.

After school, when I came back and told him, he just closed his eyes. That's it. I tried to talk to him, but he wouldn't even make a sound, so I touched his penis with my hand until it got hard, rubbing the underside of the tip with my thumb like he'd shown me. "That there is the sweet spot" was the way he put it. Logan didn't look at me or say a word while I did all this, but he didn't stop me either. After a minute or so, he grabbed me by the shoulders and rolled me on my back. Then we had sex using one of Dani's condoms.

"Just one more thing," he said after he finished, just as calm as you please. "One more Goddamned thing."

Dirty Wild Indian

ogan's state of mind changed a little every day, going sour like milk left out on the counter. I knew it'd gotten serious when I came home from school on Thursday and found him messing about in my bedroom. He was squatting down behind the door and poking through the dirty laundry basket. The blinds were open and anyone passing by could easily of seen him. Like my mom, for one. His lips stretched into an awful smile when he saw me. If I squinted, I could still see the cute, sweet Logan I first met, but he was doing a damn good job disguising him.

"Oh," Logan said, "it's just you." He wore a pair of my faded yellow panties on his head like a hat.

"Yes," I said, edging around him to close the blinds, "it's me."

"Good, yeah, good." He whipped the panties off his head and tried to stuff them back in the basket along with one of my T-shirts before I noticed. But I noticed. "I thought it was your mom," he said quickly, pretending to wipe some sweat off his forehead. "Whew. That's a relief."

Standing there naked in my bedroom, Logan looked so completely out of place he might well of been something I'd hallucinated. This would of made more sense than the actual truth of the situation. His hair was squashed down in the front and sticking up on the side. Dirt was smeared all over his chest and legs. In the late afternoon light, you could see where his beard stubble had come in. It looked like brown mold. The skin around his eyes had turned a bruised color. I wanted to scream. For a second, I thought my head would pop and splatter the walls of my bedroom. That's how angry I felt. I couldn't believe he would actually leave me without saying good-bye or anything. Because that's exactly what I thought he was getting ready to do—scrounge together an outfit from my dirty clothes and abandon me.

"You know that shirt would never fit you," I said in a mean voice. If I used that same voice on Dani, she wouldn't speak to me for a week. I decided to ignore the panty hat for the time being. "What are you doing?"

"I heard your mom go out the front door, so I made a quick trip to the bathroom. It weren't the kind of thing I could do in a Coke bottle." He swallowed hard and stared at his filthy feet. "Then I thought I'd get the next book in that Green Gable series you got me started on. I was only out here for a few minutes. I'm sorry." He looked more than a tad scared. His mouth tightened up into that strange grimace again, and he winced like he expected me to beat him. "It's just that . . ."

His face fell. I thought for a moment he might even cry. Seeing all this, I stopped being mad at him. Almost right away, truth be told. Even so, I knew I couldn't just leave this sit. I needed to do something to punish him in case he thought about leaving me ever again. I couldn't have that. No, sir.

"It's just—well—it's been thundering all day. I know you'll think it's stupid, but the thunder sounded like something bad. I freaked out a little bit. I couldn't stay back there anymore. All the air was gone. I had to get out. I'm sorry, Lynn Marie." Logan panted some and his eyes bounced around his sockets like Super Balls.

"Logan, honey, if you've got to go to the bathroom, you should really try and wait until I'm here." This time I made sure to speak in a much nicer voice. Later, I realized it was the same voice I used when I talked to strange dogs. I didn't think of this at the time, and it kind of freaked me out afterward when I did. "What if my mom's boyfriend came in? Then you and me would of been in a world of shit. Let me tell you."

"Your mom has a boyfriend?"

"Yeah. Hayes. He's a real dick. There's no telling what he would of done if he found you." I gave him my elementary school teacher frown.

Really, if Hayes had stumbled into dirty, wild-Indian-looking Logan, he would of screamed, turned tail and run until he puked, but I didn't tell Logan that. It was funny to think of this happening, but not that funny. If Hayes did come in and find him, I'd still be in a world of shit, as Logan had got me saying.

"Shit," Logan said again. This was his main word these days. He used it when he was startled or angry or sad or happy. The longer he stayed in the storage space, the smaller his vocabulary seemed to get. Then his face lit up. It appeared a hopeful thought had fought its way into his brain. After poking around behind my clothes basket, he turned and smiled. "I nearly forgot. I made you something." He handed me a tiny paper man about the length of my face made of dozens of intricate folds. Logan had even found a way to make the man appear to have curly hair. "It's me."

I nodded. Looking closer, I realized he'd torn a page from *Anne of Green Gables*. This made me none too happy, as it was one of my all-time favorite books. He saw right away what had come into my head.

"Don't worry. I made sure to use a boring page. It's where she's up in her room all upset about something that happened at school the day before."

I opened my mouth to say how we might disagree about what constituted boring, but I didn't see the point. All manner of feelings were wrestling around in my chest. Me and Logan stood there and stared at each other. He smiled at me in a hopeful, annoying way. I tried to quick-think of some way of punishing him without him knowing that that was what I was doing. Just something to throw a scare into him, so he'd make sure and stay in the storage room unless I told him it was okay to come out.

That's when the doorbell rang. We both shut up. Logan yanked at his earlobe as if he meant to pull it off. Something in his chest whistled when he breathed. I moved first.

"On the double, you," I said, giving him a little shove. "Get back in there."

Logan didn't react for a very long set of stretchy seconds. His face turned the color of cigarette ash. I grabbed his arm and gave him a good, hard tug. Still, he wouldn't budge. I flashed him my sternest what-the-hell look. Sweat dotted his forehead and upper lip. His eyes lost focus, like he was peering at something a football field away. I'll admit, it frightened me some.

"Come on," I said. "Get."

I reached over and pinched his other earlobe. It worked to snap him out of it this time, too. I filed away my new bit of Logan lore for the next time I needed to hustle his ass someplace quick. When he finally moved, he moved fast, faster than I would have believed. Logan turned and scrambled back into that closet like a squirrel chased by a dog. He plowed through my clothes, tripping over my nice neat row of flip-flops and knocking my black cotton dress off its hanger. Oh, Logan, my overgrown, naked first grader. His ass wiggled as he crawled through the attic door. Since I was around him all the time, I sometimes forgot he was naked. But seeing him run like that, I remembered and I couldn't help but smile.

Darling, Mind If I Step Inside?

stood there in the hall for quite some time, wincing at myself in the mirror like a Mongolian-type idiot. I wasn't paying attention the way I should of. That's where I went bad wrong. The bell rang a second time and then went silent for several minutes. Right as I moved toward the window to take a peek at the person on my front stoop, the door opened slowly. This can't be, I thought, I'm sure I locked it. A man stepped in, tucking something shiny into his jacket pocket and blinking against the dim hallway. At first he appeared normal enough. If you didn't know any better, and I didn't, you'd probably think he was the type who might work in an insurance office or sell furniture down at Badcock's on Broad Street. In the gush of sunlight from the door, the normal-seeming man's eyes were the bright blue of swimming-pool water in a TV show. He had a bushy orange mustache two shades darker than his head hair and an oversized potato of a nose with a tangle of purple veins at the tip.

"Hey," I asked, "what on earth are you doing?"

At first blush, this man gave me the impression he was a good deal more surprised to see me than I was to see him. He didn't say anything for a moment. He didn't, for example, apologize for busting into a stranger's house. Instead, he stood and gawked at me. It wasn't until I heard him breathe that I had an awful inkling of who this could be, and even then, I wasn't completely positive. Mouth breathing sounds different over the phone than it does when the person huffing and slurping his air stands about a half-dozen Bibles away. The normal-seeming man's show of surprise vanished as quick as it came, but still he said nothing, just stood there shifting his weight from foot to foot and jangling something in his pocket.

"Excuse me," I said to my visitor, not wanting to listen to his breathing any longer. I put on a stern face and crossed my arms. "What can I do for you, sir?" I found myself imitating my mom's official voice, the one she used when she first picked up the phone and didn't know yet who was calling.

"Are you the, uh, lady of the house?" This man, who might or might not be Marty Keegan, spoke in a low, rough voice, but he didn't sound especially mean. Still and all, I won't lie, the whole business had me rattled.

"No, my mother is at work." I continued to use my most proper voice.

"Darling, mind if I step inside?" Maybe-Marty pointed with his chin toward the hallway behind me in a lazy sort of way.

And here's where the situation tilted and slipped away from me. I didn't have a chance to say anything back to this, and he didn't even wait to see if I meant to. The man brushed me aside like I was nothing. With the size of those hands, if he wanted to, he could of picked me up and chucked me out on the front lawn with just one. As he stepped past, that flabby gut of his sent me banging into the wall. I saw right off there were about fifty ways this thing could go and nearly all of them were bad. It was then I went from uncomfortable to feeling well and truly scared.

"My mom don't allow strangers in the house if she ain't here," I told the man's back, forgetting to speak proper now that I'd swallowed a full dose of twitchy fear.

"I ain't a stranger, little pullet."

"Strange to me," I squeaked.

"But not to your mama. She'd know my name if you said it to

her." He smiled with his mouth, but his eyes looked as flat and gray as nickels. In the murky light of the hallway, the blue in them vanished. "Anyway, I bet your mama carries on with a lot of strange men."

I took offense but couldn't get my lips to function. I stood with my mouth open. The floorboards groaned as he traipsed into the living room and glanced around in a way that made me think he was looking for something specific. I knew he wanted Hayes, but the way he studied the room wasn't the way you'd look for a person. It occurred to me for the briefest moment he could be an undercover agent from the Army looking for Logan, or somebody from the FBI looking for Hayes; however, these ideas were only foolishness and soon tossed aside. I didn't kid myself any longer about the man. Once he shoved his way into the house, I knew this was Marty and I was in a giant, hairy fix. Meanwhile, he made his way through the house like he had it in his head to go visit my mom's bedroom next. Or, God forbid, mine.

"Do you even know my mom?" I asked, hoping to delay this possibility.

"Not to look at, no, but we have a mutual friend."

Now I had one advantage. He didn't know me, and he didn't know I knew who he was or what he was up to. A fairly slim advantage, I'll be the first to admit, but I figured there had to be some use I could make of it if I waited and kept my eyes peeled. I edged around the room slowly and put myself between him and the hall leading back to bedrooms. I worried he might already smell Logan and wonder where this stink was coming from. If Mom hadn't been working so much and been so anxious over the Hayes business, I'm sure she'd of noticed by now herself. My original plan for the day had been to scrub him down and shave him. I'd intended to do it myself with a dish tub of hot water and a scrub brush. I thought it might be fun.

Marty pulled a drawer of silverware from the china hutch and emptied it onto the floor. The sound, like a hundred tiny sword fights, shocked me more than I can say.

"Who are you?" I asked him. "And what the hell are you doing?"

The mouth breather said nothing. Instead, he snatched an uno-pened envelope from the breakfast bar and held it up to the light. Using a horny, yellow thumbnail, he tore it open and tapped the contents into his palm. Whatever the letter contained seemed to amuse him. He snorted and crushed it all into a ball.

"What's the name of this friend of hers you both know?" I asked, speaking a little louder. "See, even my mom's friends don't gene-rally go through her mail. How about you put that down and tell me what you want?" I forced myself to sound a good bit more peppery than I actually felt, but this isn't to say I wasn't pissed off. I was. Friend or not, and he definitely was not, there wasn't any call for him to be taking down books, flipping through them, and then chucking them over his shoulder like he did. Or opening up random drawers and poking his big summer sausage fingers into them, which he also did, ignoring me all the while. "Maybe I know this person," I told him, raising my voice to carry over the racket he was making. "'Cause I sure don't know you."

Marty looked over his shoulder at me, and when he saw I was watching, he hauled off and kicked the china hutch so hard half the plates came tumbling onto the floor and smashed as they hit each other. I wished I had a tranquillizer gun like the kind they use in nature shows to take down bears and such. This one here needed taking down in the worst possible way.

"Hey!" I shouted at him.

When he didn't turn around, but only smiled to himself as he flung the contents of the end table drawers onto the couch, I knew he was probably trashing our house partly to get a reaction out of me, and I made a pledge to myself that, in the future, I wouldn't

give him the satisfaction of seeing me get bent out of shape. As he
moved closer and closer to the shelves where Mom displayed her
boats in bottles, I followed his destructive hijinks with a growing
awfulness in my belly.

"What are you looking for then?" I said.

"You know Goddamn well I'm looking for Hayes."

"Well, you ain't going to find him in a drawer."

He crossed the room in three long steps and peered down at me
like I was a palmetto bug or a fire ant. Something irritating he could
squish very easily with one of his beat-up, black-tasseled loafers.
"Don't bullshit me, honey. I'll find that boy one way or another,
and if it turns out you're hiding him, you'll be as sorry as you've
ever been. Now answer me this, he holed up somewhere in here?"

"Hayes was here, but he left. A long time ago. My mom got
tired of his foolishness and tossed him out on his ear." I didn't
know if this was the right thing to say. Fear had made an idiot out
of me, I'll admit it. "Anyway, Hayes don't live here. He never did
live here and I seriously doubt if he ever will."

The mouth breather put his hand on my shoulder and squeezed.
He had the strength you might imagine a gorilla's hand having, if
he was the biggest gorilla in the whole pack. Maybe Marty didn't
know his own strength, or maybe he meant to cause me a boatload
of pain all along. Either way, his squeezing hurt like all get-out.

"Ahhh," I said, my voice rising to within a short hair of an all-
out shriek. "Owww. Stop. Let go, please. You're hurting me."

"Where'd he go?" Marty looked at my eyes. He wasn't looking
into them. He wasn't making eye contact. He was looking *at* them.
His own eyes now appeared even darker than before. The color
of a driveway oil stain. They seemed to shift and change shades
the way seawater does during a storm. It was this look that really
put the scare in me. Before it, I was frightened, but seeing those
empty, careless eyes, I became terrified. My bladder went slack and

it weren't no mere sprinkle that came out. Warm wet sopped the seat of my shorts.

"I don't know," I wheezed. There was hardly any air left in my lungs for talking. "He just left. No one explains anything to me." By now his hand hurt my shoulder enough to make tears come popping out of my eyes. He squeezed really, really hard. It felt like my collarbone might snap at any moment.

"Hmmh," he said. That was it. Just, *Hmmh*. Then he picked me up and moved me out of the way, so he could get down the hall.

Please don't smell Logan, I thought. Please, please don't smell him.

"What's in here?" he said, pointing to my mom's room.

"Nobody. It's my mom's room."

"Nobody, huh? That ain't even what I asked."

The mouth breather opened the door and went in. Right away I heard something fall over with a heavy thud. It sounded like it might be the lamp on Mom's bedside table. The place on my shoulder where he'd squeezed me throbbed. I had an awful headache and my knees didn't want to hold me up anymore. The bones had all turned to soggy bread. Back in Mom's room, something small and fragile smashed. I knew what it was without looking. The painted china clown on the windowsill. Mom had gotten it from her crazy Uncle Brett on her fifth birthday. To me, the clown was creepy-looking, but my mom loved it. I leaned against the couch and prayed.

I hadn't prayed in earnest since my father disappeared, and even back then it wasn't much more than a mumble-mix of wishes, patchwork memories of Sunday school, and bits from Sunday morning TV pastors. Back when I was smaller, I used to ask God to bring Dad back, to make Mom stop sleeping through the afternoon on her days off, to get me some flair DKNY jeans, and to blow away the dark gray smoke that sometimes clouded my brain with sad thoughts. My little tangerine-sized head imagined God to be half-Santa Claus and half-Wizard of Oz, a faceless beard with a single, giant, all-seeing eyeball that spoke in a deep Darth Vader voice. Nothing happened when I prayed then. Even so, you have to do something when a guy with fists larger than your teenage head barges into your house, almost breaks you in half, and is on the verge of finding a naked, dirt-smeared soldier gone AWOL behind your closet, and, no matter what you might of thought of yourself yesterday, you're still only a kid and your arms and legs feel as flimsy as McDonald's straws and there's nothing else left to do. That's when you pray even if you know it probably won't help.

Right then, I made it simple. God, sir, I said in my most polite inside-the-head voice, please don't let him find Logan. That's all I ask. It ain't much. I don't want nothing for myself. If you could just see your way toward doing this one bitty little thing, I'll do . . . I'll do . . . I don't know what. Something. Anything. Just please, please don't let him find Logan.

After Marty finished smashing Mom's prized clown, the room went quiet for a long time. This was nearly as worrisome as the previous racket. He stayed in her room for another fifteen minutes. I couldn't imagine there was fifteen minutes' worth of stuff in there to look at, unless he'd turned on the TV.

"What is it you really want?" I asked when he came back into the hall.

The man didn't even bother to answer. He went into the bathroom and knocked over the shampoo bottles, opened up the linen closet and threw all the towels on the floor, and then came out to kick apart the flimsy door to the fake closet that held the water heater. Once he finished destroying that, the mouth breather looked over his shoulder at me for the smallest slice of a second, strode across the hall, and threw open my bedroom door, like there might be a couple or three Hayeses cowering behind it. I followed

Marty down the hall, stopping for a few breaths at the doorway. I couldn't do nothing more than stand there and be afraid.

In order to reach under the bed, Marty had copped a squat on my throw rug. He treated me to an eyeful of ass crack so hairy it would of shamed a bear. In those few minutes I'd been trembling in the hall, he'd already managed to scatter the little girl stuff hidden under the bed all across the room. When the mouth breather finally noticed me in the doorway, he sniffed loudly and wrinkled up his nose.

"Something's spoiled in here, girl." The surprise in this came from the way he said it, as though nothing strange had been going on and he was only giving me a bit of uncle wisdom.

"What?" Coming out of my mouth, the word sounded like it had rust on it. Did he mean me? That I was spoiled?

"I expect you just left out a dish of something, and in this heat, it's gone south in a hurry." Marty peered around the room and then lifted each of his scuffed loafers and squinted at their soles before his frown zeroed in on me again. "You really need to start learning how to keep house, honey, especially if you ever hope to hold onto a man longer than a night."

A bit of clumsiness was the only thing that protected Logan from certain awfulness. Were it not for that cute little wiggle Logan's ass made as he squirmed back into the storage room, my black dress wouldn't of fallen in just the right way, so that it covered the storage room door with barely an inch on either side to spare. Marty was right about one thing. Logan put off a furious stench. His calling attention to it made me realize how bad it really was. A mixture of dirty socks and sex-sweaty crotch and overripe armpits and old shrimp shells and a few other dark and nasty flavors of stink. This never seemed to bother Logan any, or at least he hadn't said so if it did. If and when I get through this, I told myself, I have to clean that boy up first thing. It's only a matter of time before that smell gets us caught.

The mouth breather seemed content to let stinking dogs reek. He picked up my old jewelry box, the one Dad bought me for Christmas when I was seven. The box was covered in pink satin and had a ballerina inside. When opened, tinkling music played and the little dancer turned in circles. Brahms's "Lullaby," Dad said it was.

"This is my house." My voice sounded stronger now, not so pipsqueak as before. "You hear me? This is my room. Hayes ain't even allowed in here. Get out! What do you—?"

"Shut up," he mumbled, pushing me aside with one of his huge pink paws.

"You shut up. Come into our house and smash my mom's clown. How'd you like it if I came over to your house and smashed your— whatever nasty shit you care about? Huh? Huh? You ain't nothing but trash, you hear me, tra—"

Without even looking at me, without even turning around, he swung his hand out and backhanded me across the cheek and sent me stumbling into the wall.

"I think you broke my jaw," I said.

Something scrambled and creaked in the closet. I tried my best to sit up. A head peered out from beneath my old church dress. I made frantic motions with my hands and mouthed the words, *Go back! Go back!* Logan watched me for what seemed a dangerously long time with a pair of woeful eyes and then vanished. He was naked, weaponless, and barely bigger than Marty's right leg.

The man was a troll waiting under the bridge for billy goats. He was a rusty-haired version of Bluebeard with half a shave and on his way to a head-chopping. He was the big, bad wolf turned the color of squash, sucking in his mouthy breath so he could blow the house down. He said the words *shut up* like they meant *I'll kill you* in some other language. Troll language.

Finally, after one last peek behind the drapes, Marty straightened up and brushed something invisible off his pants, took
another long, hard look around the room, and left. I followed
him but made sure to stay out of paw's reach. When he paused
to kick one of the slats from the broken door to the water heater,
he might as well of kicked me. That thick stew of piss and vinegar, hot sauce and black pepper still simmering in my brain
boiled over again and another steaming dollop of crazy came
spilling out. I pushed him with both hands as hard as I could.
Which, considering the bulk this man carried, didn't do a hell
of a lot, but it still felt good to do it. A fierce urge to shout came
over me.

"Get out," I told him. "Get out!"

I'd pretty much lost whatever sense I had left at this point, seeing
as I knew what I could expect from this kind of behavior. I pitched
a good, old-fashioned fit. I punched one of his ass cheeks. Twice,
thrice, five times, maybe more. This was like slugging an extra-
large pair of pantyhose filled to bursting with Velveeta cheese. I
kept on with the yelling throughout. I'm not sure what all I said,
but I expect I told him to get out of my house in every and any way
I could think of, adding a choice swear word here and there for
flavor. I didn't have even the tiniest crumb of self-control left and
I smelled of stale pee.

That ass-hat Marty turned around in the doorway to the living
room and laughed at me, a heaving wheeze that looked and sounded
more like an asthma attack than any fit of the giggles I've ever seen.
This little burst of fun didn't last but three seconds before he took
me by the shoulder again and squeezed even harder than before.
He leaned over and put his face right down next to mine, so close
I could feel the scratch of his mustache on my cheek and smell his
breath. Rotten meat and whiskey and overripe bananas. And then
he squeezed. And he squeezed. God did he squeeze. I didn't want

to give him the satisfaction of making me squeal or beg, but finally, I just couldn't take it anymore.

"Stop it . . . please . . . stop . . . "

He grinned wide to hear me say it, the way a man might when he hears a few bars of a dearly loved tune from his teenybopper years. But this smile only creased his face for the briefest flash and then his mouth fell back into its usual rut.

"You best be sure your mama gets this." Marty pulled a grey business card out of his jacket pocket, placed it on my palm, and then closed his fingers around my hand and squeezed it tight to make sure this little scrap of cardboard stayed put. I didn't even look at it. "You tell her this: You can fool your old Unkie Marty once, but you try to do it twice and by God you'll be sorrier than you ever thought you could. The deal has changed. You got that?" He shook me. My head jiggled atop my neck like a bobblehead doll. "Every day he don't come through with them pills, the vig doubles. You got that?"

"What's the vig?" I asked, and then wished I hadn't before the taste of the letter *g* even left the tip of my tongue.

Marty pressed my arms against my sides and slid me up the wall until I was a good three feet off the ground and the two of us were eye-to-eye, a hand's breadth apart. I know it don't sound all that bad, especially when you compare it to the other things he'd just done to me—slapping me and squeezing me—but his eyes were not a place any sane normal person would like to dwell for long. I knew it wasn't so, that it couldn't be true, but it felt like he was sucking something important out of me, something that lived way down deep, something I needed to keep. I did my best to stare at his forehead instead, right between his eyes.

"Why won't you leave?" I said, the words sounding odd and misshapen to my ears. "Ain't you done yet?"

"Not quite, little pullet." Marty tried on a smile. He wore it like a bad-fitting suit, something several sizes too small, painful and slightly disturbing to look at.

I went away for a spell. Somewhere gray and fuzzy. When I came to, I was flat on my back.

"Look at me, girl," he said, kneeling in front of me now, his voice loud but not quite raised up to a shout. "You awake? You all the way here? I lost you for a little bit. Worried me some. You remember what happened?" He didn't seem all that worried to me, squinting down as though sizing me up for something, a noose, maybe, or a body bag. I didn't like the feeling one bit.

"Hey, quit playing possum. I know you're awake. Let's not make this any tougher, huh? You remember that message for your mama I told you before?"

I must of paused too long to suit him. Marty sat me up against the wall again and gave me a shake. Not as hard as before, but I had more hurts than before, too. The tears came gushing out again. They kept coming and coming until my chin dripped like the broken showerhead in our bathroom. I'm still embarrassed I cried so much. I wish I could tell you I acted different, braver, but I can't.

"Oh, the waterworks again." He sighed. "Let's try this one more time. You look like one of those smarty-pants kids the teachers are always cooing over. Pretend it's a spelling test. Tell it back to me."

I did. Stuttering with sobby little sucks of breath between the words. I thought for sure my shoulder was about to come off in his hand like the wrenched-off arm of an abused Barbie doll. The pain was such I could barely think my way through it. It took all the brain I had left to reply to this simpleminded request to recite his orders back to him.

"Fucking A," he said when I'd finished, and then he let loose of me.

I collapsed into myself and slid to the floor. Not caring anymore. You'd of thought I'd run out of tears by now, but there were plenty left for me to squeeze out, and I did. My sodden shorts felt cold and nasty and the stink of my own pee came up and shamed me just that much more. He had got me and broke me down. That much was sure. But tell me this: what kind of accomplishment of bravery is it for a large and fully overgrown man to reduce a young and skimpy girl like myself to shoulder-squeezed crying fits? Not much, I say. Not much at all.

"Good," he said finally, with all the airs of a man who thinks a job well and truly done. He shot the cuffs of his sports coat and dusted off some imaginary dirt he got on him from squeezing me. "Remember, he and your ma got till tomorrow. After that, anything bad happens, it's their own damn fault." And then Marty did something really strange. He barked at me and growled like a dog. "You do that to Hayes and see what he does." Whatever this meant, it cracked him up something ferocious. He laughed a few long and ugly seconds about it. Then that mouth-breathing troll turned around and walked off into the sunshine. Not even bothering to shut the door.

It was a beautiful day. Eighty-nine degrees, cool for August in Metter, Georgia, a decent northeastern breeze and not a cloud in the sky. A bird twittered in the holly tree beside the stoop, as if it were any old day. A car passed one street over. When I felt like I could stand up, I went back to the bathroom and threw up.

Business Card

arty's card was the color of a fresh-dried scab with lettering raised in gold.

Martin Keegan
Manager and Co-owner
Bow Wow's
Register, GA 31225
Ph: 912-556-9875
Fax: 912-556-9876

On the right was a bad drawing of a dog's head. It was so sloppy you couldn't tell what kind, only that it had a spiked collar and big, sharp teeth. Drool came out of its mouth in golden drops. Underneath the head were two crossed bones. All in all, sort of like a retarded version of a pirate flag.

A Misdiagnosed Stomach Bug

Logan's face looked as tight and twisted as a convenience-store Halloween mask. He sat in the far corner of the storage room gouging a circle into the plywood floor with an old tin Christmas ornament. A dented red wise man. I waited a good long time before I came back to see him. Long enough for me to round up and lash down all the escaped emotions running wild in my head. Or so I thought.

"What the fuck?" he said when he got a good look at my face.

"Not so loud, wait—" I started, worrying Marty might still be somewhere close enough to be dangerous.

"I'm going to kill him." Logan threw the wise man across the room and stood up as much as he could in that cramped space. "Where is he? Where is this asshole? If I'd of known he was doing that, I'd of killed him right then. Even if he is your mama's boyfriend."

"Logan, it ain't what you think."

This only seemed to make him angrier, if he'd heard me at all. He closed his eyes and sucked in a furious breath. The squeaky fan in the corner did its level best to cool things down. My hands were so slick with sweat they slipped off the little doorframe as I crawled through and I tumbled in with a double thud. Logan clenched and unclenched his fists. His bare toes curled against the floor.

"Anybody who could do that to you don't deserve to be walking around taking up space. Shit, a man who'd do that to a little girl, there's bound to be more and worse in him."

I couldn't help but cringe at "little girl."

Logan grabbed a ceiling beam with both hands and pounded his forehead against it.

"Hey, listen to me." I took his sticky cheeks in my hands and pointed his eyes toward mine. "That wasn't Hayes. It was some-body much, much worse. He and his are after Hayes for money or pills he owes them. He wanted Hayes. I just had the shit luck to be here when the man couldn't find him."

Logan stopped trying to pound his head against the beam and started to pay attention to what I was telling him. "What do you mean, not Hayes?"

It all came out then. The whole pot of shrimp. My head was still a blurry mess of a place, so it was all I could do just to spit the story out in fits and starts, sometimes having to back up to tell him a bit I'd forgotten to tell in its place. Fake dog dope, bloody ears on the door, Hayes's chopped pinkie, Heckle and Jeckle and Unkie Marty. All of it.

When I'd finished with this sorry tale, I finally looked up to see what he made of it. I'd pretty much kept my eyes pointed at the floor while I'd told him the whys and whats and whos. Now I wanted to know what he'd say. But Logan said nothing. Instead, he cried. The tears drew jagged lines of pink skin on his cheeks. He made no sound. His eyes might of looked red and raw, but they were full of a generous kind of sad. A look that was absolutely new to me. I knew then that whatever else might happen between us after he finally left my attic storage room, good or bad or nothing at all, I would always love him for these ten tears. Ten. I counted five on each side. It didn't matter to me what I'd just gone through to buy them. Right then, and maybe even now, they seemed to me a bargain.

"What's his name?" Logan asked, his voice a croak.

Neither of us breathed a word about the tears. I knew this would only ruin them.

"It don't matter, Logan. He's gone."

He stared at me until I looked down.

"What," he said in slow, careful voice, "is the man's name?"

I showed him the crumpled card.

Logan glared at it for a long time, his lips moving silently. I sat there blunt-brained. That terrible afternoon had hogged up all the space in my head. There wasn't room for extra thoughts of any kind. I could of sat there like that for a cat's age, all nine lives of it. I believe Logan must of said my name a few times before I heard him. He handed back that mean bit of cardboard.

"Why didn't you tell me all this before? I could of helped. Protected you. If I was worth half a shit, I would of anyway. That fucker was slapping the shit out of you five feet away and I just sat there with my hands under my ass. I'm sorry."

"There wasn't a blessed thing you could of done, Logan. And it was me who told you to go back. I thought I could handle him. You ain't got nothing to be sorry for."

"Still."

"You got more than enough problems of your own to sort out. I've already caused you plenty of trouble. I didn't want to give you any more to have to worry over."

"The one who ought to be worrying is that fat fuck Marty. He comes back while I'm here it'll be the last time. If I had a pair of pants, I'd—"

"See, that's what I was afraid of. You'd go out and get yourself in trouble over this, get arrested or worse, and it'd all be my fault. You sure as hell don't need a dozen more burdens loading you down."

"You're no burden, Lynn Marie."

"And you're sweet to say it, but I know a burden when I see it in the mirror."

Logan puffed through his nose and shook his head. I saw something then, maybe in the way he set his lips or the cast of his eyes. I had a feeling I'd made a giant mistake telling him all this. If I'd only waited a half-hour longer or at least until I'd gotten my head together a little more before I came rushing back here, looking for him to say, *oh, poor little Lynn Marie*, then I'm sure I would of had the sense to keep my mouth shut. Ten minutes ago, these two separate lives of mine, even if they were only about five feet and a piece of sheetrock apart, were completely separate, unmuddled. Each had its own problems, sure, but mixed together as they were now, they were like a lit fuse on an atom bomb. Right as he opened his mouth to keep on with this angry, self-disgusted talk and work himself up into doing something we'd both sorely regret, I cut him off.

"Listen now, Logan, honey, we already said it all. There's no point in driving ourselves crazy with it. The egg's been broke, the milk's tipped over, so instead of smearing it all into a terrible mess on the floor, let's us see if we can't bake a cake." This was something my mom always said and I was shocked it'd come out of my mouth. But he smiled to hear it, so I guess it was okay.

I moved in to kiss him and add a little sugar to this batter I was talking up. It will probably sound more than a tad strange considering the timing, but my body surprised me by wanting to get with Logan's body in the worst way. But before I could make good on this, something new and drastic happened inside Logan's head. What little color I could see under the grime on his face fled to some lower portion of his body. The pink tear trails went ashy. He took my hand in both of his. And what cold and clammy things they were, too. He looked about to puke. I feared he must of drawn some fresh and horrible conclusion from all of this crazy shit I'd unloaded on him.

"Lynn Marie," he said, his voice a rasp so low I had to lean in close to make it out. "I know what it is now."

"What *what* is?" I said.

"I love you." He blinked at me. "So it makes sense now, all the other stuff. The you know . . ."

"No."

"Me puking and all the rest."

"Puking?" None of this made a lick of sense.

"Oh, right, you were at school."

"What now?" I was truly alarmed.

"Which part, the puke or me loving you?" He coughed out a laugh, looking more surprised by this statement than I imagine even I was.

And I was floored, this having been the absolutely last thing I ever would have imagined coming out of his mouth at that moment.

Seeing my look, he said, "I know, I know, it's crazy." Logan laughed again. His color came back and then some. The blush of blood showed in his ears. "For a while I thought I was coming down with a stomach bug."

You Clean Up Nice

I made sure the water in the two salad bowls was warm, but not too hot, and I brought along some liquid soap that smelled like limes, and a fresh towel. It's alright for men to smell like limes. Limes are an either/or smell. As I put together Logan's bath kit, I got to worrying more and more about the crazy behavior of his I'd seen before Marty came. It troubled me, I'll tell you. I couldn't have him strolling about in the altogether for the entire world to see the next time he got it into his head to sort through my dirty laundry for disgusting headgear. I figured giving him some kind of discouraging punishment, no matter how much I hated having to do it, was even more important now that I knew Marty might come back any time.

When I came to give him his bath, I knocked Logan in the head with the doorknob by accident. For some reason he'd gone back to cowering in the corner behind the door and scratching the floor with his dented, red tin wise man. He didn't recognize me at first, which worried me more than a little, especially after our love talk. Did that mean he was lying when he said it?

"Jesus," he said, once I'd calmed him down. "What was all that? I thought we were under . . . I didn't know what the hell was going on."

My Specialist Loy sounded nearly as scared as I did when Marty squeezed my shoulder. This irritated me. I wanted Logan to be strong and sure and capable in an emergency, and it seemed pretty clear this wasn't going to be a dependable trait of his, but what confused and confounded me was I also wanted him to be the little boy I kept an eye on and took care of. I never knew which one I'd find when I opened the closet door.

"What was *what*?" I said carefully.

"The shooting. Somebody fired off a gun. Not just once. Five times. I counted."

What was he talking about? There hadn't been any thunder. Or any other loud sounds I'd heard. Then I got an idea of how I could use this to my advantage. This is going to sound cruel. I know it better than anybody. But you got to remember, I did what I did to protect him. If I couldn't count on him to be a soldier, I needed a way to protect the little boy from his own mischief.

"They're looking for you," I told him. "Those weren't guns you heard. The police have been knocking on every door around here. You know the way they do, knocking on doors like they hold a grudge against anything with a knob. Didn't you hear me talking to them out front?"

"Uh-uh," he said.

I made him sit down on several sheets of clean newspaper and then I took a washcloth and soaped him up. I'd watched my mom do this at the hospital many times. I started with his face. Careful downward strokes. First the left cheek, then the right. Logan was so agitated by what I'd told him, he didn't seem to notice what I was doing at first. Somehow he'd managed to get grime in his ears, but I washed it all away. I made sure to be methodical about it. One bowl for scrubbing, one for rinsing. This was how I managed to keep the brittle bits of my brain together on that unhappy day. Without someone else to look after, I feel certain I'd of come to pieces in under an hour. In this way, Logan saved me. He served me more by sitting and allowing me to scrub his dirty hide than he would of done had he leapt from the closet and served Marty up with a mighty thump on the head. And besides, Marty would of turned and done something even worse to Logan. Maybe even given him the gift of nine grams, as Logan himself was always saying. I noticed, just before he left, that Marty carried some sort of firearm beneath his sports coat in a shoulder holster. And nine grams is the weight of your normal workaday bullet.

"God, you're dirty," I told him. "How did you get so filthy dirty?"

"Now I think about it, maybe I did hear somebody talking. You swear that wasn't a gun?" Sweat and soapy water drew lines through the dirt on his chest.

"Yeah, I'm sure. Last time it was Mr. Cannon's door set you off, remember?"

"Right," he agreed, with an extra-sad look. Logan had taken to tapping each of my toes three times in quick succession every time I came into the room. I can't recall when this practice started. But instead of the usual one time through, he kept at it over and over as I washed him. "How'd they know to come looking for me here? You said it was safe."

I knew I had him now.

"Remember that man we saw when you bought the wine? Mr. Jenkins?"

I took his left arm and rubbed it down, rinsed the cloth and washed the soapsuds off. Then I did the other arm. He had a faint star-shaped scar on his shoulder. I kissed it.

"Oh, shit," he said. "That old guy from Cobbtown?" The one who called my sergeant? Damn, I knew that'd come back and bite me on the ass. What's he done now?"

I washed his chest, scrubbing in circles. He had a dusting of hair there, darker than the hair on his head but lighter than the hair on his boy parts. Dirty lint had collected in his belly button. I lifted his arm and gave his pits double washings. That's where he smelled the ripest. There and down between his legs.

"He went and told the police he saw us together. I guess snitching to his brother wasn't enough."

"What did you say to them? The police, I mean?"

"Turn around," I said, so I could get at his back. The grime was smudged in the shape of an upside-down bottle. I'd only now begun to really scrub and already the water in both bowls was filthy. "I told them I got a ride from you. I didn't really know you all that well and that was the last I saw of you. I don't think they believed me. That's why they wanted to search the house. I said they'd have to wait for my mom. They know you're around here somewhere because they found your car."

"Who was it that found it? The hardware guy again?"

"A policeman. Don't you remember? I told you all that."

"Shit, shit, shit," he rubbed his hands against the tops of his thighs. "What am I going to do? I knew I should of brought my rifle." Then he mumbled something about bombs. I didn't like the way his eyes looked. If I hadn't of known first hand, I'd never of believed this was the same Logan pitching me woo only an hour before. He wasn't a bit scared of Marty, the one who was worth worrying over, but a couple of handclaps drove him to distraction.

"When I'm back here all by myself," Logan said, "I have to listen out for every sound. Just in case, you know? It makes my neck hurt, and my back. Today, all those sounds about drove me crazy."

For some reason, being the source of common sense soothed me, even if I was the one who'd set these fears in motion. My own shoulder ached down deep in the bone, but telling Logan the simple fake-truth like this somehow made even the worst of my hurts feel better too. I can't explain it.

"I'm fucked." He took a deep breath and let it out with a long, wheezy squeak. "I am *so* fucked."

I washed his thighs. This went more quickly. They weren't as dirty as the rest. The washing soothed him, but not enough to make him sit still.

"Calm down. You're safe in here. I told you that a dozen times. They didn't find you, did they?"

Logan shook his head, still jittery with worry.

"And believe me, mister, they questioned me pretty hard. This is as good a hideout as you're likely to find." I held his chin in my soapy hand and forced him to look at me. I made my voice go soft and low. "You're still here with me, right?"

"Right."

"And you feel safe here with me, right?"

"Mmmm," he said.

"And you love me, right?"

"Mmmm," he said.

"What's that?"

"I love you. Of course, of course."

Then I went on to his feet, which were black on the bottoms and took some serious scrubbing. The big toe on his right foot was crooked. I'd forgotten about it until then. Logan told me the story the first night he spent behind the closet. He'd broken it the day his base was overrun in Iraq. The insurgents had caught him napping, literally, and in his rush to put on boots, he'd stumbled against a cot and cracked that little bone in two. If you knew his alphabet of scars, you could read Logan's body like a book. Slowly, I was learning the ABCs of Logan Loy.

"I don't see you being taken away from here in handcuffs any time soon, sweetie."

"I guess." His breathing slowed a little, hitched, then slowed a bit more.

"You can hide out until things have calmed down, as long as that takes, and then you can ride my bike to Statesboro and catch a bus." I washed between his legs, taking my time. I did it slowly.

Over and over. I used a lot of soap. His little guy hardened in my fist. Like a turtle's head with a long, pink neck.

"Yeah," he said, but not like he believed it. He looked down at my hand and then back up at me. "It might be better for me to go tomorrow morning before they really get serious about looking for me."

"Nah, that's crazy. It's way too late for that. If you tried to bike or walk there now, especially during the day, they'd catch you for sure. Statesboro's the closest Greyhound station and it's still a fair hike. They'll give up looking for you around here after a few more days. Don't forget, you've still got a pile of Green Gable books to get through."

I lifted his heavy, wrinkled sack of skin. In the bright light, it looked like something deformed. It occurred to me then that a boy's equipment had its uses, but it really wasn't much to look at once you got over the thrill of seeing it out in the open.

"I guess," he said.

I put the washcloth back in the water and looked at him. I smiled.

"What are you smiling about?" he asked.

"You clean up nice," I said.

But It's Really More Like a Dozen

The first thing Mom said to me Thursday night after work, as she came in through the kitchen door with a brown paper sack in each hand and a carton of Virginia Slims Menthol 100s tucked under her arm, was, "I saw Mr. Jenkins today."

There, under the bright twitch of the fluorescent lights, I got a good look at Mom's face and I didn't much like what I saw. She had about twenty pounds of frown dragging down each corner of her mouth and her eyes had sunk into deep, dark caves beneath her eyebrows. Still, those eyes of hers flashed at me as she set down the bags and told me what Mr. Jenkins said.

And since these were the first words to come out of her mouth—never mind a *Hey* or a *How you doing?*—my first fast thought was I must of brought this on myself by lying to Logan. I'd had this happen to me before. Tell someone a hard lie, and in return, someone else might tell you a hard truth. A string stretched between these things. Mr. Jenkins told her about what you'd expect. "And now," she said, "they're looking all over for him. Some people have it in their heads he might even be hiding here."

"In our house?" I fairly screeched this out. My God, look what my lie has done.

Mom, God bless her, just laughed at this.

"No," she said, "nobody thinks you're a tramp, honey. Just a foolish child who maybe made the very bad decision to ride around in a strange man's car."

I couldn't keep the blood from rushing to my face. It went there without my permission. And my cheeks flushed hot and guilty. I had to cut Mom off at the pass before she tripped me up or caught me in a lie. Frantic thoughts bounced around my skull like flies trapped in a bottle. The lies had gotten so thick and tangled, I near about had to write them down to keep track.

"Something bad happened," I said, after a too-long moment.

My mom's eyes widened and I could see she thought the very worst. "God, Lynn. Did he do something? Did he touch—?"

"No, no, Mom." I shooed that idea away with my hand. "That's not what I'm talking about."

"Then what?" she said, putting her hands on her hips. When I didn't speak up right away, she stepped across the kitchen to fetch her quilted cigarette bag from the counter. The motor in the fridge *chug-chugg*ed and stopped. The room went dead still. The metal clasp on her bag sounded like a Black Cat firecracker when she snapped it shut again. Mom knew something was up, so I decided I'd best walk on tiptoe from here on out. She blew a thin blue jet of smoke at my chest and stared me down with her shiny black eyes. There was nowhere for my own to slip away to. When I glanced off to the safety of the tablecloth, she snatched up my chin and made me look at her. Mom hadn't done this to me since I was ten years old and she thought I'd messed with one of her boat bottles. "Don't you look away from me, Lynn Marie. I know something's happened. You've gone red as a beet. What? Please don't tell me you're pregnant because I don't want to hear it. Not now, anyway. Not tomorrow either." She turned my face to one side. "And what in God's name happened to your cheek?"

"It's two things, really." I took a breath.

"Jesus," she said, pacing back across the room and throwing her cigarette bag onto the counter. Cigarettes spilled everywhere. She put one hand against her forehead and the other on her hip. Then she pushed out her lower lip and blew at the bangs hanging over her eyebrows until they fluttered. "Tell me. What is it?"

"Rhonda said for you to call in is one."

Her eyes flashed at me. "That's not what—"

"No, I think it's important. Really important. She seemed pissed." *Slow down*, I thought. She knows I babble when I'm spinning stories. "She said Dr. Drose wants to talk to you. Right away."

"Oh." She dropped her hand from her head and hugged herself. "What's two?"

Then I took the mashed and sweat-limp business card out of my pocket and held it out to her like a pet that'd died. When I opened my mouth to steer this conversation toward safer shores, suddenly, without me meaning to or even expecting it, the tears came popping out one after another and dribbling from eye to nose and nose to chin. Touching the card again was all it took for the fear to squirt out of that fresh crack behind my left cheek and go juddering down my spine. I thought I was over it, but I guess the bad feelings were only hiding out and waiting to ambush me when I least suspected it.

"What, baby? What happened?" When she came across the kitchen to hug me, I handed her the card. This brought her to a full stop. Her eyes turned to slits as she read.

I told her what Marty'd told me to say about the deadline and the money and all the rest. And then I told her what he'd done. I lifted my shirt and showed her the mess he'd made of me. I was surprised myself at how ugly the marks looked. I could see the reflection of it in the microwave door. My shoulder was seriously puffed up by then and an ugly blue-red color. The prints left by his sausage-link fingers couldn't have been clearer had he drawn them on with a marker.

"Oh, baby, I'm sorry." She sucked in a breath and winced. "He did that to you?"

"Yeah," I said, quietly, "he did." Then I told her about what he'd done to the house.

She ducked her head under the cabinet and looked across the breakfast bar at the living room.

"God-damn-it," she said. Each syllable came out of her mouth with a hiss, like water dripped in a hot skillet.

Mom kicked off her shoes and slid back and forth across the linoleum in her stockings. She gnawed at her lower lip. She did it in small, hard shuffles, like she was cleaning grime off the floor with her feet. This odd sort of pacing was usually her standard operating procedure for thinking over a serious financial jam. Half a dozen expressions made the muscles in her face jump and twitch.

I sat at the table and tried to stay still, following her around the room with my eyes. After a couple or three minutes of this slide pacing, she made as if to pick up the phone and then decided against it.

"Damn it," she said finally. "This has got way out of hand."

Mom stopped to look at her scattered smokes in the sink. After three long sighs, she snatched up one of the unbroken ones, put it in her mouth, and lit it with the big pink lighter from her cigarette bag. Then she went to the phone and picked it up again.

The sky outside the kitchen window slowly turned dark orange. An ambulance screamed through the parking lot on its way to the emergency room. The entire room filled with red light for a moment and then went dim again. After the ambulance turned the corner, it seemed a whole lot darker in the kitchen than it had before.

"Hey, Rhonda. Yeah. No, I didn't. What'd he say?" She took a drag off her cigarette. "When was all that? No. Yeah?"

Rhonda's voice scritched and scratched in the receiver like an angry cricket.

"If that's what he thinks, why'd he have you do it then? Damn,

I should of known Carla would say that. Uh-huh, I've been thinking that for years now." She laughed an angry laugh. "Like hell
she will. She'd sooner get that man to look at her then fly. Thanks.
Yeah, page Dr. Drose." She stabbed out her cigarette, gave me a
curious appraising look, and shook her head. "This is the last time
I—" Suddenly her voice dropped a pitch and became softer. She
gripped the phone with both hands. "No, Dr. Drose, I wasn't talking to you. I'm sorry. No, of course." She paused for a long spell.
"I don't believe I know." She closed her eyes and bit down hard on
her lower lip. I recognized it as something I did when I tried hard
not to cry. "Is that what you think of me, Dr. Drose? Alright, well
is that what *they* think of me?" She blinked her eyes twice, hard,
and grimaced at the ceiling. "No, absolutely not. I've never even
considered doing such a thing. That's right, I have to get the drug-
cabinet card key from *Carla* and sign everything out. She's always
right there when I'm doing it, and believe you me, she never so
much as blinks her eyes."

Dr. Drose's voice was a yellow jacket trapped in a Coke can.

"Oh, so that's what this is." She rolled her eyes and clenched
her jaw even tighter. "I'd be happy to take a urine test, but when
it comes out negative, which it will, I think I'll deserve an apology.
No, I'm not blaming you. That's right. That's exactly right. I'm
glad you can see that too. I'll be there in fifteen minutes."

Mom disappeared around the corner of the breakfast bar and
didn't speak for some time. I thought she'd hung up, so I got up off
the couch and went into the living room to find out what this was
all about. When I came around the corner, I found her squatting
on the floor with her eyes shut tight and her back against the wall.
I wished right away I hadn't seen it. It wasn't meant for me to see. I
can still picture her like that now if I shut my eyes. Something was
bad wrong at work. Something was terrible wrong at home. These
troubles pinned Mom to the wall like a wriggling bug. It wormed its

way out of the phone and then down through her body in unhappy ways. Her face went from clenched and angry to utterly blank and then mercifully softened into something vague but hopeful as she listened to the buzzing voice on the phone.

"An hour from now?" Then she actually smiled, which surprised me more than any of the expressions that came before. A nice smile. "No, Raymond, I haven't forgotten your invitation."

Raymond? I wondered. Is she talking with someone different now? Who in the hell is Raymond?

In the next pause, her eyes lit up. "Let's wait until I clear my good name, how about?" She giggled a downright girlish giggle. Under the circumstances, I took some offense over that. Here she is flirting while Metter burns. Or at least our place in it. I stood in the dark and glared at her, but she only had ears for this Raymond character. I don't even think she knew I was there beside her. "Yes, that's right, a steak the size of my head and an extra-large strawberry daiquiri."

She hung up the phone and immediately her mouth shrank down to normal size and her eyes took up a worried look again. I'll admit to feeling some satisfaction about this. After all, this was an emergency we were dealing with. Shoulder-squeezing thugs and dog butchers coming by the house on a daily basis should be given priority over steak dinners with Raymond.

"What's wrong?" I asked.

"Oh, shit," she said, taking my hands and pulling herself up. We went and sat on the couch. Spilt silverware clinked as the cushions moved.

"What, Mom?" I put my arm around her and laid my head on her shoulder.

In the dark, I heard her sniffle.

"You'd think I'd know better at this age than to think I could go and fix somebody."

"And now it ain't only Hayes, they're picking on me too. Isn't there something we can do to get out of this? Call the police, maybe."

Mom started. "Oh, God, no, honey. He's in way too deep for that. Before his accident, Hayes was playing tricks with peoples' fighting dogs. I'm not sure what exactly, some kind of half-assed cheating. The sorry man couldn't even cheat right. He lost everything and then some. To pay them back, he had to drive his truck down to Florida and pick something up."

"Drugs?"

She shrugged and looked away. "I didn't ask."

"Then drugs."

"Later, I overheard him talking with somebody at the hospital, after the crash. I guess there are people that go around to crooked doctors and get pain pills. There's a bunch of these doctors down in Florida. Somebody has to pick up the pills. It was only supposed to be the one time." She glanced at me and away.

I nodded.

Hayes told her he thought somebody was following him on the way back. A blue dump truck. Maybe one of the pill people down in Florida. He decided to make sure, so he got off on a two-lane highway just over the Georgia border. About ten miles down the road, way out in the country, the dump truck edged up and passed him. He went up over a small hill and saw rubble spilled across the blacktop. When his truck hit it, Hayes lost control. The truck went sideways and rolled three times. Four days of intensive care in Jacksonville and they transferred him back to the hospital in Metter. The cops told him they didn't find any rubble. And when they looked in his truck, it was empty. The cops thought he was lying about something, but he swore it was all true.

Dr. Peeples, one of the older doctors at the hospital, put Hayes on some serious strong pain pills. And that was fine at first because he needed them. His leg was all torn up and he'd broken four ribs. But then Hayes kept on complaining of pain. My mom didn't doubt he still hurt, but after a few weeks, you got to downgrade the medication.

"So Hayes got hooked?"

"Yeah," my mom said, putting a cigarette between her lips but not lighting it. "Hayes sadly ain't one of those men who knows when to say he's beat and stop."

"It seems to happen that way with Hayes a lot, don't it? One sorry trick leads to the next. But I don't get what this has to do with now. With us."

"Those pills were worth a lot of money." She closed her eyes. "Thousands and thousands and thousands."

One day, Mom told me, when Hayes was just about to be released from the hospital, she heard him talking to a man in his room. The man told him he'd cut his throat and leave him in a hog pen if Hayes didn't find a way to make up for the lost pills. Then he whispered something else Hayes didn't like. "I don't care if you don't like it, son," the man told him, "you're going to do it." Hayes didn't tell her what it was, but he said he was done for if he didn't find a way to pay them back, so sucker that she is for a pretty face, and Hayes, nasty as he was in almost every other way, did have a pretty face, so my mom got him a job at a pharmacy.

"That lasted about a week," I said. "Stupid Hayes."

And the threats kept coming. They got worse. Hayes begged her to help him.

"So this has been going on for almost a year now? Jesus, Mom. What did he ask you to do?"

But I knew. I knew and it made my teeth hurt.

Mom shrugged again and blew smoke toward the TV. "Now there ain't nothing for me to do but step back and let him fall down and hope he can pick himself back up. I don't intend to have—"

The phone rang and we both turned our heads, but neither of us got up to answer it.

"But you ain't going to help him get more pills, right?"

The phone rang again. And again.

"Mom? Are you?"

The answering machine picked up. "None of the Sugrues are here to answer just now. Say something nice," my mom's recorded voice said nicely, "or we won't call back." Beep.

"Hush, sweetie." She held up a hand and cocked her head to one side to better listen to what might come out of the machine's speaker next.

"Darla, are you there? This is Raymond."

Mom fairly threw me to the floor to get to the phone.

"I'm here. I was out back of the house."

It always amazed me to hear my mom talk with men. No matter the man, she underwent a change—even for the teenage boys working the drive-through window at McDonald's. I'd seen it all my life and it never failed to fascinate me. That night, it struck me that something between her and Dr. Drose had changed. Because I heard now that this Raymond character was indeed Dr. Drose. I'd known him near about my entire life and I'd never heard his Christian name until that night. I knew he and his wife had separated around Christmastime, but I'd no idea he'd started looking for Mrs. Drose number two so quickly. But this discovery also provided some relief. It meant the Hayes days were now coming to an end.

"Uh-huh, well, I'm on my way. Then we'll see who it is that's turned junkie. Just promise me this, if I got to pee in a cup, then so does Carla." She hung up and stomped back into the living room. "Sweetie, I got to go back to the hospital and clear up a few things."

"What's going on? I don't want to stay here all by myself. What if that Marty guy comes back?"

She covered her mouth with the back of her hand and choked back what sounded frighteningly like a sob. Just the way her mouth looked alone, crumpled and slack like a damp dishrag, made me want to cry. Feeling my own throat tighten up, I stepped across the linoleum to help her pick up the rest of the loose cigarettes.

"This time, Lynn, lock all the doors. Don't even turn on the lights. I'll be back as soon as I can."

She yanked open the back door and slammed it behind her, but it didn't catch. A breeze made it swing back and forth against the jamb. *Smack, smack, smack.* I doubt there's a lonelier sound in the world than a screen door banging back and forth like that. I went over and pulled it shut, but she'd broken the latch when she slammed it and it wouldn't stay closed. I had to stick it shut with Scotch tape.

And Then the Awful Quiet

Friday stretched silent and tense like a cat creeping through the tall, dead grass to pounce on a broken-winged bird.

Good Cop, Bad M.P.

They were sitting in the carport, one smoking and the other chewing gum, when I got home from school Friday, so I didn't see them until I came around the side of the house. A regular policeman with his hat tucked under his arm and a man in desert fatigues with an armband that said M.P. I nearly fell into a faint.

"Darla Sugrue?" the regular policeman asked. He was an extra-tall man with long, skinny arms poking out of his short-sleeved uniform shirt. His name badge said Watkins.

"No," I said, my voice wobbling a little at the edges, "Lynn Sugrue."

"Good," the M.P. said, a dapper little guy with a buzz cut and bright green eyes. He had a Yankee accent, like something out of a movie, and popped the gum he chewed on. He smiled in a lopsided way I didn't much care for. "Just the one we're looking for. Why don't we go in the house?"

I about shit myself.

"No, sir, my mother don't allow it. Not unless she's here."

"Not even for policemen like us?" the M.P. asked, his smile wilting.

"Not for no one, sir. She don't allow it."

"I see," the regular policeman said, running a hand through his wavy black hair. "Well, then." He put out his cigarette on the bottom of his shoe and put it in the big green trashcan by the utility room. "This'll do fine right here, I guess. You know a fellow by the name of Logan Loy? A young guy? A soldier?"

"I met him once. He gave me a ride."

"Where'd you meet him, miss?" the M.P. asked. The front pocket of his shirt was embroidered with the name Tills.

"Down at the BP station on Broad." I sat on the low brick wall at the edge of the carport and put my book bag on my lap.

"You often get in the car with strange men, miss?" the M.P. said, his voice becoming sharp.

Officer Watkins shot him a look.

"No, sir," I said.

"Where exactly did the two of you go?" the M.P. asked.

"To Cobbtown and back. We stopped out there and got a Coke. Mr. Jenkins from the hardware store saw us. Ask him."

"Oh, we talked to Mr. Jenkins." M.P. Tills smirked at me.

Officer Watkins watched the M.P. in a careful way, as though he might do something sudden and alarming. I liked Officer Watkins's sideburns and the way he turned his hat in circles with his hands. If I wasn't mistaken, he'd let my mom off with a warning once when she rolled through a stop sign. I wondered why he'd called me by my mom's name.

The M.P. waited for me to respond to this, and when I didn't, he said, "That's it? To Cobbtown and back and then he let you out of his car?"

"Yes, sir."

"You fool around with him?"

"Sir?"

"Kissing, petting—"

"Hey, hey," Officer Watkins said, holding out his hand, "come on now."

"No, sir," I said, with as much disdain as I could muster under those very stressful circumstances.

"You see him again?" The M.P. frowned at me, hard.

I shook my head.

"Jesus," the M.P. said, and snapped his gum. The crack echoed in the carport.

"What did you talk about, Lynn?" Officer Watkins said, his voice soft, almost a whisper.

"He told me he wanted to draw comic books. He told me about his car."

"Jesus Christ," the M.P. said.

"He tell you where he was headed?" Officer Watkins smiled.

"Back to Hunter," I said. "He wanted my phone number, but I said I'd only take his."

"You still have that number?" the M.P. asked quickly.

I shook my head. "I threw it out soon as he drove off. He was nice enough but too old. I only drove with him because he said he knew my cousin Bucky. Turned out he was fibbing about that, but it was kind of funny the way he did it. I didn't mind."

"So that's it, huh? Cars, comics and Cobbtown," the M.P. said, his voice turning mean. "I don't believe a word you said, little girl." He made the word girl sound like the most terrible insult ever.

I glared at the rude little man.

"How'd you like this? How'd you like to come down to the interrogation room at Hunter? If you feel like it, we could talk all night about cars, comics, and Cobbtown." The M.P. took a couple steps toward me, but Officer Watkins stepped between us and put a hand on the M.P.'s chest. The M.P. shook it off and for a second I thought something might come of it. A spiteful look went across his face like the shadow of a passing bird.

"There ain't no call for that," Officer Watkins said.

"There *ain't* no call for me to stand here and listen to this little bitch lie to me." When he said "ain't," the M.P. tried to put on a Georgia accent, but it just sounded petty and foolish. "I'm going to take her with me."

"No," Officer Watkins said, "no you *ain't*. And I won't have you cussing out children neither."

The two men squared off and looked at each other. The carport was quiet for a while. I shifted my book bag from one arm to the other. Finally, Officer Watkins took a cigarette out of his pocket and lit it. When he exhaled, the smoke seemed to fill the entire area.

"I know something isn't right here," the M.P. said. "I know it."

"Well, maybe you should wait and speak with the girl's mama." He turned and looked at me. "She works over at the hospital, ain't that right?"

"Yes, sir," I said, pointing in the direction of the hospital, about a quarter mile from the house on a grassy hill. "She'll be there till late."

"This isn't the last of it. If you know where Loy is, it's in his best interest and yours for you to tell me. Harboring a criminal is a crime. Do you understand me?"

"Yes, sir," I said, "can I go? I've got a lot of homework for tomorrow."

"Homework." The M.P. made a sound of disgust. "I bet."

"Come on, now. Let's go. There ain't no need to keep harassing the girl, sergeant." Officer Watkins smiled at me and put on his hat. "Have a good afternoon, Lynn." He turned and then stopped short and looked back over his shoulder. "But if you think of something that might be helpful, you see this soldier has gone missing and might even be in need of help, make sure and call down to the sheriff's office, you hear?" He handed me his card.

"Yes, sir."

Officer Watkins winked. It was a strange wink, as if he also knew something wasn't right here. Only he went about figuring it out in a different way. Or maybe it was just a friendly wink.

"One last thing, Miss Sugrue," the M.P. said without looking back, "somebody took a dump at the end of your driveway."

"You just can't quit, can you?" Officer Watkins said.

They crossed the backyard and walked through the stand of pines that separated our house from the large, grassy strip below the hospital parking lot. The police car was parked over by the entrance. I wondered if it'd been their plan all along to sneak up on me or if they just wanted to talk to my mom too. The muscles in my neck felt as though they'd been wound around a stick. God, I thought, that was close.

The 175-Pound Three-Year-Old

Once those policemen were safely away, I decided to check on Logan first thing. All this talk about him had me feeling nervous. When I came inside, I found him out in the living room picking through the ashtray. He must of heard me coming because he made a mad scramble to hide behind the couch. I picked up a throw pillow on my way around the couch. He crouched in the corner, clutching a handful of cigarette butts. I chucked the pillow at his head.

"What are you doing?" I said. "Are you crazy?"

"I am." He made a fake-crazy face that really did make him look a little insane. "I'm loony. Ha, ha. Bippy as a beaver hat."

"No, really. What the hell are you doing, Logan?"

Out in the daylight, he looked even dirtier than I remembered, and I'd just given him another bath. The rash on his inner thighs had spread to his chest. I noticed he had scabs in the corners of his mouth.

"Nothing." He chewed on his lower lip and smiled with his mouth only. His eyes looked glazed and empty, like my mom's after she's had her fourth beer. "Just getting some air."

"Well, I just spent the last ten minutes talking to a mean M.P. and a policeman who were looking for you."

"Shit," Logan said, looking suddenly bashful. "Again?"

"Last time it was only the regular police, not the M.P. type," I said. "You know they know you're around here somewhere. And what do you do? You hop around the living room with the blinds open."

I grabbed his arm and dragged him back to the closet. He came along without any trouble, but he wouldn't speak to me at all. My room reeked of cigarette smoke, which was better than Logan stink but still worrisome. So he'd been sneaking out and swiping butts before. When we got inside his little room, the smell was overpowering.

"You can't smoke in here. There's nowhere for it to go. You'll choke to death," I said. "Besides, you don't smoke. I thought you said you hated open flames."

"I'm trying to get over my fears," he said, grinning with half his mouth. He'd already stuck another little butt between his lips. "And besides, I've got to do something with myself. You ain't got a fucking clue how bored I am."

He lit up, but the butt was so short he burned the tip of his nose with the match. When he saw me watching him, he wheeled around and hunched over. It was a strangely chimp-like move.

"Alright," I said. "Let's talk about it. Just put the cigarette out."

"It's out," he said, grinning that strange grin again. He held up his arm and showed me a red mark on the inside of his wrist. It took me a second to realize what it was.

"Jesus, Logan, why didn't you just put it out against the wall?"

"And mess up your painting? Shit."

I gave him a worried look.

"I hope you don't mind, but I borrowed these." Logan held up an old bleach bottle with part of the top cut off. I'd kept my crayons in there when I was a kid. He shook it so it rattled.

"Where'd you find that?"

He gestured at one of the boxes against the wall and then picked up a half-dry felt-tip pen and started scratching out lines on his thigh with it.

"Just wait till you see my masterpiece when it's done," he mumbled, jerking his thumb at the wall behind his head.

I hobbled over and lit up that side of the room with my flashlight. He'd turned one wall into a cartoon strip. In the first panel, men in turbans chased a girl who looked a bit like me. In the next, they cut off her breasts. The blood formed a huge waterfall down the wall and he'd even colored a bit of the floor red. It looked like he'd melted a red crayon and let it drip and pool. In the final panel, the turban men chucked the girl's boobs in a bonfire. The drawings were crude and brightly colored. The turban men had fangs. I felt sick.

"Jesus, Logan," I said.

"I told you it ain't finished," he said, his voice small and sullen. "I have two more squares to fill. Just wait."

He Ain't What I Expected

"Look who's here," my mom said, presenting Dani with both hands. It was just about seven thirty.

I must of looked as though I'd swallowed a live tree roach because Dani piped up quick. "I'm only allowed over for a little while. Just long enough to get my social studies homework from you." As my mom couldn't see her face, Dani also allowed herself a giant wink.

Oh God, nothing good could come of this.

The moment I shut the door to my room, she let out a little whoop. "You didn't think I'd let you get away with not giving me get at least a peek at him. He's still here, isn't he?"

"Well—"

"I knew it. This has to be quick. That story about homework was complete bullshit, but homework's like a magic word, you say it and you automatically get a little parental slack. My parents are actually playing bridge over at the McKinleys'. I got about an hour before my mom calls to check on me."

That, at least, was a relief. But still.

"This ain't the best of times, Dani. He's not feeling too well."

"I guess I'll have to cheer him up then." She zipped into the closet before I could move in front of her. The door to the attic croaked.

"Wait, Dani, if he doesn't know you, he's like to—"

Dani let out a shriek. I went in after her as fast as I could, thinking, Oh Christ, he's gone and killed her. But by the time I ducked in, they were on either side of the attic, both looking scared half to the grave.

"I didn't do nothing to her," Logan said, pointing at Dani. "I thought she was the cops."

"What in the hell's wrong with him?" Dani's lips tightened and the skin between her eyebrows wrinkled up.

I'd gotten so used to seeing Logan naked and grimy, it took me a moment to understand what she meant. Logan looked like something out of *National Geographic*.

"This is too much," Dani said, backing away from him. "And the smell, ugh!"

"Who is this fat little girl?" Logan asked me. He clutched his red wise man ornament like a hatchet.

"Hold up a second, Dani," I whispered.

"What," Dani said, pushing me out of the doorway, "did you do to him?"

When I got back in my room, she had her hand on the door to the hall. Dani took quick, shallow breaths and squeezed herself with one arm.

"Let me explain," I said. "It's not what you think."

"I don't know what all you two have been doing back there, but . . . he ain't what I expected." Her eyes were red with tears. "At all."

With that, she was out the door before I could say another word. If I'd of had even one more tear left, I would of cried it right then.

A Stink Even Febreze Can't Fix

I thought we were going to have sex, but he couldn't get it to work. He wanted to. It was his idea. But it wouldn't get hard. I rubbed it and put it in my mouth for a little while when he asked me to, even though the last time I tried this it made me gag.

"What's wrong with it?" I said. I wasn't trying to sound mean, but I guess it came out that way. I didn't understand what the problem was. It always worked before.

By this point, we were both naked. Two candles sputtered in the corner. After Dani had left, I'd given him a fast sponge bath, but he was already completely filthy again and his eyes were almost swallowed up by charcoal-colored pockets of wrinkled skin. If they sunk any deeper into his head, they'd disappear. He said he couldn't remember the last time he'd slept more than a few minutes at a time. The little room seemed to smell even worse than it did before, but I thought maybe Dani's visit had made me more aware of it. I made a note to buy some Febreze the next day at the Piggly Wiggly. But this was a stink I wasn't even sure Febreze could fix.

"Nothing's wrong with it!" he yelled. He took it into his hand and shook it at me. "Something's wrong with *me*. With *you*."

"Shhh," I said. "My mom's still awake." I pulled my T-shirt on. Something black was smeared on the sleeve.

"I don't care if she is," he said. "I'm getting out of here tomorrow. Even if I have to go naked." He shook his dick at me again. "You've been lying to me this whole time."

"About what?" I said.

"About the clothes, for one."

"No, that's true," I said, but this sounded like a lie even to my own ears. My voice came out flat and unconvincing.

"Right," he said, folding his sweat-shiny arms across his chest.

Out in the kitchen, my mom shouted, "Like hell I will, Hayes!"

I shifted my attention to her phone conversation, so when Logan spoke again, it made me jump a little. He sounded levelheaded and clear. "What ever happened with all that? That mess with the boyfriend? That's who she's talking to, right?"

I didn't think he'd been keeping track of this. But of course he could hear Mom's voice as clear as I could. I'd noticed many years ago it was easier to hear the rest of the house from back here than it was to hear the attic from the rest of the house. He'd probably heard more about Hayes than I had with all that time on his hands and nothing to do but listen to my mom and make whacked-out cartoon strips on the wall.

"Yeah, probably."

"She don't seem to sleep much, or else she can do it in front of the TV. I never could sleep with people talking like that. The only time I can close my eyes is when she's off at work."

"I'm sorry, sweetie. You got to believe that."

"I don't got to believe anything. My brain ain't doing what I'd like. I don't know." Logan tapped each of my toes three times. "I don't know."

"Well, I know you've been outside, so you know I'm not lying about your car."

"What?" he said, trying to act all innocent, but I could tell he was surprised.

"A girl at school told me on the bus this morning she saw you running around naked in the yard the other day. Lucky for us, everyone thinks she's full of it. I can't believe you did that. This whole time I've been trying to protect you. You think it's easy, hiding you like this? Well, it ain't. I'd get in a lot of fucking trouble if anyone found out. As it is, people are getting suspicious."

"Ah ha," he said, making his fake-crazy face again. It wasn't even close to funny this time. Just scary. "Ha, ha, ha."

"Do you want to go to jail?"

"I'm in jail!" he near about shouted.

"Quiet," I said, "hush."

Logan stopped making faces. He cocked his head and looked at me. "Okay," he said. "Then let's figure a way for me to get out of here if *you're* so worried about getting into trouble."

"That's not what I meant and you know it."

"When your mom's gone, I sleep all the time 'cause it's dark. But only for about five minutes at a time because I have these *dreams* you wouldn't believe, and then since it's dark, the dreams just kind of slip into my awake time. Everything's getting mixed up." His eyes were red and shiny, like they'd been coated with a thick layer of varnish and had yet to dry.

"Fine. Leave tomorrow."

"*Leave tomorrow. Leave tomorrow*," he screeched in a piss-poor imitation of my voice. "You say that every Goddamned day. What if I left right now?" He crab-walked toward the door.

"You take one step out of this house and I'll call the police." I waved the card Officer Watkins gave me. "Three-eight-three, four-four-four-three. Here, take it, I memorized it already."

Logan held the card up to the flickering candlelight and peered at it for a good, long while before saying anything. "You wouldn't do that."

"Go ahead and see."

"I'll tell them you've been keeping me prisoner, that you stole my clothes."

"Yeah?" I said, squeezing my hands into fists. The nails dug into my palms. "Yeah?" Something sizzled inside my head. My anger glowed inside me like a lightbulb filament. "And I'll say you overpowered me and then forced me to have sex. That you climbed in through the *window* and raped me."

"Bullshit," he said, but it got him to thinking. I could see it in his eyes.

I stared at him.

"So, okay, now I see where we are. I get it." Except he didn't. He didn't get it at all. His voice cracked. "I liked you. The most. What the hell happened?"

I saw I'd broken something between us. I thumbed my eyes to keep from crying.

"I'm sorry, Logan. I didn't mean that. It just came out. I swear."

"Sure," he said, "whatever."

"I mean it. I do love you. I do." And I did. When I said it, I did.

"Maybe," he said, "but that's the first time I've heard you say it. And it don't change nothing."

He turned away and picked up a crayon. I touched him on the shoulder, but he shrugged me off. After that, I saw there wouldn't be any more talking. At least not that night. I crawled back out into my room.

"You can't watch me all the time," he said.

After I climbed out of the storage space that night, I moved my dresser into the closet. I didn't push it all the way against the door. I wanted him to be able to breathe, after all, and escape in case of emergency, but there was no way he was getting out of there tonight without me hearing him. Anger made me shiver. Whenever things got tough, I was the first thing people dropped. Just like with Dani, my mom, my dad. And now him. If he really tried to leave tomorrow, I knew just what I'd do. I'd go to the school nurse and sham a bad case of PMS. They always let you leave for that. Then I would call the police with an anonymous tip from her office when she went to tell the front office, so the police couldn't track my cell phone. And then I'd come home in time to wave and smile as they dragged little Logan off. Yeah, that's what I'd do. But even as I pictured all this in my mind, step by step by step, I knew I'd never do it. Plus, I remembered: tomorrow was Saturday.

Shitty Mothers

It was a little after two in the morning Saturday when I heard a trashed-out car pulling up into the driveway. The exhaust backfired with a bang like a shotgun blast and echoed off the front of the house. That ought to be driving Logan just this side of crazy, I thought. Nothing good could come of a visit from anyone at this hour. I slipped my cell between the elastic of my panties and my hip. Just in case. I left the lights off in my room, but I cracked the door.

"What the fuck do you think you're doing driving here?" my mom yelled. It didn't even sound like my mom's voice, but it was. Shrill and ragged, loud and drunk. "We had an agreement. Now anybody passing by is going to see that piece of shit you stole out front and know you're here."

"Borrowed," a man mumbled. Whoever it was talking spoke so low it took me a moment to puzzle the sound into a word. There was only one person it could be.

"Goddamnit, Hayes, what's wrong with you? Are you stupid as all that?" There was a wet sob in her voice that made my own throat burn with held-back tears. I wanted to go out there and hit him in the crotch with the first heavy object that came to hand.

"Do you want me to move it?" His voice was thick and slow and sad.

"What I want you to do is to get the hell out of here. I almost lost my job today because of you and your stupid shit . . . ah, damn it, Hayes." The yell left her voice. Now my mom's words sagged in the middle and stumbled at the ends. I don't remember ever hearing her sound like this before, so defeated.

"I'm sorry," Hayes said. He sounded like a beat dog. "I was trying to help us."

"Us? Us? You're such a fucking liar," my mom said. The refrigerator door slammed and the bottles on the inside shelf clanged together.

"Darla, wait."

"*Darla, wait,*" Mom mimicked back in an ugly falsetto.

"I'm in over my head with this one, Darla, I really need—"

"No, Hayes, no. I won't."

"Wait till you hear me out."

"It don't matter what you say. I'm done, Hayes. Got it? Through."

Hayes didn't say anything I could hear, and this was probably a smart move on his part.

"Well," Mom said after taking a noisy slurp of beer, "did your cousin lend you a hundred and fifty grand?"

Hayes mumbled.

"I guess that means you're shit out of luck."

The closet door thumped against the dresser. Oh shit, not now. Thank God and all his angel buddies Mom and Hayes were too wound up to hear it. I tiptoed over to the closet and poked my head in. Logan's hair stuck out around the drawers.

"Lynn, are you and your mom in trouble?"

"No, sweetie, just my mom breaking up with Hayes."

He made a raspy laughing noise. "Don't sound like he's taking it so well, huh?"

"Nope."

Hayes spoke very, very quietly. Soft, sorry syllables that sounded an awful lot like an apology from where I stood behind my bedroom door. This went on for quite a while. I couldn't make out one word of it, so I edged out into the hall until I could match the sounds to words and put the words into sentences—all the while careful as hell not to get too close.

I felt sick and sorry. Listening to Hayes, I heard myself—trying to spin bullshit into something shiny and believable. I slumped against the wall and slid to the floor, yanking my T-shirt over my knees. In some strange and awful way, I had this powerful feeling it was me that brought this entire mess into our house. I tied the strings to each trouble. Me seeing Hayes that night at the Bow Wow club was a big one. I felt sure it had been this that caused Marty's creeps to come to our house. They'd only reeled in that string, whether they knew it or not. And Marty would never of tried sneaking into the house had I not tied the next one. Bringing Logan home and keeping him locked up behind my closet brought Marty here. See how they match up? The causes and effects were too clear for me to ignore. I knew these things were true the way I knew the sun would come up in the morning. If not for me, Hayes would of seen the end of his bad behavior somewhere far from our house. If I'd only left well enough alone, my biggest worry right now would be the Algebra II exam next Friday. Who knew what other ugly, ill-intentioned people were reeling in the different lines I'd tied right that very minute?

"Darla," Hayes said, so strenuous in his pleading that his voice trembled, "listen to me, please. I fucked up. I know that. I can't undo it. But the man is going to fucking kill me. You do get that, don't you? Not beat the shit out of me. They already done that. *Kill me dead.* Jason told me—"

"Who?" Mom wailed.

"The one what let me use his car. The beater out front. I've been sleeping in it different places every night. Jason, he told me he saw Butthole Gibbs parked outside your house today looking for me. You know what he brought with him?"

"Great. Now you've led yet another asshole straight to my house. Lynn is here for God's sake. Use your head." Something crashed against the wall. "Get the hell out of here now or I'll call the police myself."

"You wouldn't call the police on me," he said, but he didn't sound so sure. "Wait. I didn't tell you yet. Butthole came in a panel van and parked across the street. Stayed all afternoon just looking at the house. And he left a great, big pile of shit down at the foot of your driveway. You can make me leave, and I will, but it's not only me they're after anymore. They think we're partners. All of them think that or they wouldn't be coming by and fucking with you and Lynnie the way they've done."

Mom laughed like a frog. *Croak, croak, croak.* This didn't stop Hayes one bit. He kept on and on, but he spoke in that low, mumbly voice again and I couldn't make out enough of the words to puzzle any sense out of them. Pills, dogs, fucking, trouble. After a while the words sputtered out and someone started sobbing, but I couldn't tell whether it was him or my mom or both. The refrigerator door opened, rattled and shut. And then a couple of minutes later it opened again. But the door to the house never opened, so I guess she let him stay, or at least didn't make him leave. There's some difference there, but not all that much. I wanted to go out and talk with her, but I knew very well my mom's anger could easily turn on me. I sat down next to my bedroom door and thought, Jesus, has there ever been a day when I haven't been the mother around here. And then I thought, We're both shitty mothers. I didn't raise her right.

Wet Wiring

'm not sure if it was Logan banging on the little door or the thunderclouds crashing against each other in the sky above my house, but something woke me up with a start that made me knock my head against the bedroom door. My cell phone told me it was 3:12 A.M. A huge sheet of lightning lit the front hallway like a camera flash. I waited for the bang, but it never came. Heat lightning. My Earth Science teacher, Dr. Yarbrough, once told us true lightning is hotter than the surface of the sun, but heat lightning isn't even as hot as the surface of your skin. It's trick lightning. All flash and no bang. And I felt something very much like it, all bright and fake.

My neck hurt and my mouth felt gummy. In the closet, Logan whined like a chained-up dog. A high, lonesome sound. It made my arm hair bristle to hear it. I hushed him, but it did no good. When I leaned in through the door and whispered for him to quit, he said something I didn't understand about hajjis and started to cough. I smelled cigarette smoke again and it pissed me off. Mom and Hayes murmured. The TV yammered behind their voices. Then a heavy thump shook the floor behind me. I knew exactly what made it.

Logan sat on my bed wearing a pair of jeans a good two sizes too big and nothing else. Laid across his knees was a pink Wiffle ball bat with a jagged piece of metal tied to the fat end with a shoelace. It looked as though he'd dug up my crusty old Easy-Bake Oven from one of the boxes back there, disassembled the thing, and weaponized it. With his right hand he stropped what looked to be a butter knife against a ragged leather belt. The cutting side was shiny and sharper than a butter knife has any business being. Before I had a chance to say something about all this, he held up a hand.

"Just wait," he said, without looking away from the knife, "and hear me out."

Clearly, something had changed. He sat up straight. His hair still looked messy, but he'd done something to it. Maybe patted it into place. Even his eyes looked clearer. The knife made throat-clearing noises as it scraped the leather. Logan whipped it back and forth five more times. Then he raised his head.

"Keep your voice down. I seen one out there, but there may be more. If they don't know we're onto them, we keep some tactical advantage."

"Who?"

"Hajjis. I knew it was only a matter of time before they found me. You'd think I'd be scared, but I ain't. I aim to be free of this shit once and for all."

"Logan," I said, trying to keep my voice down, "what the hell? Every time a door slams it's hajjis."

"That's right. Before I only heard them. This time I've *seen* them." He pointed to his eye with the butter knife. "One I spotted had an M-4. Ain't no mistake about it."

Suddenly, he hunched his shoulders and held up both hands, commanding silence. Without meaning to, I went to one knee and listened. Logan widened his eyes at me and smiled. This smile had nothing to do with me. His head swung back and forth, following some imagined sound.

"Hear that?" he asked.

I nearly said no, but then I did hear something. A leaf clawed against a window screen. For half a moment, he had me going there. I let my breath out through my nose.

"Wind," I said, but I whispered it.

"Nuh-uh." Logan smiled that faraway smile again. "Not possible."

I tried to think of something I could say to calm him down, but he was up and past me before I'd even managed the fuzzy outline of a thought. I made a grab for his newfound jeans, but he twisted away. Logan opened the door wide enough to slip through sideways, settled the bat against his shoulder and disappeared into the hall.

"Logan, don't," I said, but it was too late. The boy was beyond listening to anything I had to say to him. Some bit of wet wiring inside that pretty head of his had truly gone awry. It shouldn't of shocked me, but it did. And it was even worse knowing I'd been the cause of it. I didn't find him this way. I made him this way. There wasn't a thing to do but follow him out into the trouble.

It Ain't a Tea Party

"What in the hell?" Hayes said, but he didn't do much more than lean forward.

My mom stood. She looked from Logan over to me, and then back to him. I had no idea what she made of him in his falling off jeans and his pink Wiffle weapon. A tipped-over beer gurgled across her bare toes and onto the carpet.

"As if your mama don't have enough shit to deal with, but you got to lay this on her. Couldn't you of waited till—"

"Shut up, Hayes," she said.

"You're all in grave danger," Logan told her. "As of—" He glanced down at his naked wrist and frowned. "As of a few minutes ago, a group of armed men surrounded this housing structure. I'm not sure of their intentions, but being as they're hajjis, it ain't a tea party."

I flinched when he said "hajjis."

My mom noticed. She glared at me until I looked away. "Who is this man, Lynn Marie, and what is he doing in my house?"

"He's my friend."

"I knew something weren't right with this picture," Hayes said, only now setting down his beer. His eyes were glassy and rimmed with pink. "This bozo's wearing my pants. Ain't enough wrong in the world but that you got to go and steal a man's pants."

Mom turned toward him and snapped her fingers four times. Hayes shut up.

She turned back to me. "What's he doing in my sitting room

half naked at God-fucking-knows-what-hour of the morning?"
Her voice rose with every word until she shouted out the last one.

"I . . ." There wasn't a reasonable answer to this question. I
opened my mouth but had no sounds to fill it.

"And wearing my Goddamned pants to boot." Hayes attempted
to stand and caught his knees on the coffee table.

Logan went to the window, lifted a corner of the blinds and
peered out.

"My favorite ones," Hayes said.

"What in the name of God is he doing now?" my mom asked me.

"He's checking for—"

Logan held up a clenched fist, still monitoring his made-up
men through the window, and hushed us. Amazingly, it worked.
My mom worried her forehead into a maze of wrinkles but said
nothing. Hayes drank what was left in the bottle Mom knocked
over.

"Ma'am," Logan said softly, moving to one side of the window.
His movements were so precise and efficient, so professional, they
demanded your attention. He might of been insane, but he didn't
look it. "I suggest you and your friend get behind the couch. This
could get ugly fast."

Something unsavory occurred to my mom. Her lips tightened.

"Now Logan—" I said, hoping to keep him from scaring her
completely out of her wits.

Mom took a step forward. "What is it you think you're doing
over—"

"Yup," Logan said, "here they are. Get ready."

Someone knocked at the front door.

We all four of us went still. The silence afterward fairly screamed.
First one side of Logan's mouth curled up, and then the other,
completing a satisfied smile. He nodded once and positioned himself at the end of the front hall. I tried to catch his eye.

Ten long seconds. The second set of knocks were much louder, more insistent. Me and my mom jerked at the sound. Logan made some sort of signal to us behind his back with a hand, but his attention never wavered from the door.

"Hello?" came a small voice from the other side.

"Is that . . . ?" Mom whispered. She put a hand to her mouth.

"Please. I know it's late, but I need to speak with you." It was Mr. Cannon, our neighbor. Three more meaty thumps. Then a shoulder slam, like he meant to bust the door down. "Really, I must insist you answer your door. It's urgent."

"I thought he was out of town," I said, as quietly as I could.

My mom shrugged, but it looked more like an involuntary muscle twitch.

"Is it locked?" Hayes asked. In the thick quiet, his voice seemed bullhorn loud.

"I can hear you in there. Please open the door. It's a matter of life and death."

Still nobody moved. We all listened to the door handle twist. But my mom had thrown the bolt when Hayes came.

Outside, Mr. Cannon began to sob. This sound roused something in me. The man was in trouble and here we sat on our hands, listening to him cry. Enough. Logan had them spooked, but I knew just how ridiculous this actually was. Before it could get any worse, I stepped around Logan and into the hall. Mr. Cannon made a wet noise that could of been the word please.

"*Lynn!*" Logan hissed.

I turned the bolt and yanked open the door. Mr. Cannon must of been leaning against it because he fell on top of me, knocking me to the floor and collapsing on my legs. The hall light was off, but even in the gloom I noticed Mr. Cannon was naked but for a short green robe made out of some shiny fabric. Blood ran from his ear to his chin.

"Hajji motherfucker," Logan said, quiet but pissed off.

He jumped past me and Mr. Cannon and swung his bat. Another silhouette lurked in the doorway, a tall man with a long, thin neck. He shouted as Logan's makeshift club caught him on the shoulder. The hall flashed orange and the whole house shook with a noise so loud I almost couldn't hear it. It rattled my teeth in their sockets. Something warm dripped off my earlobe. Mr. Cannon screamed until he choked, squirming against my feet. The air tasted bitter. In the doorway, Logan wrestled with the tall man. Sharp grunts and puffs of breath. My ears rang. Mom yelled my name in a muffled way, like her mouth was filled with cotton balls. Even in the dim light, I saw the flash of the butter knife as Logan pulled it from the waist of his pants. He lunged. Something happened to tip him off balance and the tall man swung the butt of his rifle into the back of Logan's head. He went face-first onto the floor. For a long moment, nothing at all happened. Smoke drifted out the door. When Logan didn't get up, the man felt his neck and then stepped over him, oddly careful not to tread on his body.

Mr. Cannon panted. Each time he exhaled, a small shrieking sound came with it. The tall man pulled Logan just far enough into the house to close the front door. Then he flicked on the hall light. With it came a flood of red. The wall beside me dripped with Mr. Cannon's blood. My arms and shirt were splattered with it. Mr. Cannon took three quick breaths and screamed. I tried to slide out from under him, but I was trapped. My own breath came so hard and fast it made me dizzy.

"Now this," the tall man said, "has got to stop." His voice was high and nasal and the words came out slurred, but not like he was drunk. It sounded off somehow, more like when a person sings way out of tune.

Mr. Cannon's head quivered and jerked.

"Please don't kill him," I said, still trying to squirm out from under his back.

"Not *please don't kill me*?" The man laughed. He would of been handsome but for the mess somebody had made of his ear and the space around his temple. The skin appeared melted and shiny, like congealed cheese dip, and in the time since it'd cooled, hair had refused to grow there. His left ear was a collection of irritable red nubs. "What's this sorry sack of dog mess to you?"

"Just don't," I said.

The man appraised me. His eyes were the chemical blue of drain cleaner. I watched him make a calculation. I was a column of numbers.

"You're the girl, then."

It wasn't a question. I wouldn't of answered it anyway.

"Shut him up," he said, picking his way down the hall.

As soon as he walked into the other room, Hayes sputtered. An empty bottle fell over and rolled across the coffee table. The man laughed again, a joyless noise, cockeyed and scary as a bag of copperheads.

"Shit, Mr. Gibbs, I can explain," Hayes said.

"That ain't what I come for."

Hayes said something about deals to be made.

"Don't tell it to me. I ain't the one pissed off at you." Butthole Gibbs whistled and stepped back into the hall. "Hey, jellybean, wrap the fat man's leg with this." He tossed me a roll of duct tape and smiled when I caught it with one hand.

Bright and Blank and Terrible

M r. Cannon hushed when I told him the man would probably kill him if he didn't shut up, but I honestly don't think he knew what was happening to him anymore. The skin on his face had the blank, yellowish color of buttermilk, and he kept blinking his eyes and grinding his teeth. His leg was a gob of red mush below the knee, the foot turned nearly backwards. On first sight, my stomach rolled over. Bile seeped up to the back of my tongue. I didn't know what all I could do about this with a roll of tape. Blood cooled in a puddle around him, stinking like burned metal. I did my best to stop him from bleeding anymore. Duct tape doesn't work well with wet surfaces. It kept sliding away. Finally, I pulled out the belt from his dressing gown and tied off his leg above the knee. His boy business flopped about as I tried and tried to twist the tape around his ruined calf. I put as much pressure on the wound as I could. Bright yellow fat oozed out. Finally, I got the idea to tie the tape in a knot around his leg and then wrap it. When I yanked the tape tight, he moaned until his face went slack. Then he fell against the wall with a heavy thud. I would of thought him dead but for the vein twitching on his forehead. This was a small mercy for both of us.

In the living room, my mom said she was a nurse and asked if she could tend to Mr. Cannon. Nothing happened, so I guess the answer was no. Logan snored. His right hand flexed and relaxed. The butter knife lay a few feet away. I snatched it up and tucked it into the other side of my waistband from the phone.

"You about done with fatty?" The man appeared at the doorway to the living room half a beat after I smoothed my T-shirt down over the knife. The rifle rested in the crook of his elbow. His eyes moved about the hall. When they found my face, I wanted to run. They were bright and blank and terrible. He shook a fistful of shoelaces at me. "Time to move this show outside. Smells like shit in here."

I didn't notice the smell until he said it. Then I couldn't smell anything else. At first I thought it might be coming from me, but no, Mr. Cannon had shit himself. Maybe when he passed out. His one remaining sock was smeared in it. The other foot had stayed bare and pink and clean.

"Come on, then. I got a chore for you."

"Are you Butthole Gibbs?" The words came out at the same moment I shaped the thought.

Instead of shooting me, he laughed a new laugh. It sounded like someone balling up newspaper.

"Yeah." He smiled. His left dogtooth was a bluish color. "But how about you call me Leon?"

Shoelaces and Duct Tape

Butthole "Call me Leon" Gibbs watched as Hayes and my mom dragged Logan through the kitchen by his feet. I held up his head, so it wouldn't thump against the doorjamb. Blood clotted in his hair. Outside in the dark, it looked black against the white of his neck. When we set him by the clothesline, my hands were speckled with dry shards of it.

First, Butthole told my mom and me to prop Logan up and tie his hands behind the metal pole that made up one end of the clothesline. Then he dragged me by the sleeve to the other end and showed me how he wanted the last three shoelaces looped around Hayes's and my mom's hands and feet. Butthole had them sit down face-to-face, so the pole sprouted up between the outstretched Vs of their legs. One shoelace for each pair of their feet, and the last one for their hands. He made certain I didn't leave any slack and yanked the one around their hands so hard my mom cried out. Then he had me wrap their wrists together with duct tape.

"This way, you two can always see how the other one's feeling," he told them.

What about me? I wondered, but had sense enough not to say. Still, he somehow saw the question in my face.

"I ain't got nothing special in mind for you, but don't worry, darling, I happen to know there's something been planned." He pulled over a rusty porch chair and sat down. "There's nothing left to do but wait." He pointed to a spot midway between Logan and my mom. "Stay there."

I crouched in the damp grass and stared at his clothes. He wore a navy-blue blazer and gray slacks and a shiny pair of black penny loafers—a bright orange Lincoln head stuck into each one. Butthole reached inside his bulging side pocket and pulled out what looked like a purple plastic cordless phone with a smiling girl's face on the back. A child's walkie-talkie. He grimaced before putting it up to his good ear and telling it, "I got them all trussed up and ready for you, chief."

A static-warped voice shouted, "Roger. We're on our way."

I hugged my knees against my chest and thought about whether I could run fast enough to get around the side of the carport before he fired his gun. He caught me looking at the end of the house.

"No," he said.

Five minutes later, Logan's head moved. I glanced over at Butthole, but he only had eyes for his walkie-talkie, which he whittled at with a clasp knife. God knew what he'd do to Logan once he came to. But, Logan, being nothing if not determined to get his ass in trouble, opened his eyes. One, then the other. A few experimental blinks. When he saw me, he smiled sweetly. What could I do but send him one back?

"The man his self. Awake at last," Butthole said, sounding downright happy to see it. Not mad at all. "You pack a hell of a wallop with a plastic bat. I'll tell you what, I'm going to be feeling that one tomorrow."

"You speak English?" Logan asked, his face the very picture of perplexed.

Oh, no, I thought, not this shit again.

"High school teachers might tell you different," Butthole said, amused. No matter how many times I heard it, I could not get used to that high, wandering voice of his.

"Well," Logan said, chewing this development over, "I guess you'd have to. Pretty good at it too. If I didn't know any better, I'd think you were from Bulloch County. How'd you get all the way here from Iraq?"

"What kind of dumb shit are you?" Hayes chimed in.

"Oh, Mr. Hayes." Butthole made *tsk-tsk* noises and rubbed one forefinger against the other. "It's good to know some things don't change much. You are still the same retard I remember."

Hayes opened his mouth to say something to this, but my mom hushed him and yanked on his wrist by leaning back.

"At least your woman here knows when to shut up." Butthole turned his attention back to Logan. "You, sir, are a genuine sur- prise." He drew the vowels out in the word genuine. "A kink in the plan. A fly in the ointment. Nobody said nothing about a soldier. Fact is, you nearly got the drop on me. I know, I know, big of me to admit it, but it's God's own truth. I came to the door expecting a girl, a nurse, and one certified pudding head. What I got instead is you. Fatty in there will limp to his grave because of that balls up."

Logan's face crumpled into a look of deeper confusion.

"Wondering how I figured you, huh?"

"I thought you were here gunning for me." Logan scooched himself backwards and up, so his spine ran straight along the clothesline pole.

"No doubt you pissed somebody off before I made the scene. But looks like I'm the one you'll have to deal with. Landed yourself in something of a jackpot here, friend."

"A soldier?" Hayes said. No one bothered to answer this.

My mom gave me one of her patented mom looks. *Now I unders- tand*, it said, *and I don't like it one bit. We'll be talking about this later.* And I sent a look back that said, *In the middle of this shit storm, you're worried about something like this?*

"Look, I just got to ask, 'cause you don't look like the type that

usually teams up with dumbass over here." Butthole folded his
knife shut, stuffed it in the front pocket of his pants, and stood,
pinching the pleats to keep them sharp. "What in the hell are you
doing mixed up in all this?"

"Is this a trick question?" Logan asked. The gash on the back of
his head reopened. A small trickle of blood ran down his neck and
into the sparse hair on his chest.

"Might well be a trick answer." Butthole walked over and
inspected him, nudging his leg with a shiny shoe.

Back in the house, Mr. Cannon let out a long, low groan. Then
the yard went silent but for regular summer sounds. The box on
the telephone pole beside the house gave off a high-pitched hum.
Tree frogs barked. A breeze up at treetop level rattled the dry pine
needles like stick pins in a jar.

"So?" Butthole rocked back and forth on his spiffy loafers.

"Name, Logan Loy. Rank, specialist. No, well, by now they've
probably busted me down to, never mind. Serial number . . ." He
shook his head. Droplets of blood flew. Butthole avoided them
with a quick step back. Logan mumbled out a list of numbers.

"Son, do you even know where you are? I must of rung your
bell pretty good." Butthole dropped down into a squat. He poked
at something on Logan's chest with the walkie-talkie's antenna.
"Mmm, shrapnel, huh?" His voice strangely sympathetic now.
"Got a couple of them myself."

"He don't have nothing to do with Hayes and his stupid trouble.
He's just my friend," I said. My own voice was small and meaning-
less out there in the big, sticky dark.

Mom twisted her body so she could look over at me again, wondering about something. Her face was a jumble of hard lines and
wrinkles in the porch light.

"That right, jellybean? Just a gentleman caller calling on the
worst night in the world?" Butthole measured me again with a

quick up-and-down of his eyes. For what, I didn't know, but worried about it and wanted to fight it. He let out a large and dramatic sigh. "Up to me, I'd cut him loose, but I ain't the boss of me in this . . ." He paused to smile toward the sky. ". . . this here endeavor. Only a paid employee." He laughed at the idea, and this seemed to make those last few words into a lie. Somehow this reassured me. Not much, but some.

Logan grumbled at him. All I heard was the words "ass kicking."

"I'd like nothing better than to see if you could manage it. Don't mind the occasional challenge. But it ain't to be, friend. I'm on the clock tonight."

Butthole went back to the porch chair and sat. He took off his jacket to fuss with the tear that Logan's weapon had made in the shoulder. I thought about the butter knife digging into my hip and what I might do with it and when. I wasn't tied up yet, and that was something at least. Moths flew back and forth above the kitchen door, casting monster shadows on the patio. A mosquito nibbled at my ankle until I smashed it into goo. The time between the flashes of lightning and the rumbles of thunder got smaller and smaller. From eight seconds to seven, and then from seven to six. The first I heard of what would happen next was the barking of dogs.

Those Dogs Looked Like
They Were Fixing to Eat Us

The purple walkie-talkie chirped once and then a familiar voice said, "The dogs are approaching the kennel. I repeat, the dogs are approaching the kennel."

A second voice broke in, somewhat softer but definitely irritated, and said, "Stop fucking around with that and give it here, you—"

Dogs barked in the background. And then continued to bark somewhere on the other side of the house. A big car, maybe two, pulled up on the street. A door slammed. Another two doors followed, almost on top of each other. The dogs went crazy, howling now like crazed women.

Butthole grinned. "Ready for the greatest show on earth?"

"Jesus fuck," Hayes said.

"That's right," Butthole said, "Jesus fuck."

"I knew there were more, Lynn. I told you." Logan nodded his head, pleased about this for reasons only known to him.

I tried to hush him with my eyes.

Metal rattled and clunked on the other side of the house. The sounds the dogs made changed, their voices quieter but more intense. Butthole stood up and turned toward the carport. I knew I had to move. My mom craned her neck to watch me. Three steps, two seconds. I slipped the knife out of my waistband and put it into Logan's hands while I hugged him. For whatever reason, Butthole hadn't made his bindings as tight as the others. His hands had a little play.

"You know what to do," I whispered against his neck, having absolutely no idea myself.

"I won't let them," Logan said. His eyes shined. He smiled.

I kissed him on the mouth.

"Hey, now," Butthole shouted, all the jolly out of his voice, "none of that shit."

"I just wanted—"

"Sit your ass down. Don't make me—"

"Leon," someone yelled, all hale and man-friendly, "I knew you'd wrap this shit up. 'Bout fucking time, too." It was that bastard Marty. But I'd known all along he'd come, even if I hadn't thought it outright.

"Yup," Butthole said.

Marty came striding around the corner of the house and looked for a moment as though he might wrap Butthole in a bear hug and then thought better of it. Instead, he brought his hands together in a porkchop clap to give him an excuse for the silly gesture. The man looked even bigger than I remembered. Fat, yes, fat as hell, but with a broad back and big arm muscles underneath all that padding. A few steps behind him, four or five dogs strained against leashes. With all their jumping and yipping, I couldn't keep them straight. They pulled my old friend Travis so hard he slipped and nearly wiped out coming around the corner. Burns trailed behind, hands stuffed in the pockets of his bomber jacket. A drop of rain hit my arm, but none followed.

"Hey, Leon." Burns waved a hand, wearing a grin so wide and tight it nearly split his lips at the corners.

"If you ever call me that again, I'll cut your dick off and make you eat it," Butthole said.

Travis laughed.

"You neither." Butthole pointed his purple walkie-talkie at him. In his hand, it looked like something vicious.

"Don't worry about them, but—" Marty frowned and pointed at Logan. "Who the fuck is that one?"

"Come here, chief." Butthole led him around the corner into the shadow of the carport.

"I'm glad we ate," Travis said, speaking over his shoulder at Burns. "This looks to be a long one." The dogs yanked so hard he slid a couple of feet in the damp grass. Those dogs looked like they were fixing to eat us.

"Nah," Burns said, sitting on the porch chair so hard it screeched and shed flakes of rust, "he'll fold up faster than that little girl. We'll be out of here in under an hour. Tops. Look at him over there. He's crying."

"Fuck you," Hayes said, but it sounded more like a question than a curse. And the man was right about the tears.

Burns jerked forward in the chair with his arms spread boogey-man-style, playing like he was coming to get him. Hayes flinched away so hard my mom let out a little gasp of pain. She muttered something to him. Hayes hung his head and stared at their feet.

"See what I mean?" Burns said.

"Hey, Hayes. H.K. got drunk and accidentally ate your finger." Travis giggled.

"Shut up," Burns told him. "That's stupid."

"Well, he almost did. That's what Benny said."

Burns shook his head.

"New plan," Marty shouted, rubbing his palms together as he marched around the corner. "Come over here. Leon'll fill you in."

"He's the one, ain't he? That fat one. The one who came over the other day," Logan said, voice raspy and tense.

"Yeah," I said, trying not to move my lips because Marty stared at me as he came across the yard.

"Alright, then." Logan nodded his head. "Alright."

"You!" Marty bellowed, pointing a finger in my direction. "With me. We got some things to discuss."

"Leave her the fuck alone!" Logan yelled, spittle flying with the words.

Marty paid no mind. He stooped over and pulled me to my feet by the crook of my elbow. Halfway to the kitchen door, my mom made a noise and he stopped to look at her.

When the time comes, I've got to move, I told myself. No matter what.

"Please," my mom said, her voice ragged and pitiful, "let her go. She ain't got nothing to do with this."

"That depends on you, ma'am. I don't get any pleasure out of hurting little girls," Marty said.

"Bullshit," Logan said.

Marty glared at him for a long moment. Then he dragged me into the house. All the time I worried about what he meant to do with those dogs. The dogs themselves seemed to know. Their joyful, angry barks told me they were ready to go and happy to do it. *What's the holdup?* they barked to Travis, who had a hell of a time holding onto them. *We're ready to eat these people now!*

As Marty closed the kitchen door, I heard my mom ask a question and Logan answer.

You All Got Anything Cold to Drink?

ear slapped my senses, like Logan's makeshift strop against
the butter knife, putting a pretty keen edge on them. I could
count each and every pore in Marty's big, vein-busted nose. I
smelled the barbeque he'd had for dinner. I heard the coins jingle
in his pocket as those belly laughs shook his pants. The smile he
showed me was so big with horrible delight that every tooth and
hole showed. Marty was missing two of his bottom teeth. It made
his smile a true troll's grin.

A long smear of blood ran down the hall to the front door. Mr.
Cannon was gone. Poor man, all he did was answer his door. I
pointed to the hallway and started to ask him about it.

"Don't worry. Your neighbor's getting the proper medical
treatment he needs. If you act nicey-nice," he told me in sing-song
baby talk, poking me in the belly with the antenna of his monkey-
shaped walkie-talkie, "I won't have to give you any boo-boos.
Okeydoke, artichoke?"

I nodded, still thinking on when and how I could make my break
for it.

Marty must of been thinking along some of the same lines but
reversed because he waggled a finger at me. "Don't be hatching up
something stupid and maybe painful. Let's us sit down and chew a
little fat. You all got anything cold to drink? A tall glass of strawberry
Kool-Aid would be about perfect right now. This heat is something
terrible. But I don't expect you all have any of that, huh?"

I stood in the doorway to the living room and looked at him, arms folded across my chest. I wished I had some shorts on. I'd taken them off when I heard it was only Hayes at the door earlier that night. Without any AC, the house felt hot as a stove element and sucked empty of air. But right then I wouldn't of minded cords and a winter coat. I felt next to naked in panties and a T-shirt, even with the shirt coming down to the tops of my knees. Goosebumps pimpled up my legs and arms.

Marty patted his dark-blue sports coat in a few places. It was almost exactly like the one Butthole wore, but whereas his looked tailor-made, Marty's jacket fit him like something picked out of the trash. Too tight across the shoulders and too long in the sleeves. It took him quite a few seconds of hunting before he found a crumpled pack of strawberry Swisher Sweets hiding in an inside pocket. He pulled one out of its cellophane and gave it a long, satisfied sniff, running the little cigar across the flabby groove between his nose and upper lip. The fake strawberry flavor came clear across the room and it reminded me of bubble gum and puke. He stuck out his yellow tongue and licked the little cigar from one end to the other. Then he bit down on the plastic nib and wiggled it at me, trying, I guess, to be comical, but I wasn't in much of a comical mood.

"I weren't kidding about the cold drink," he said. "What you got?"

I opened the fridge and poked about, wondering if I could knock him out with a bottle of ketchup.

"Milk, Diet Dr Pepper, Clamato, and Wanker," I told him, not turning around.

"What the hell is Wanker?" He sounded offended.

"Some kind of beer."

"I'll take the Clamato, if it's cold."

I went to the cabinet and poured him a short juice glass full. He sniffed it three times before taking a sip and then let out a long, exaggerated sigh. He was chock-full of funny gags, this one. God, how I hated him.

"I expect you must be wondering the reason I dragged you into the house, huh? Very mysterious. Spooky even, huh? What you think, little miss?"

I answered him with a sour look and hoped the Clamato had gone bad and would poison him.

"Remember our chat a while back about your good buddy, Hayes?"

"Hayes ain't no friend of mine."

He took another sip. "To tell the truth, I don't much care for him myself. We know him and your old ma are holding out on us. Got a little stash hid somewhere on the homestead here."

"That ain't true."

"You know how I know? A dirty little birdie told me the two of them had business ideas of their own. A woman who knows your mama."

"Who told you that trash?"

"One of them nurses over at the hospital, name of Carla, is a cousin of mine. A second cousin, maybe. I forget. Said your ex-friend Hayes thought to cut me out of the deal and sell the shit on his own. Him and your ma both, that is."

"My mom doesn't have anything to do with Hayes's stupid plans. That's all on him. There ain't any pills here. I heard Hayes begging my mom to help him get some more and she said no."

"Mmm-hmm," Marty said and knocked back the rest of his Clamato in a single gulp. "That might could be. But we got to make sure. You understand, don't you? It's just good business practice. You hear them dogs?" He swung out his arm and shook the empty glass toward the back door. A large red drop of Clamato landed on the linoleum at my feet. "Sound angry, don't they? They ain't been fed for a day or two. Makes them jumpy and pissed off.

And from the sound of it, my associate Mr. Gibbs is getting to the nub of the matter right this minute."

"You mean Butthole." It just slipped out.

"You and the bad man swap stories and jokes and the like, did you?" He frowned at me and cocked his head to one side. "That's strange. A young girl like you, I'd of thought it'd show on your face. Bruises and shit. He ain't known for being gentle. The sad fact of the matter is the man just don't know how to talk with women. Or girls. The fairer sex baffles him. I think it's got something to do with all the time he spent in the infantry and then that stint in the state pen."

I hugged myself and backed away, not realizing I was doing it until I came up against the counter with a painful thump.

"Well, you've met the man, so I know you don't want to have to spend any alone time with him." He gave me a curious look. "Do you?"

My lips had amnesia. I shook my head no, believing what he said about Butthole to be true. The microwave pizza I'd gobbled down a few hours ago gave me a few sharp elbow jabs to the gut. I tried to swallow.

"See, here's where you come in. If Leon—" He smiled his snaggle-toothed grin. "I mean, if Butthole can't get the truth out of those two using his usual encouragement methods, we got you as our ace card. You, little miss, are plan B. If it makes you feel any better, his usual methods usually work."

I turned then and puked in the sink.

"Truth to tell," he said, "it don't set well with me neither. That look his face gets when he's messing about with young girls? Terrible. Nobody knows what it is he's got against you ladies. It amounts to a kind of crazy with him." He frowned down at his smoking cigar before ashing into the sticky, red juice glass even though there was an ashtray beside his elbow.

Out back, the dogs barked louder. The thunderstorm blew closer and closer to the house, bringing with it jagged forks of electricity and big house-shaking booms. I watched lightning carve
the sky into slices through the window above the sink. It looked
like the end of times. I put my head under the faucet and splashed
my cheeks with water, all the while tripping over a tangle of busy
nowhere thoughts. What to do? What to do? I turned around and
gave him a level look.

"Can I have one of those candy cigarettes?" I asked him.

"These ain't candy, little girl." A flash of anger crinkled up his
eyes. "Might be they'll set you to puking again."

"Nah," I told him, "I smoke them all the time. Since I was a
little girl."

Marty reached into his jacket pocket and dug up the half-
crushed box of Swisher Sweets. I stepped across the room to pluck
one from the pack. As I reached for it, he took my chin between
his thumb and first finger and turned my face toward the twitching
overhead light. I tried to pull away, but he took a hold of my arm
and yanked me closer. This pissed me off to no end and the bright
flare of my anger made my cheeks feel more than a few degrees
closer to real lightning. Then Marty turned my face the other way
and studied it even closer, like a man speculating on the ripeness
of a peach.

"Could be I know you from somewhere? It struck me when we
talked before. I know your mama's name is Darla. What's your
family name again?"

When I didn't answer, Marty slapped his lighter onto the table
with a loud crack. A Zippo engraved on one side with a dog's head
above two crossed bones. It made me jump, but I reached for it all
the same. He grabbed my hand as soon as I touched the lighter and
gave it a squeeze. The lighter pressed hard against the underside
of my knuckles. It hurt. I pulled myself loose and flicked the wick

into flame, sucking hard on the sweet little cigar to get it lit. I don't care what he said. It tasted like candy to me.

"What's he doing out there to my mom?" I pointed to the kitchen door, walking across the room as I did.

"Don't worry. The man likes a psychological approach. It's Hayes who'll be hurting right now. If I know Butthole, that boy will be trying to throw the fear of God into your mama. He'll figure she won't be able to watch Hayes getting punished for very long before she gives up the goods. It's the psychological approach that often gets the best results. And he takes his time." Marty glanced down at the chunky gold watch on his wrist. "Anyway, it ain't been long enough for him to of moved on to your mama yet."

We both looked at the window. I realized I hadn't heard the dogs barking for a while. I wasn't sure how long. Someone shouted, but I couldn't tell who or what they said. My tongue tasted like a hunk of bitter meat too big to swallow. Guilt made my chest feel hollow. I didn't believe Marty. I wanted to believe my mom was okay, boy did I ever, but I didn't. He'd tell me whatever he thought would keep me from rushing out the back door. I walked to the sink and leaned across it on my tiptoes to get a better view out the window.

"Hey," Marty said, actually getting to his feet now, "get away from there. You don't want to be watching all that."

Him saying this only clinched things that much more.

Lightning flashed. Travis held my mom back. Someone else stood aside with the dogs. Hayes slumped over with his head against the ground. Storm light is shaky, and I only got the briefest glimpse, but this much was clear as day: something bad had happened to Hayes. I wasn't sure how I felt about it. It was him, after all, who'd gotten us into this mess. Still, it didn't mean I wished something horrible on him. Thunder rumbled.

"What are they doing to Hayes?"

Marty grabbed me by the elbow. "Sit your ass down."

I didn't fight him when he led me back to the table and pushed me into a chair.

As Marty opened his mouth to tell me something else, some new line of bullshit, lightning struck again. The house seemed to slip off its foundation. The juice glass rolled off the table and smashed. This time there wasn't any gap between the flash and the boom. I'm almost certain it hit the house. Or somewhere close enough not to make a difference. The lights flickered twice and went out. The fridge's motor rattled and died. This sudden dark gave me a burst of foolish courage and I used it while I had it—these things being uncertain when it comes to length. I pushed away from the table so hard my chair clattered over backwards. I only got the chance to take three steps. The legs of the chair hit my shins. I went down in a painful heap of barked bones and bruised elbows. Marty gifted me with a Santa Claus smile and then produced the ugliest-sounding fart I've ever heard. I pulled a face. This tickled the hell out of him and he let go with a hacking laugh. If I could of, I would of killed him right then. I swear it.

All this happened in a handful of seconds. The lights flickered a few more times and came on, at least some of them, and they brought with them a rude lesson about power. Marty had some. I had none.

Marty went through his whole jacket-patting routine again, but this time he pulled out a little pistol, which looked like a dollar-store stocking stuffer in his meaty, overstuffed paw. Four plump ballpark franks and a nectarine for a thumb. The way he waved it about explained he wanted me to go back to my seat, so I picked the chair up and sat. My cigar still burned in the ashtray.

"You smell something?" Marty lifted his chin and gave the air a few delicate sniffs. From the way he spoke, simply curious and happy tempered, you'd of thought us two had been chatting away, as smiley as a couple of cherrystone clams, all the livelong night.

"Smell what?" At first I thought he was making funny over his obnoxious mule fart. I couldn't get that lightning snapshot of my mom in the backyard out of my head. When would Butthole get tired of waiting for her to feel sorry for Hayes and start . . . what?

"Smells like burning plastic." He pointed with his chin to the living room.

A very thin layer of smoke drifted along the ceiling in the living room. If not for the smell, it could of been from the cigars. Acrid and oily, it reminded me more of an overheated car engine than cheap tobacco. Mom's car blew a gasket earlier in the summer and this was what it smelled like.

"Are they trying to burn our house down?" I asked him, serious.

"Nah," he said, making one of his I'm-the-boss-around-here faces, "not with me in it." He paused and frowned toward the back door. "They best not be, anyway."

"Smells like it."

Marty chewed on the plastic nib of his cigar. "Not before we get them pills, they ain't. That I guarantee."

I didn't much care for his guarantees.

A hand rapped on the window. Two fast knocks and then two slow ones. Marty shook his head and gave me a gloomy look.

"That ain't good news for you," he said. "You and me, we got to go outside. Seems Hayes and your mama need more convincing. Sorry, missy, I really hate to have it come to this. You could end all the bullshit right this second, you tell me where they got them pills stashed."

We stared at each other.

"No? Well, then for your sake, I hope Mama loves you more than that worthless piece . . ." Marty trailed off, looking not at me but at the window. Someone outside had shouted.

The monkey-faced walkie-talkie on the table shrieked. "We got trouble, man." The rest came out in squawks and gobbles. A male voice, but otherwise unidentifiable.

"Goddamnit." Marty pushed himself back up. All this sitting and standing was probably more exercise than he got in a week. He wheezed a little and his face turned the color of an unripe plum. The table shook with him. For half a second, less even, the tiniest of expressions crossed his face. An uncertain squint crossed with a frown. Was he afraid of something?

The back door swung open and Burns burst in. He panted, spittle flying on the exhales. You'd think he'd sprinted for a mile and not just loped across the yard.

"Sorry, sorry, sorry." Burns cringed like the man might shoot him. "Even Butthole don't know how he did it."

"What?" Marty shouted. "Done what?"

I reached back to check that the cell phone was still tucked tight against my hip inside the elastic of my panties. It was pure luck it hadn't fallen when I had.

"The soldier. He slipped loose. Cut Butthole a good one on the forehead."

I laughed, but neither seemed to notice. Marty pushed him to one side, hard enough to slam both Burns and the door against the wall, and moved onto the top step of the back porch.

"One second he's tied up and the next he's spinning around with something sharp," Burns told Marty's big, old walrus back.

"Where's Butthole?" Marty yelled out the door.

"Took off after him," Burns said. "He said—"

"Butthole!" Marty bawled into the monkey.

"That slick fuck," the monkey said after a moment of static, "slipped off just like a rat snake."

"Get him, Goddamnit! I don't give a fuck how," Marty said, pressing the monkey into his cheek hard enough to leave a mark. Then he turned to Burns. "Get your ass back out there. We need to end this shit now."

Burns didn't need to be told twice.

Marty glanced over his shoulder at me, his face half dark from the doorway's shadow. All the angry gone now, vanished in the time it takes to blow your nose. "This kind of thing just happens sometimes, honey. All there is to do is grit your teeth and get through it. I won't let them go too far, but I can't promise it won't sting. You know, the way the doctor always does?" He managed to give me a sickroom smile. "And hell, ain't the doctor always lying anyway? Come on, missy, guess I'll have to bring you out here for Butthole . . ." Marty scratched his neck and turned his head away.

I'll give the man this: he didn't seem all that happy about his chore. His mouth sagged and his eyes looked dull.

"Okay," I said, quiet and docile, but the thoughts in my brain were anything but. My head was in mad-scramble mode. I took one last drag off the sweet cigar, making the cherry burn bright.

"That's the way. I like you, missy. You're a tough little pecan. Maybe it ain't clear now, but we got more than a few things in common."

I wanted to scream. Instead, I blew two lungs full of strawberry puke smoke at him.

He reached over to take my arm. "You got sand aplenty and that's saying—"

As Marty bent toward me, I smiled hard and pushed the hot end of the cigar into his left eye. It sounded like bacon dropping into a hot pan—a mean sizzle and a sharp pop. The smell I can't describe, nor do I much care to. He let out a yowl of pain so loud it near about burst a tunnel through my head from ear to ear. I didn't wait for it to end before I screamed Logan's name with all the air left in my lungs. Marty didn't waste no time. He followed me right across the kitchen for some payback, swinging his arm behind his shoulder for a go at my head. But I saw his open hand coming and ducked away as best I could. Liked to of backflipped into the sink if I could of managed. Still, he connected. The kitchen turned half a dozen different hues of blue and yellow. The overhead light sparkled and shimmered like the sun seen from underwater. The next thing—I'm looking up at the bottom of the table with a sound like angry bees in my head. Swaying there under the table was my old cowboy Weeble, my favorite toy when I was a kid, bobbing back and forth and hissing for me to run. But it was all I could do right then just to suck myself some air.

What are you doing down there, Mr. Weeble? I thought. I left you on the dresser.

"You little bitch!" Marty shouted so loud it rumbled the linoleum. "You half about blinded me!"

It wouldn't be long before one of his thug boys came in here to see what the problem was. That'd finish the question and quick.

I rolled over on my side, scrabbling about for a way to get back on my feet. The world around me—kitchen, clock, and floor—moved incredibly slowly and, in a senseless way, very, very fast. I blinked hard, trying to clear a bit of the blur out of my eyes. That was when I caught a glimpse of another thing that made me think I'd had both the sense and air knocked out of me. A lamp looked to be floating across the living room. Marty stepped around the fallen chair and reared back his leg to give me a kick. The lamp sailed into the kitchen behind him. It was bright yellow and had a picture of a boat painted on it. I laughed. Scared as I was, I laughed. I hated that lamp and here it was coming to save me. Marty held off on that kick just long enough to frown at me. The lamp shattered on his head and he toppled over, knocking the chair across the room. The last thing I saw was his empty face heading toward mine.

The World in Ashtray Colors

"Lynn, Lynn Marie, Lynnie."

A warm hand patted me on the cheek. My eyes didn't want to work.

"Come on, Lynn Marie." The breath smelled like cigarettes and microwave pizza, but the voice I knew.

I squashed my eyelids shut with my thumbs and tried again. Above me, a blurry Logan Loy peered into my face, trying to tell me like a saucer of tea leaves. Something pricked my neck. I blinked and blinked again. His nose came clear. A smudge of something gray on his cheek. Some joker had painted the world in ashtray colors. Holly bushes pressed in on me from three sides.

"I pulled you out and hid you in the shrubs." Logan spoke through his teeth. "You fainted or something."

"Or something." My throat felt clogged with mud.

"What now?" he asked, tilting his head and smiling a normal smile, like we two were sitting on a park bench having a laugh in the sunshine. But a couple of feet below his face, I noticed the handle of the butter knife tucked into the waist of his jeans and it glittered when he moved.

A dog barked. Then two more answered. A man shouted. Somewhere in the other direction, a car engine revved and glass shattered. The smell of that oily smoke became very strong. Logan tensed and squinted through the bushes at something I couldn't see. All business now. I put a hand on his leg and felt the heat of his skin through the denim.

"I'm alright," I told him, feeling anything but, and tried to sit up.

"Stay down." He pressed the tips of his fingers against my chest. "They got that Asshole character looking for us. He ain't nobody to fool with."

Everything that could hurt did.

"Butthole," I said.

"Exactly," Logan said, nodding. "Stay here, I'm going to reconnoiter."

I blinked once more and he disappeared.

The Time
for Fucking Around Is Done

The sky tore open, letting loose raindrops as big as quarters. A slot-machine jackpot of a storm. My hiding spot smelled of pine sap and wet cement. Dead leaves stuck to my legs. I tried to sit again. My head swam. I explored my cheek with a careful finger. It felt puffy and deformed. And it hurt. It hurt like all get-out. It took a while to remember how I ended up lodged in the shrubbery, but not much longer than that to start worrying about what had happened since.

A gun fired twice. The shots muffled by the rain, impossible to tell which direction they came from.

I felt for my cell phone, but it was gone. If you'd looked in my mouth right then, you'd of seen my heart thumping away on my tongue. A whole different kind of scary took up residence in my chest and double-dared me to move. The time for fucking around was definitely done. We needed help. We needed the police.

I wished then I'd told the police earlier. The nice one. Officer Watkins. Mom might be in jail, but she'd still be around. Now I didn't know if I even still had a mom.

I took a deep breath, clenched my teeth and sat myself up. It felt like two bees stung the backs of my eyeballs. Bricks, a shutter, holly leaves, my blood-streaked legs, the dark-green clouds. They all came unglued to swirl together for a moment and then, after another breath, stayed put. Paisley shapes swam on the surface of my eyes. Next step, legs. I went to my knees and tried to stand. My

belly heaved up its last few drops of stomach juice. No, hands and
knees it would have to be. And it was a good thing too, because
half a minute later someone ran past the front door and around the
side of the house at a fairly good clip. Had they seen me standing
then, sitting duck would of been dead duck. I crawled to the front
steps and took a quick peek at the yard. Empty, except for a dark
curtain of rain, which seemed to seal the house off from the rest of
the world. The front door swung in the wet storm wind, thumping the wall of the hallway. Water dripped off my nose and chin. I
closed my eyes, counted to three, and then forced myself up onto
the stoop and rolled into the house.

Mr. Cannon's blood stuck to my palms, tacky as drying paste. I
scrambled to my feet as best I could, woozy, and slid along the wall
to the kitchen. Marty was gone. All he'd left were some bloody
smears and a pile of broken lamp. I'd forgotten all about him
falling on me until I saw the mess. Smoke drifted across the house,
through the kitchen and out the back door. Someone had left it
open as well and turned the kitchen light out, or broken it, but the
porch bulb burned bright enough for me to see two of the dogs
yanking at leashes tied to the clothesline pole where Logan had
been. The rest of the dogs were gone and so were the men. Hayes
leaned limp against the other pole. My mom rested her chin on his
head. Something was very wrong with him. Mom's head moved, as
though she was speaking, but I couldn't see her face. Over on the
far side of the house a gun went off three times. Couldn't they hear
the damn thing from the hospital? Thunder rumbled from one
side of the sky to the other.

I went to my knees and felt around for the phone. It had to be
someplace in the kitchen. I hadn't seen it behind the hollies or in
the hall. I found my cigar under the chair, still smoldering and
burning a brown rut in the linoleum. When I picked it up to take
a drag, a piece of the broken juice glass cut my thumb. A lot of

painful panic passed before I discovered the phone stuck between the fridge and the Tupperware drawer. Cowardly thing, hiding like that. I huddled under the table and dialed 911. An elderly black woman asked about my emergency.

"Some men broke into the house." Tears blurred my eyes. Telling about it made it true in a terrible new way.

"Yes, dear, and where are you? What's your name?"

"Lynn Marie Sugrue." I forgot my address for a moment, then mumbled it out. "They're going to hurt her. They got dogs. And they shot our neighbor in the leg. I don't know where he is. They hid him someplace. Please, hurry."

"We're coming, honey, you just hold on tight. Are you someplace safe?"

A figure slipped through the rain and knelt by my mom. When he turned and faced the house, I saw it was Logan. One of his eyes had swollen shut. A gash oozed blood on his back. I crawled to the doorway.

"Honey, you still there?" the kind lady asked.

"I got to go," I said.

"Wait—"

I hung up.

"—that's right," Logan told my mom. "That's all I ever wanted. You see now, don't you, ma'am? It wasn't like that at all."

"We'll take care of the rest later. Just don't let them hurt her," my mom said, her words slow and muddled, barely coherent over the wet clatter of the rain.

"No, ma'am," he said, straightening, "they'll have to deal with me first. Now you're loose."

Mom raised her arm. I think she told him she couldn't move.

"Logan," I said. "Mom."

They both looked over. Feet pounded around the side of the carport. Logan said something more to my mom and made a break for the pine trees in the back of the yard. A gun went off with a lick of flame and a muted slap. I backed into the house, wondering what the hell to do now, and came up against something hard where there shouldn't of been anything at all.

"There you are, jellybean," said that terrible, wrong voice. "I been looking all over creation for you."

Butthole took a handful of my shirt and yanked me up.

I screamed. I didn't have much left, but I put it all into that one sound before he clapped a hand over my mouth.

Shadow Puppet Show

"So now," Butthole said, taping my wrists to the kitchen chair with the same roll of tape I'd used on Mr. Cannon. He'd already done my mouth. "You had everybody worried and here you were all this time. I near lost my patience. Time you set things straight, so we can wrap this mess up. Don't you want to be finished with all this?" He took a handful of hair and nodded my head, putting on a high, whispery voice as a stand-in for my own. "Yes, Mr. Gibbs, I sure do."

The smoke in the house thickened and made it difficult to see more than a few yards. Something orange and unpleasant glowed from the direction of my mom's room. My eyes watered and every few minutes I coughed through my nose. With the tape over my mouth, it made my sinuses sting. Butthole turned the chair so I faced away from the back door. In the porch light, his shadow stretched over my head and out across the kitchen floor. He put his face down next to mine and pressed his melted ear stubs against my cheek.

"I'm going to tell you a story. Don't worry, it's a quickie. Keep your eyes on the wall over there." Butthole straightened up behind me and smoothed my hair with a hand.

Because of the tape, I couldn't do anything but look straight. The shadow of his head moved aside and, in its place, a shadow monster made of hand and wrist wriggled across the wall. A nasty sort of snake with giant fangs.

"The old gardener pulled out his red hanky and blew his nose." His laugh rattled like a handful of shook pebbles. "My mama always says that instead of 'Once upon a time.' In this story, there was a bad little girl, and this bad little girl knew a secret. A big secret." A mushy-headed figure with flapping arms and legs danced across the wall. A pretty sorry looking excuse for a girl. "This was a dangerous secret, a deadly secret, because more than anything else in the world, a monster wanted this secret for his own." The monster snake wriggled in from the other side, rearing up in front of the shadow girl. "The first time the monster asked the girl about this secret, he used his nicest voice. 'Please tell me where the magic beans are,' he said. But the girl was stubborn. She didn't want the magic beans, but being hardheaded, she didn't want nobody else to have them either. This made the monster irritable, but he tamped down his temper and asked again. This time in not so nice a voice. 'Where are the magic beans?'" Butthole thumped me on the back of the head with his bad-girl hand.

Something heavy and metallic clattered onto the floor, but I couldn't turn my head to see it. Both shadow puppets vanished for a moment.

"Mr. Asshole, you shouldn't of taped her up like that." It was Logan. From his voice, I could tell he must of been in the doorway to the living room. My lips tried to smile under the tape. All my numb brain could think up at that moment was: I'm sure glad he's not saying "hajji" anymore.

The snake and the girl reappeared. "The third time the monster asked about the beans"—Butthole made a growling sound—"the girl just shook her bad little head." The shadow girl swayed back and forth.

"Let's us see how well you do without your rifle, huh?" Logan stepped forward. The knee on one side of his jeans hung torn. Soot covered his chest. His left arm was red and blistered. "What you think?"

"When the girl told him no the third time, the monster said, 'Fuck the beans, I'm going to eat you.'" The shadow snake gulped her down.

Logan stepped in front of me and winked. "Don't worry, baby."

"Fuck the girl," Butthole said, "I'm going to eat you."

He jerked my chair aside and the kitchen floor rose up to punch me in the shoulder. Logan's bare feet moved past my head. The black loafers lashed out at him. Logan grunted and tripped over the back legs of my chair, falling and breaking one of them off. He picked it up and threw it. From the thud it made, I knew it'd hit something soft. I hoped to God it hurt.

Butthole yanked my hair. The chair slid backwards, and I screamed through my nose, a sorry sound like a kitten drowning in a sack. He shook my head back and forth. "No, I won't tell you where the beans are." This in his whispery girl voice.

"I knew you'd hide behind her like a REMF pussy," Logan said, edging out of my vision.

My head slapped the linoleum. Tears made a blurry mess of the kitchen cabinets and everything else. My head throbbed so bad I didn't know what to do with the pain. For a while, I saw nothing but heard a lot. The slap of bare feet. The gritty sound of leather sliding across the floor. Puffs of breath. The moist smack of skin hitting skin. Swallowed groans. The table fell on its side. A pepper shaker rolled over and bumped my nose, filling it with a sharp, dusty smell. The fighting noises moved away. Maybe into the living room. Something brittle smashed.

During all this, the smoke went from filling the kitchen with a haze to pushing out all the breathable air. I'd known before something had caught fire, but with everything else going on, I hadn't thought much of it. Now I felt the heat on my legs and listened to that heavy breathing sound a fire makes when it's getting big. It panted and roared. I couldn't get enough air through my nose.

In the other room, a giant crash, followed by a bunch of smaller ones. I imagined my mom's boat bottles falling one by one onto the coffee table and bursting into tiny shards. Each bottle meant a month of her life. I had to get out.

Using my free leg, I pushed against the linoleum. My sweaty foot slid at first, then caught traction. Blood rushed into my head and pounded in my ears. Each push cost me. I felt middle-aged by the time I made it past the fridge. My hair went white and I grew a thousand wrinkles by the time my face moved over the doorjamb. The cool metal felt as good as a glass of iced tea. For a time, it was enough just to hang my head out and suck in the cool, wet air through my nose. I was a hundred years old and dying. Raindrops smacked my cheek and ear. I wanted more than anything to open my mouth and catch them. I wondered, Am I dead?

I Forgave the Rest

"Flipper," a person croaked.

Something tapped my neck and fiddled with the back of my head. The duct tape came off with a crackle. Hair came with it. I wanted to shout but didn't.

"You're mama ain't doing so good." Hayes lifted the chair and pulled me out of the house. It took some doing on his part. My legs hit the last two steps.

"What?" I tried to say, all sandpaper and sawdust.

The tape on my wrists didn't want to come off. Hayes picked at it, swearing quietly. His sweat smelled sweet and putrid, like a morsel of hamburger left to rot in a sugar bowl. I could move my head now. My mom sat with her back against the clothesline pole, eyes closed, wet hair stuck to her cheeks. Please don't be dead. The second strip of tape came off with a bit of skin. All I could do was whimper.

The barking of the dogs got closer. The sound made Hayes's hands shake. Even in the rain I could tell he was crying. He muttered "fuck" over and over again. His face crumpled up on itself. I knew by looking at him all he wanted to do was run. But he stayed. For that, I forgave him the rest. All of it.

"I seen them both—Butthole and the Army guy!" Burns shouted. "They're going at it in the house!"

"We should get," Travis said, closer now.

"Fuck no," Marty said. "That little bitch stole my eye. I'm going to see her hurt."

My legs jittered and shook. Hayes's fingers skittered like crab legs across the tape. One of his ragged fingernails slipped and took a piece out of my arm. The dogs howled and screamed. Not being able to crane my neck far enough to see, I imagined them slavering at the smell of my blood, desperate for a taste of me.

"Hayes, get off that child. I'll shoot you in the head if you don't get out of my way." Marty fired a round to show him this. A dollop of mud and grass splattered the two of us. "Let them loose, Travis," he said. Then after a moment: "Sic her, Blitzen. Chew her fucking head off."

The first dog ran so hard it slid past us. Its nails clattered on the cement apron below the steps. Buried beneath all the barking and Marty's shouts to sic me and the openmouthed chewing sound of heavy rain, something keened like a fucked cat. A ghost whine. As the first dog jumped, Hayes covered me with his body. I thought maybe he made the sound, or even me. I wasn't sure at first if he meant to protect me or if he'd been shot like Marty threatened. A second dog worried at his shirt, tearing the wet cotton. Hayes shouted for it to leave us be. A third went at my neck. I pushed its face away with my free hand. It bit through the webbing between my finger and thumb. I screamed. And screamed. Rain fell in my open mouth. Logan still didn't come.

"Kill her, Donner! Goddamnit!" Marty shouted, hoarse now but louder than before.

All the dogs were on us. Hayes moaned and covered my face with his hands. I felt teeth tear my legs. My earring ripped through my earlobe. Hot breath in my face. More than anything I wanted to tear Marty's throat out. I didn't need a weapon. I'd use my teeth. Be my own dog. No more barking once the dogs really set to, only yips and growls. Hayes tried to hide my head in his chest.

"I can hear them coming, Flipper," Hayes mumbled into my hair. "Hold on—"

Two flat cracks and the dog biting my ankle collapsed. Then Hayes let out a long, gurgling breath.

"The hell with this," Travis said. "I ain't facing a murder rap."

"Get your ass back here!" Marty screamed.

That keening sound grew louder. It'd been floating in the rain above me all this time, but I couldn't hear it for what it was. Now I understood what Hayes meant. I felt a couple of lifetimes away from the girl who'd made the 911 call. I slapped one of the dogs in the neck. It only growled and looked for a new angle. I tried to curl up under poor Hayes. The dogs kept on. They didn't give a shit about police sirens. Teeth went into my shoulder, my arm. A hank of hair got torn off the back of my head.

A different gun went off. So loud I thought I might be hit and just not know it yet. Then another. This one farther away. My first thought was that Butthole had come back and he'd decided to end all this. The dog on my other leg quit biting. I couldn't hardly breathe for the weight of Hayes on my chest. I squinted past his head at the pouring rain. Blue lights flashed in the grass, orange lights throbbed in the trees. Another shot went off somewhere behind me. A dog screamed. That's exactly what it sounded like—a girl's horror-movie scream. I listened for Logan. Where was he? How long had it been? Glass shattered over near the house. A gruff voice demanded someone stop or he'd shoot. Shoe soles slapped the pavement. Another man yelled, "Get that fucker!" Wheels squealed. Followed by the crunch and screech of tearing metal.

I don't remember the exact moment the dogs stopped chewing on me. My right mind picked up and left me, and what went away didn't come back for a while. I lay perfectly still. I was afraid to lift my head and let the dog get at my face again. I'd seen a dog catch a squirrel once down in Forsyth Park in Savannah when I was little. And this was the picture in my head. That dog whipping me around in its mouth and snapping my neck like a squirrel's.

Someone touched me on the shoulder, asked if I was okay. I don't know what I said. I don't think I actually said anything. Just made a sound.

"You've got to get up, honey." It was a man's voice.

My other hand came free of the chair, and once loose it carried a new and evil sort of pain. The man rolled Hayes off my chest. When I saw rain splashing Hayes's open eyes, I knew, and something important tore itself loose from my chest and flew up into wet sky. The man with the gentle voice tried to pull me up by my armpits, but I kept my knees locked tight against my stomach, my eyes closed and my chin down. "This house is on fire." He truly did have a gentle voice and I wanted to believe he meant well, but still I was afraid. "We got to get you out of here, darling. It ain't safe."

And that's when I opened my eyes. It looked like the whole fucking world was on fire. Flames did pirouettes in the trees. Flames dripped down off the roof and spilled onto the grass. Fire chuckled and guffawed. Timbers popped and crackled. Glass cracked and crashed. Above it all, the clouds dropped gobs of hiss on everything. I looked around for Logan and my mom. I yelled for them.

"Come on, now," the man said. I recognized him as the policeman who came and spoke to a school assembly about drugs last fall. A squat man with a short, black mustache. He seemed mean and no-nonsense at the assembly, yelling at us to not get mixed up with drugs and showing us slides of a woman insane from LSD, but now his voice was soft and kind. A TV show father voice. Somehow he'd managed to escape out of some terrible nineties sitcom and here he was to help me.

"Come on, now," he said again. "Let's go."

The policeman took my hand and dragged me up. This time I let him. My legs felt numb and then they felt like what they really were: something that had gotten the shit bitten out of them. My arm screamed bloody murder, but only I could hear it. I made an *ahhh* sound, high-pitched, almost like a bird, and he apologized. My hands were bloody and my jaw felt cracked open and raw. When I stood up, it seemed as though I'd gotten my hearing back and I hadn't even known it was gone. Everything became so loud. The heat licked at my face. A jumbo jet could have crashed into the house and it wouldn't of looked any worse or sounded any louder. The fire hissed with the loudest static you've ever heard. A million TVs tuned to empty channels. How did the house go up so fast? I'd only really seen the smoke before. Now even the holly bushes were on fire. An explosion went off somewhere in the middle of the house. Loud enough to make my ears ring. Bits and chunks of the house came flying out. A piece hit me in the chest, but it just bounced off. What could hurt me now? I thought. Nothing can touch me now.

A man out front in the driveway yelled, "It's got to be the furnace—must of been an oil burner!"

I found my mom leaned up against a police car in the street. She was wrapped in a blanket. Blood covered her face and the collar of her shirt. Her uncovered elbow dripped black onto the pavement. Absently, she daubed red squiggles on the white hood of the car with her fingers. Rain turned it pink. Sirens whooped several times and stopped, as though somebody had decided they needed to raise an alarm. Bright light flashed across my mom's cheeks and neck—blue, then white, then blue. She stared at the house, her mouth open and blood smeared as if it'd been made with the slash of a steak knife. Her eyes looked black and empty. The policeman's hand on her arm was the only thing keeping her standing.

When she saw me, she made a shrill sound and tried to pull away from him. "There she is," she shouted. "Baby," she shouted.

"Did you hear me, ma'am? It's important you think about this clearly," another policeman said to her. "I asked you, is everyone out of the house?"

I didn't even think of it then, with the words being spoken a few feet away from me. Instead, I thought, Where is Butthole? Where are the dogs? And then the man asked her again and I suddenly understood what the words meant.

"No, no, no," I said. I ran over and grabbed him by the shirt with my less hurt hand.

The assembly policeman who'd been helping me said, "Whoa, now. You need to be looked at, little lady."

"In the house. Someone. A boy in the house," I said, the words tangling up in my throat.

"Where?" the policeman beside my mom said.

"In the living room maybe."

My mom squeezed me. "Baby," she said. "Oh, baby. Your face." She sounded like she was crying, but there was so much blood on her face I couldn't tell.

"My soldier. He's still in the house!" For a flash, I know I saw him in the living room window, flailing his arms, calling me, then he was gone. I tried to blink it away, but I saw him burning even with my eyes wide open. Arms and legs in flames, fire spurting from his hair, his whole body going up in smoke. Logan projected on the burning trees. Logan flaring across the bright orange sky. "Please. Please. He's going to burn up!"

"Hey!" the policeman shouted. "There's another one in there."

"No, there ain't," my mom said, shaking her head. "She's just shook up."

"Hey, wait," a second policeman said, turning me toward the police car's headlights and leaning down to look into my face. "Ain't you the one who went riding around with the missing soldier from Hunter? Is that the one you mean?"

"Yes, yes!" I said, shouting right into his ear. "He's still in there. I never saw him leave. Please—"

My mom pulled me away and pressed me up against her side. The second policeman, a younger man with blond hair and a bristly mustache, kept looking at me, unsatisfied about something. My last "please" was muffled by Mom's arm.

"There's no one in the house," my mom said finally. "She's had a bad time. She don't know what she's saying. Believe me."

"Why do you keep saying that?" I yelled at her. "You saw him."

I still wonder about that. What had she and Logan said to one another? What sort of deal had they made?

The policemen looked at her, then at me, and lastly at each other. The older one made a gesture with his head, a sort of twitch that the younger one seemed to read because he nodded and moved off toward the house. An ambulance pulled up across the street and two men jumped out. There was a noise like someone puking behind the cop car. A person in the backseat yelled and banged on a window. I couldn't make out who it was because the window was smeared and blurry. The dog truck had crashed into a telephone pole across the street and one of its doors hung open. A man's leg stuck out. The foot was missing its shoe. I wondered in an absent way when this had happened, who it was. At the end of the driveway, a dog lay in a pool of black blood. There was a trail of blood from the backyard where it had dragged itself.

One of the ambulance men wrapped a blanket around me and I fought loose. My arm throbbed and my shoulder ached and my head pounded, but I made a break for the house. Like I would of been able to do anything if I'd gotten there, but I wasn't thinking like that. I was just thinking, *Logan Loy, Logan Loy, Logan Loy.* A fireman grabbed me by the back of the shirt and swung me around and down into the wet grass.

The house burned. The fire was hungry and it ate the house. Another man tried to put me in the back of the ambulance and I bit him on the arm. His partner grabbed me from behind and the two of them dragged me away kicking and screaming for all I was worth. I wasn't worth much by then. The house burned down.

I yelled his name once more. I screamed it. But I couldn't make the words loud enough for them to hear what I meant. And then I was tied down on the stretcher and I couldn't move my arms or legs anymore. My mom whispered something in my ear, something soft and stupid.

"He's going to die," I told them and her and everyone else who could hear me. "If you don't do something, he's going to die. Then it will be your fault."

But I knew whose fault it really was. I knew and it scorched my brain as bad as any burning house. Try to keep just one thing as yours and only yours and the world burns down. You can't own anything. You can't own anything but your own faults. You can't own anybody but your own self, and sometimes even that isn't yours to keep.

And then the doors closed, and the ambulance pulled away from the curb, and then we were rushing somewhere very fast in the dark. I closed my eyes.

Ashes, Ashes, We All Fall Down

I got fifty-seven stitches, a cast on my arm, and a week's stay in hospital room 212.

Hayes died. Instantly, they said. Shot in the head in our backyard.

Marty died too. The newspaper said he had a heart attack and crashed his truck into a utility pole. No one was quite sure which came first, but it all amounted to the same thing. Him dead. I wondered if he'd get his eye back in hell.

Travis and Burns went to county lockup to await trial on manslaughter charges. No one listened to their "crazy" stories about what "really" happened. It was their word against my mom's, a respected local nurse. Finally, they made a plea agreement with the district attorney and went off to the supermax upstate. As far as I know, they're still there.

Carla the nurse, Marty's second cousin, tested positive for pot and lost her job at the hospital, screaming bloody murder all the way out the door. "Sour grapes," my mom said, and after saying it enough times with a reasonably straight face, she got the tag to stick.

Somehow, amazingly, my mom wasn't hurt all that much. She had a slight concussion, a few stitches on her arms, and a bruise or two. Whenever the anger rose up in my throat like bile before puke, I tried to remember her raising her hand when Logan cut her free, unable to move, him bending over to whisper something to her. What deal did they make?

Logan died. Burned up in the living room of our house with an ashtray still in his hand. They found the glob of melted glass. Many are the nights I dream of him fighting off the fire with nothing but a glass ashtray. I can see him right now if I close my eyes. Head like a torch. Skin bubbled and black. I don't care what anybody says. I killed him. I'll have that lodged beneath the skin of my heart forever. My guilt smells like burning plastic.

Butthole Gibbs vanished.

The story of what happened got bent so far backwards that it broke in half. Mom claims she never told any real lies, but she sure as hell didn't tell them the truth either. The truth was too messy. "Justice," she told me over and over, "was done. Ain't that enough?" Hayes got blamed for stealing the pills. The police found a copy of the hospital pharmacy key in his borrowed car. Mom let him take the blame. I still don't know the whole truth about her part in the stolen batch of pills, but I have my theories. Hayes wasn't smart enough to do much of it on his own—that I know to be true. The police told the story as a drug deal gone wrong. Hayes chose to meet the buyers at his *ex*-girlfriend's (Mom insisted on this, and a reluctant me backed her up) house. Mom claimed no knowledge of his arranging a drug deal that night, which was true only in the barest sense.

Poor Mr. Cannon burned up too, although the coroner said he'd bled to death long before. One of those assholes had dragged him back into his house and left him there to die.

When Logan's body was found, the police jumped to the conclusion he was part of the drug gang. He'd already gone AWOL and was known to be suffering from Post-Traumatic Stress Disorder. They always spelled it with capital letters like that in the paper. I tried more than once to tell them different, but no one listened to me. Everyone thought I'd cracked up under the strain of what happened, and my mom helped spread this idea. She knew this business about Logan wasn't true, but she kept her mouth shut. Whenever I tried to talk to her about it, she'd say one of two things: "The dead are beyond caring about their reputations" (I expect this applied to Hayes as well) or, "Don't kick a dead dog, Lynn, it might just be sleeping."

The last I saw of Logan Loy was a cardboard box. His father came to recover the cremated remains. A nurse told me he was in the building. I watched his father leave the hospital with the box. He came up out of the basement, where the morgue is located, and walked it out to his car. It wasn't much bigger than a medium-sized suitcase. The parking lot was right below my window on the second floor. A woman waited for him in the front seat. She looked far too young to be his wife. Logan's father looked nothing like him—a bald man with a thick circle of padding around his waist, hunched-over shoulders, and a slow trudge of a walk. He put the box in the backseat, and then he did an odd thing. The man walked away. Slowly. He stopped behind three pine trees and covered his face with his hands. I guess he didn't want the woman to see. I hoped that Logan Loy saw, wherever he was. His father cared enough to cover his face with his hands. I cried so hard I didn't see him leave. Once I'd wiped my eyes, the car had gone.

Dani came and visited every day. She brought a question on her face each time, but I never answered it. She knew something wasn't right. Logan, after all, had been partly her idea. But for once, she let it lie. At school, she told me, I was a celebrity. Dani brought back news releases from the hospital to my adoring fans. I remained famous for about a week after I returned to school. My stitches made me a high school superstar. Wayne Keegan signed my cast. But after that week was over, most people forgot. Or moved on. There was a big bonfire pep rally and we beat Statesboro High 7–0 in football. A very big deal in our town. This was the first team to do it in a decade. The news was enough to crowd out what had happened at our house that night. That's the kind of town it was. But believe me, I wasn't sorry to see it go. Dani kept a little distance after I got out of the hospital. And even more after my celebrity ended.

The strangest news she brought was about the Angry Eyeball. Two nights after my house burned down, her father heard something outside and found poor, pimply Wynn hunched over by the window to Dani's room with his pants around his ankles. Mr. Dunham dropped his shotgun, pulled off his belt and beat the living crap out of Wynn. His parents tried to sue Dani's parents, but Dani brought out the e-mails and Wynn admitted everything. He said he'd tried his best to be her friend and all she gave him back was cruelty and spite. Dani smiled when she told me this. Wynn's family settled it with the Dunhams out of court. Wynn wasn't allowed to be within a hundred yards of Dani, which must of been hard, considering the fact they were neighbors, and the following week he transferred to Christian Day School in Garden City. Dani never told her parents the whole story about The Game, which was probably just as well. In the end, there were really only three people playing, and if it hadn't of been for Wynn's sloppy peeping skills, he would of won The Game hands down. He had Dani running scared. Dani stopped playing The Game while I was in the hospital, and the day I was discharged, she calmly informed me The Game was officially over. She wasn't playing anymore. When I asked her if her quitting had to do with the Angry Eyeball e-mails and this whole sorry business with Wynn, she said, "No, it was getting old anyway." And so the night my house burned down, The Game died too. Dani and me stayed friends, but only just. I stopped spending the night at her house. And then later, she teamed up with a new girl from Macon named Sally Fraser.

I didn't have a house to come home to. Just a pile of ash. I can't say I missed it all that much, but it was my home. The only thing I ever heard my mom complain about was the loss of her bottled boat collection. While I was in the hospital, she moved in with Dr. Drose. So that's where I went when they gave me my discharge papers and set me loose. It wasn't so bad. I had my own room with my own TV and cable connection and my own bathroom. Dr. Drose never raised his voice. Or his hand. But I sometimes caught him giving me odd what-the-hell looks. That's about as much as I could ask from any of my mom's men. It lasted through Christmas and then we found a place in Savannah. Mom got a job at St. Joseph's Hospital. I got a new school. None of this touched me. Nothing much would for a long time after.

One thing kept me up at night. Or I should say, one thing made me keep a steak knife beneath my pillow, gasp at shadows, and jerk awake at tiny sounds. Butthole Gibbs disappeared. No one made mention of him. Not the police, not the papers, not Travis or Burns. He just disappeared. I never once even saw his face after I dragged myself out of the house. He was just a voice whispering about magic beans. A shadow-puppet monster. And when I walked down the street or through the mall or across the azalea-choked Savannah squares, he was every tall man I saw. I stopped asking my mom all those other questions. Down in the dark-red, mushy part of my heart, I knew the answer to all but one. I made sure to ask my mom at least once a week.

"What," I would ask her, "about Butthole?"

She never had a good enough answer to suit me.

Four and a half months had passed since Logan died. I thought maybe I'd put some of this terrible shit behind me. A new house, a new school, a new town. I began to think maybe, just maybe, a fresh start was possible. And then I went to the doctor. After the fire, Dr. Drose told me it was a perfectly natural response to serious trauma. I shouldn't worry about it. My mom told me to enjoy it while it lasted. My new doctor, Dr. Patel, told me something different.

"You're pregnant," she said.

Hide and Seek

t was October and I was five years old. I woke up with this idea. It was like an egg I dreamed in my sleep. Perfect and whole and waiting for me when I opened my eyes. I would hide today. I knew a place my parents would never find me. I would go there and I would hide, and when they were having their breakfast, I would pop out and surprise them. There was a huge package of paper towels under the kitchen sink. It was exactly my size and very, very soft. The sky outside was the color of iced tea. Everyone was asleep. I crawled in and shut the door. It smelled like soap and chemicals. I don't know what happened, but I must of fallen back asleep. When I woke up, I couldn't hear anyone. I crawled out. No one was there. I went to my parents' bedroom and no one was there either. This was my old house with an upstairs and a downstairs. No one was anywhere. The doors were locked and dead-bolted. I was stuck inside. Sometimes, as I waited, I thought they had gotten angry and left me forever, and sometimes I thought they had died. I lay down on my back on the polished wooden floor in the front hall and closed my eyes and waited to die myself. I wished out loud I would die. Over and over. I've asked my mom about it and she says it never happened, but I remember it clearly. I remember it as clearly as anything that has ever happened to me. And sometimes I feel that way still.

Acknowledgments

The initial inspiration for this novel was a tiny single-paragraph story in the Nation section of the *New York Times* I read sometime around 2001 and no longer have, so, first of all, thank you anonymous *New York Times* reporter. Because I fiddled and drafted and fiddled with this book over the course of a decade, there have been numerous readers and helpful advisors, so please forgive me in advance if I leave any of you out. My heart- and head-felt thanks goes to: Avi Neurohr, for that great, tough read; Nancy Dessomes; Matthew Miller; Dr. Joseph Thomas; Patty Pace; Carol Houke-Smith; David Starnes; Dennis Thompson; Imad Rahman; Tamara Guiardo; Jack Gantos; Bronwen Hruska; Juliette Grames; the inimitable Aileen Lujo; Justin Hargett; my beloved, brilliant, and extraordinarily patient editor Mark Doten; Steve Pett; Deb Marquart; Val Helmund; Dennis Thompson; the ever remarkable Scott Yarbrough; Charlie Kostelnick; Ben Percy, all of my other helpful and friendly colleagues at Iowa State University; my sisters Amy, Karen, Beth, and Lisa, and sisters-in-law Ann Marie and Gina Marie, from whom I stole girlishness shamelessly; my brother Patrick Zimmerman for his superb reading skills and continual encouragement; my large and boisterous family-at-large, from Amalfitanos to Zimmermans and all the marriage-made surnames in between; and of course, Tina, child whisperer, Confederate-in-arms, and delight of my life.